BLOOD AND MAGIC

MELISSA SERCIA

CITY OWL
PRESS

BLOOD AND MAGIC
Blood and Darkness, Book 1

CITY OWL PRESS
www.cityowlpress.com

Cover Design by Mibl Art and Tina Moss. All stock photos licensed appropriately.

Edited by Amanda Roberts.

For information on subsidiary rights, please contact the publisher at info@cityowlpress.com.

Print Edition ISBN: 978-1-944728-95-3

Digital Edition ISBN: 978-1-944728-96-0

Printed in the United States of America

To my strong and beautiful grandmothers
Violet Campbell and Agatha Sercia.

You will always be a part of me.
I miss you both more than you could ever know.

"Demons have many faces, like shadows, if you look close enough. In the light that casts a glare between them, you will find the exquisite truth."

ONE

THE ROOM VALENTINA HID ME IN WAS THE SIZE OF A CLOSET, BARE
except for yellow curtains and an old cot in the corner.

Pacing around, I tugged at a strand of my dark hair, pinching it
tight around my white knuckles. The vein above my breast throbbed
and pushed through my skin like a fresh tattoo.

"You still haven't told me what happened." My throat ached.
Every breath I took scratched my lungs.

I needed blood.

Valentina lowered her eyes and bit her lip. Ribbons of curls fell
upon her shoulders, blood red and scented with lilac.

She stifled a sob. "I...I'm sorry, Gray. I couldn't stop them." Her
voice trailed off into a whisper.

A lump formed in my throat. I swallowed hard to keep the bile
down. A thousand questions raced through my mind. My muscles
were stiff, clenched and aching. "How long was I asleep?"

Valentina wiped the tears from her eyes. Black eyeliner smeared
across her cheeks. "Three years."

Every hair on the back of my neck stood up. I leaned up against
the wall to keep the room from spinning.

"I don't understand."

Her lower lip quivered. "It was Dragos... He betrayed us to the Consilium."

Dragos. The room was spinning. *Do you still love him now, Gray?* The wounds were old but as fresh as the salt being poured on them. Like a fire in my veins that I couldn't put out, the fury was growing. He made a fool of me. I locked my knees to keep them from shaking.

"What did he do to me?" The thought of Dragos creeping around my lifeless body made my stomach turn.

Valentina gazed out the window, her eyes red and swollen. "He was with Pythia. She put you under with one of her spells. You weren't dead, but you weren't alive either. She trapped you in your own mind."

My skin prickled into a cold sweat. *How could I not remember anything?*

"How did I wake up?" Pythia's magic was dark and ancient. It would have taken an entire coven of Witches to break me out of that spell.

"I...I don't know. You just did." She scurried around the tiny room, gathering our belongings. We didn't have much, except for a few trunks of clothes and weapons. She avoided my gaze while she packed.

"I have been sleeping for three years, the man I love has betrayed me to my enemies, and you don't know? *What* aren't you telling me, Val?" As my fists tightened, my nails dug into my skin, drawing blood. A sinking sensation formed in the pit of my stomach.

She waved me off. "That's all I've got, Gray. I'm as surprised as you are. What I know for sure is that when they found out you were planning to go against them, they wanted you out of commission. All that matters now is that we keep moving. Once the Consilium finds out you're awake, they will come for you again."

The Consilium had always been one step ahead of us. I had been tracking them for the last four hundred years, but every lead always led to a dead end. Their organization stretched all over the world and their resources were limitless.

I watched her shove our things into a bag like she was shoveling dirt onto a fresh grave. "I'm assuming you have a plan?"

Her eyes shifted to the ground. "Yeah, but you're not gonna like it."

My shoulders tensed. Valentina's methods were not always rational. She took a deep breath. "We're going to go talk to Lucien."

My blood curdled. "*Lucien?* You must be joking. How do you know he won't double cross us?"

As the leader of the London Dhampir coven, he had direct ties to the Consilium. I'd never met him, but I knew enough not to trust him.

Valentina sighed. "Gray, I promise, I'm not going to lead us into another trap."

A pang of guilt stabbed at my chest. "I'm sorry. I didn't mean to—"

"No. You're right to doubt me. We both trusted Dragos, but he is *my* brother. I should have seen it coming."

The sound of his name didn't always make my stomach turn. It used to send tingles up my spine, sending me into a state of breathless anticipation for his presence. Those days were long gone. "I don't want to talk about him anymore."

Valentina nodded, her eyes glistening. "Look, Lucien is an old friend. He won't turn us over to the Consilium."

Guilt clawed at me again. "You've kept me safe for three years while I've been sleeping. I'm not going to start doubting you now."

Valentina tossed me a straw and a blood bag as she moved toward the door. "When we get there, let me do the talking. Lucien doesn't like surprises." She shivered, grabbed her coat, and sauntered out into the dark London fog. It was going to be a long night, and dealing with Lucien would only make it darker.

The pavement was slick. Cold and wet with dew. The mist followed us as we stomped through the dark. The streetlamps glowed, dim and muted, casting faint particles of dust between the shadows.

Sliding down the sewer entrance to Lucien's compound, my chest tightened. The walls of the tunnels that wrapped around the city in a maze were slimy, coating the palms of my hands with a thick sludge. No human would ever make it down here, but as a Dhampir, I shimmied down without difficulty.

Valentina advanced with ease, leading us through to each checkpoint, and past the guards Lucien had stationed at each one. Dhampir soldiers. Young, but well trained. Created solely for a life of servitude. They let us pass without hesitation.

Approaching the last checkpoint, a guard motioned for us to wait. Beads of sweat gathered on my brow.

A few minutes passed before Lucien emerged from the dark, stretching out before us. His lips curled into a smile, but his eyes were as black as night and hinted at madness.

"Valentina, my darling. To what do I owe this pleasure?"

She twirled a lock of her red hair. "Lucien. I don't need a reason to pay a visit to an old friend, do I?" She winked, batting her eyelashes. A signature move she displayed when she wanted something.

Lucien grimaced. His skin was sallow, reeking of musk and sewer water.

"You've brought a friend. You must be the infamous Gray I have heard so much about." His hands twitched as he took a step toward me.

I stiffened. The way he surveyed me up and down made my skin crawl.

Valentina chuckled through gritted teeth. "The one and only. She is a woman of few words, I'm afraid."

Lucien's lips quivered as if he had just tasted the sweet nectar from fresh blood. "I see the stories are true. She *is* enchanting. I hope that we can all become *very* close friends." His eyes trailed down to the peak of my breasts.

With clenched fists, I leaned in close to him. "I want the

bastards that did this to me. I'm cranky, hungry, and *really* pissed off. So, if you could be so kind as to tell me what the Consilium is up to, I might not rip your head off."

His guards rushed toward me, weapons drawn. Lucien raised a hand for them to halt. "Ah, so the stories are true. You *are* feisty. I like that. But still, holding a grudge against the ones who made you? Tsk, tsk. That was centuries ago. *Get over it.*"

My hands shook. I wanted to wrap them around his scrawny neck. "Unless you start talking, the only thing I'm going to get over is your dismembered body."

Lucien smirked, but his eyes narrowed down at me like daggers. "The thing is, you seem to forget you are far outnumbered. However, I don't want to get your blood all over my floor. It draws the rats."

I started toward him. Valentina stepped in front of me. "Let's all just calm down. We don't want any trouble. You'll have to forgive my friend. She just woke up from a very long nap and is not herself right now." She shot me a glare.

Lucien's hands twitched again. "Yes, of course. Perhaps I can forgive and forget. What do you want?"

I drew in a sharp breath. "Where can I find the Consilium?"

The tension was thick. His guards stared straight ahead, blank, but fixated. Their eyes were dark and hollow, like black holes.

Lucien erupted into laughter. It echoed through the tunnels, scraping the air like knives carving into pavement.

Blood rushed through my veins, hot and erratic. "Did I say something funny? Because I'm pretty sure I just asked you a serious question."

He rolled his eyes. "No one can find the Consilium. They find you. They are nowhere, and they are everywhere."

"You must know something, Lucien," Valentina snapped. "Don't toy with us."

Lucien chuckled. Annoyed, I kicked a hole into the tunnel wall. Chunks of rock and dust sprayed out around us, soiling Lucien's shirt.

He snorted, flinging dirt off his collar. "I have no idea how to find them. If I need anything, I call my handler. She comes to me."

My jaw tightened. "This is a waste of time. Val, let's get out of here."

Valentina clasped his hands. "Then point us toward someone who does know something. Give me a name. Anything. *You owe me.*" A look passed between them that I couldn't place.

Lucien flinched, but nodded, reluctantly. "There have been whispers of something brewing across the pond. In New Orleans. Some of the Witches have spotted unsanctioned Dhampir activity in the French Quarter."

My pulse quickened. This had to be the Consilium. No one else would be stupid enough to stir up trouble with the Witches.

Valentina cleared her throat. "So, where can we find these whispering Witches?"

Lucien feigned a yawn. "The Wolf and Crescent. Ask for Josephine DuMaurier. She leads the coven there. But be quick about it. Everyone must check in with her when they arrive. Trust me, you don't want to get on her bad side." He paused to lick his lips. "Now, I have better things to do. So, I insist that you take your leave."

I cringed as Valentina made a spectacle out of thanking Lucien for his help. There was a strange energy between them. The way their polite courtesies dangled between icy handshakes and loaded glances. Dragos used to tell me it was the words that we didn't say that spoke the loudest. I didn't understand until now.

"Farewell, Gray. I have no doubt you will find what you are looking for." His lips pursed like his mouth was full of bitter fruit. Spinning on his heel, his guards encircled him, and they disappeared down a dark tunnel.

Gulping back stale air, I couldn't get out of there fast enough. With dirty hair and cheeks, I scrambled up the sewer drain like a hungry rat.

My hands hit the cold pavement and I breathed a sigh of relief. The crisp London air filled my lungs, easing the ache in my chest.

The silence was welcoming, but I couldn't hold my tongue any longer. "What's the story with you two?"

Valentina shrugged. "Not much to tell. We had an arrangement that worked for a while, and then it didn't. So, it ended." Her tone was sharp and final.

I decided not to push the issue. Some cards were better kept close to your chest. We all had our burdens to bear. Especially in the world we lived in.

Valentina placed a gentle hand on my shoulder. "Gray...you all right?"

They will all be dealt with.

I was far from all right. The Consilium had taken everything from me. My humanity when they turned me into a Dhampir. My only family when they converted my mother. They even turned the man I loved against me. They stole three years of my life that I could never get back. But I was done being their pawn.

Valentina waved a hand in front of my face. "Gray...?"

My chest heaved, adrenaline coursed through my veins. "They should have killed me."

TWO

I HAD NEVER BEEN OUT OF EUROPE BEFORE, AND I DIDN'T KNOW IF I would ever see it again. It never felt like home, but it was the only place I'd ever lived. A twinge of sadness crept up. *You can't miss what was never yours to begin with.*

We arrived in New Orleans just before dawn. A black town car waited for us on the tarmac. A portly, grey-haired driver stepped out, avoiding eye contact. He opened the passenger door, fingers fumbling. The scent of his fear was palpable. *Did he know what we were?*

As we drove into the city, echoes of celebration rang through my ears. Glasses clanked together amidst music and laughter. Voices were layered over trumpets and saxophones. It seduced me and crept into my bones. My ears tingled from the chaos.

Valentina's eyes lit up, wide with wonder. She leaned out her window to get a closer look. Painted faces sang and danced around each other with wild abandon. Some wore masks and colorful feathers. Others hardly wore anything at all. Their bodies rocked and swayed against one another.

Turning down Bourbon Street, a strong wave of magic hit me, followed by the sweet scent of magnolias. As a Dhampir, my senses were always heightened, and magic was something I could trace. The presence of it meant only one thing. *Witches.* Their whispers followed us. It was only a matter of time before Josephine DuMaurier would learn of our presence.

Inside the Garden District, our car came to a stop outside a Gothic two-story house. With its arched windows and ivy-covered balconies, it reminded me of an estate in Italy I had stayed in. The estate had belonged to the Striga, a Romany coven that Dragos was tied to. The three of us stayed and indulged with them for a while. There were nights I thought the blood and wine would flow forever.

The driver set our luggage on the curb with trembling hands. As he tossed me the keys to the house, a crescent moon necklace peered out from under his shirt. A symbol only Witches wore. They also had heightened senses. He knew exactly what we were.

On guard, we approached the house. Over the years, I had learned to be cautious everywhere I went. There were things made from nightmares that could be lurking in the shadows. Creatures, deadlier than us, waiting to pounce and drag you away without a sound. I took a deep breath and opened the door.

Stepping inside, my fears vanished. The house was magnificent. Crown molding framed the ceilings, ornate and detailed with bronze etchings of fleurs-de-lis. The floors were handcrafted with repurposed wood. Light and dark swirls of walnut, maple, and oak filled the cracks.

On my right, a curved staircase sprawled up toward the second floor. Stately, with its mahogany steps and iron railing. To the left, a small parlor room housed a cream-colored couch and marble fireplace. A large painting hung above it.

All the hairs on the back of my neck stood up. *What an odd choice of artwork.* It was a portrait of Lamia, draped in the skin of a snake. Known for kidnapping human infants and drinking their blood, Witches called her the "mother of Dhampirs." Some also called her

Lilith. To me, it was just an old wives' tale. Most Dhampirs, including myself, believed that we were created by the gods. Molded by Apollo himself.

Valentina lit a fire in the hearth. The flames contorted the painting of Lamia's face even more. I shuddered but could not look away.

Valentina followed my gaze. "*Who* did you rent this house from?"

I shrugged. "An agency. The owner wanted to remain anonymous."

She shivered. "Creepy. Should we be worried?"

I shook my head, shrugging off the feeling of dread. "Not yet, but keep your eyes open."

I sank into the couch, head pounding. My thirst gnawed at me, but blood wasn't the only thing we drank. I pulled a bottle of bourbon out of my bag and took a swig. It slid down my throat, warm and peppery.

Valentina raised the bottle over her head. "Let us celebrate our arrival. May the gods guide us and strike down those who dare to stand in our way."

Morning came faster than I'd expected. Sunlight poured in while we explored the rest of the house. Upstairs, there were three lavish bedrooms. Small, but luxurious. Furnished with four-poster beds, antique dressers, and crystal chandeliers. Tapestries of rich colors splashed throughout each room. Purple and red fabrics made of silk and velvet adorned all the beds.

Downstairs, the basement was stocked with wine and bourbon. *How hospitable.* I tore open one of my blood bags instead. "We should head into the Quarter today. See if we can find anything out about the Wolf and Crescent."

Valentina nodded in agreement, slurping her blood bag with a straw. "I doubt they'll tell us anything. The Witches don't like our kind. Never have."

I threw up my hands. "I've never understood that. We come from the same source. The same gods."

Valentina shrugged. "They have their own ideas about us. Their own stories."

It saddened me to think of the divide between our races. The Consilium forcing them to link to us only added to their hatred. Unfortunately for them, my patience was running out. "Let's hope they don't make us prove them right."

Valentina smirked. "Let's go."

This city was unlike any other. There were those who embraced the supernatural, and those who despised it. Witches ran the streets and Dhampirs were not welcome. They were jealous of us. We had no weaknesses. Created by the sun god Apollo, we could walk in the daylight. That terrified them because they could not control us.

Walking through the Quarter, the weight of their suspicious stares tickled the back of my neck. They slithered into corners and shadows to avoid our gaze.

Valentina fumed. "How dare they look at us with such contempt. We should remind them just how low they are on the food chain." Her cheeks flushed bright pink.

I placed a steady hand on her shoulder. "Val, we have to be smart about this. Our fight is with the Consilium, not the Witches. Just be patient. One of them will lead us to Josephine."

Valentina snapped, "Fine, let's go lurk in the shadows then."

I let out a deep breath, muffling my curses. "Don't be upset. They don't know any better."

She bit her lip and looked away. "Don't worry, I'll behave. I know what's at stake."

We both did. Our existence depended on it. Valentina had a short fuse, but I'd come to trust her with my life.

"We wait for nightfall, and then we track them."

Hours passed into darkness while we waited. Valentina was not convinced that this would work, but it had to. There were no other options.

It was almost dawn when I spotted them. A young group of

Witches with...*human companions*. The scent of their blood hit my nose, rich and decadent like chocolate. A drug I hadn't tasted in years. Not like this. Fresh and straight from the vein. My body ached.

I closed my eyes and took a deep breath. The human blood was laced with magic. It was a different kind of craving. Mouthwatering. Intoxicating. *Stop, you can control this.* Another deep breath. Hints of honey and whiskey tickled my senses. I dug my fingernails into the palm of my hand, drawing blood.

My shoulders released as the tension left my body. I glanced over at Valentina. She was frozen in place. Her eyes changed to a shade that matched her hair.

"Remember to breathe, Val."

When Dhampirs became emotional, whether from blood or battle, our eyes changed colors to reflect our shadow self. Mine would shade to black. Valentina's always turned blood red.

Her chest heaved up and down before settling into a slower pace. Her eyes blinked, shifting back to brown. She nodded. "I'm okay. C'mon, they're on the move."

The group of Witches and humans stumbled past us, drunk and oblivious to our presence. They were heading toward the bayou. *Of course.*

Witches preferred to be surrounded by nature. Their magic was stronger there. The bayou was well outside the city limits. It was the perfect place to hide a coven.

We kept a safe distance, following them through the lush, Louisiana swampland. Not that it mattered. They were so drunk, they wouldn't have noticed if we landed on top of them. The group cackled, and zig-zagged through the marsh in booze-filled delirium.

Thirty minutes had passed when I noticed a light up ahead. Moving closer, a large plantation house came into view. Music and voices poured out of it. Flirtatious banter. Laughter. Seductive whispers.

A clear path emerged, lined with torches. The flames flickered and danced under the moonlight, illuminating their flesh like fireflies. A banner hung over the entry with just two symbols. A crescent moon and the head of a wolf.

So, the stories were true. I had heard tales of Witches luring humans into their parties for amusement. They would cast enchantments and feed them love potions. Showing them the time of their lives, only to leave them dizzy and heart broken by morning. To think, they thought we were the cruel ones. We drank blood for survival, not sport. Well, most of us, anyway.

I lowered my voice. "Let's sneak in on the back of that group. Just act drunk and try to blend in."

Valentina chuckled. "Shouldn't I be saying that to you? You haven't let loose since—"

I snatched her arm. "*Don't.*" I didn't want to think about those days right now.

She looked away. "Sorry. Forget I mentioned it."

I nodded and moved ahead of her. The group stumbled inside, giggling and groping each other.

I paused in the doorway as a prickling sensation spread through me. Something dark hovered above the entrance. I looked up. There was a couple perched on the balcony, draped around each other. He nuzzled her neck as she moaned and cried out. I drew in a sharp breath. *He was looking right at me.* A chill ran down my spine. His eyes glowed bright red.

Valentina grabbed my arm. "What's wrong?"

My heart raced. "It's nothing. I just thought I saw..." *A Witch with blood lust in his eyes.*

Her eyes darted around in a panic. "What?"

I glanced up again. He was gone. My hands trembled. "Nothing. Never mind. Let's get inside."

Inching toward the door, we brushed past another group of Witches, too distracted to notice us. They doted on their human playthings, slipping oyster pearls into their drinks. A powerful aphrodisiac that caused fits of wild nymphomania. My stomach turned. The Wolf and Crescent was a den of thieves and miscreants.

I stepped in and scanned the room. Witches from covens from

all over the world lazed about. Not all of them were as distracted. Within seconds came the whispers. All eyes were on us.

Valentina snickered as I pulled her to the bar. Behind it stood a tall, lanky girl with silver hair and a long beak. A Harpy Witch, half girl, half bird. She looked us up and down, contorting her face in disgust.

"We don't have any blood infusions on the menu here." Her voice was as sharp as the beak on her face.

Valentina leaned casually over the bar. "I guess we'll just have to drink from your throat then."

The Harpy stiffened and glanced around the room.

Valentina chuckled. "What's the matter little bird? Did I ruffle your feathers?"

Valentina had always been quick to provoke. In 1614, she had a fling with the princess of Sweden. Convinced it was true love, the princess let Valentina drink from her. Over time, Valentina lost interest and left the poor girl devastated. Due to her irrational behavior, her family believed her to be under some sort of spell, triggering one of the biggest Witch hunts in history. All the women they executed were human and possessed no magic.

The back of my neck tingled. Footsteps quickened behind us. The Witches were closing in. It was time for a different approach. I whipped around.

"Well, now that we have your attention. Which one of you wants to tell us what the Consilium has been up to?"

No one moved a muscle.

I raised my voice louder. "Anyone? Do you even know? You do seem to be preoccupied with other...*distractions*." My eyes rested on a table of humans, their eyes glazed over from some sort of toxin.

Valentina stepped forward and planted her feet hard, shaking the ground. More Witches emerged from every corner, shrieking and hissing at us.

The male Witch from the balcony came forward. His icy smile sent shivers down my back. I searched his eyes. No trace of the bloodlust I saw earlier. They were just...empty. He moved closer, inches away from my face. Valentina clenched her fists.

I wrapped my hands around the daggers stashed on each side of my waist. "We didn't come here to fight, but we will if we have to."

He raised his hands. "Oh, I think that's exactly why you came here." The other Witches scurried behind him.

Crouching beside me, Valentina's eyes shifted blood red. Her lips snarled back, baring her fangs. Daggers out, I took a deep breath and braced myself.

"That won't be necessary. *Samuel*, that's enough."

Everyone came to a halt. All eyes turned toward the woman at the top of the stairs. They bowed their heads as she made her way down. *Josephine*. She was striking, with dark eyes and almond skin. The male Witch, the one she called Samuel, looked just like her.

"You'll have to excuse my son. He is not accustomed to uninvited guests. You are brave to come here. What brings you here today, Gray?" She sauntered through the room while the other Witches scrambled to get out of her way.

My heart was thumping out of my chest. *How did she know my name?* "As I said, we did not come here for a fight. We need information. Lucien said you might be able to help us."

Josephine cocked her head to the side. "Lucien? How nice of him to appoint me."

Valentina huffed. "Look, he said you might know something about the new Dhampir activity in the city. Is it the Consilium?"

Josephine's eyes widened. "Not exactly. You must be Valentina. The creature with the blood eyes."

Valentina winced, then stiffened.

My impatience was building and turning to rage. I snapped, "Don't change the subject. You need to decide which side you're on. I'm going after the Consilium. One by one, *I will* take them down. Either help us or stay out of our way. But make no mistake, they are coming for us all."

Josephine's eyes fluttered and rolled back into her head. With hands trembling she fumbled for the railing. The Witches gasped.

Her head twisted up toward the ceiling. My skin prickled. *She was an Oracle.*

"What do you see?" Sweat dripped down my brow.

Breathless, her eyes snapped forward. "Come. You will get the answers you seek."

Valentina and I exchanged a puzzled look. We followed Josephine up the stairs and down a muted hallway. Samuel trailed close behind.

She ushered us through a heavy door, closing it behind us and in Samuel's face. I shuddered. His sinister gaze left an imprint that seemed to etch itself into the wood.

Josephine's study was well lit, with candles and a fire blazing in the hearth. A white wolf slept in front of it. I froze. He perked his head up and let out a low growl. With just a flick from Josephine's hand, the wolf put his head back down and closed his eyes.

Josephine placed her hand on the door. "*Dissumlare.*" *To conceal.* A spell that sealed sound. She smiled sweetly. "For privacy."

There was one thing that was still nagging me. "How do you know my name?"

Josephine sat down next to the wolf and gazed into the fire. "From Jane. She's an old friend. I saw you in her vision. I've always kept her secrets, and you my dear, are her biggest one."

A bead of sweat dripped down my back. I couldn't remember the last time I had heard her name spoken out loud. A bitter taste filled my mouth. "I'm surprised that she has not burned all her bridges."

Josephine's eyes darkened. "Your mother is the greatest Witch I've ever known. She had her reasons for joining the Consilium. You'll understand someday."

The bile was rising in my throat. "She stopped being my mother the moment she ended my human life. Do not refer to her as such."

Josephine nodded. "Forgive me. It's not my business. I am curious as to how you broke Pythia's spell, though. *Ligaveris* is from the *Sang Magi* spell book. None of *my* Witches would have been able to break it. Yet, here you are. Wide awake."

If only I could answer that. I looked over at Valentina. She was fixated on the white wolf. "We don't know. Val said I just...snapped out of it."

Josephine bit her lip. "I see. Well, I guess anything is possible."

A gnawing ache formed in the pit of my stomach. Valentina was keeping something from me. I could feel it. Josephine didn't look convinced either. All our unspoken secrets hung over us like a dark cloud. They were the breathings of madness and despair. They threatened to pull apart our very existence, and yet I understood why we kept them.

Josephine cleared her throat. "I also understand that you were betrayed by Dragos. You must be heartbroken."

My cheeks burned hot.

Valentina snapped, "We didn't come here to talk about my brother. He's *also* none of your business."

Josephine bowed her head. "My apologies."

I wanted to slap her for her insolence, but I needed information. "What's the unsanctioned activity going on in the city?"

Something flickered in Josephine's eyes. "Some of my Witches have spotted Elemi Bannister slipping in and out of the Quarter. She has always passed through here from time to time, but in the last few weeks, it has become more frequent."

My pulse quickened. I hadn't heard the name Bannister in a very long time. "Just Elemi? What about her brother, Nicholas?" Another name that made my blood curdle.

"So far, there has been no sign of Nicholas. Believe me, I would be the first to know if that monster stepped one foot inside my city." Josephine's eyes narrowed down at the flames.

A chill crawled up my back. "Do you know why she's here?"

Josephine nodded, a smirk forming on her lips. "To protect her bloodline, of course. Her *human* bloodline."

My stomach dropped. Magic was inherited through blood. Once it was awakened, the Witch would become immortal. Elemi was also a Dhampir, and like Jane, a linked Witch. There shouldn't be any humans left in their bloodline. "How is that possible?"

Josephine shook her head. "He's off the books. The Consilium doesn't know he exists either. Elemi keeps him cloaked at all times. They would kill her if they ever found out."

My lungs tightened, shortening my breath. *A human descendant?* The Bannisters became immortal centuries ago. Elemi must have been protecting this bloodline since the beginning.

Throwing one more glance at the wolf, Valentina pulled me toward the door. "Let's go, Gray. We got what we came for." She was still seething at Josephine for bringing up Dragos.

I paused at the door. "I assume we'll have safe passage out of here?"

Josephine nodded. "Be careful, Gray. The path you're on is a treacherous one. If you stand in their way, they will kill you too."

I erupted. "They should have taken their shot when they had the chance."

Josephine looked deep into my eyes and shivered. And for the first time all night, she was afraid of me.

THREE

Witchcraft was as old as the existence of the Dhampirs. Blood magic was even older.

My mother, Jane, never referred to herself as a Witch. She called herself a healer. I knew this was only to protect herself from persecution. She was a good Witch. At least, I *used* to think so.

I'd help her gather herbs in the forest. We'd spend all night making tonics and tinctures to cure the sick and comfort the dying. I wanted to be just like her. Jane said magic had to be awakened. I begged her to awaken mine, but she claimed I wasn't ready. She turned me into a Dhampir before that day could ever come.

The thirst for blood was unlike anything I'd ever felt. It spread through me like a disease. I was erratic and unpredictable. Killing for survival soon turned to sport. I relished it. I became a monster.

Many years later, Valentina and Dragos found me and showed me how to control it. How to live with it. It was because of them I was able to hold onto the last shred of humanity I had left. But I had not forgotten the old ways. They were still a part of me.

"I need to consult the cards."

Valentina looked as if I slapped her in the face. "Please tell me you're joking. You know how I feel about all that Witchy stuff."

I paced as she gawked. Magic was not something I could tap into, but tarot cards were a conduit for messages from beyond the veil. I had to try.

"It's a part of me, Val, and we need answers. The gods will guide us."

She groaned, rolling her eyes. "*Fine*. What do you need me to do?"

A burst of energy moved through me. "Make a circle of candles in the center of the room. I'll get the cards."

Valentina huffed as I ran upstairs. I hadn't looked at my cards in years. I never needed to. I got them in Italy, a gift from a one-eyed gypsy. She told me that someday, they would serve a purpose. I shrugged it off then, but now I thought she may have been right.

Once inside the circle, I closed my eyes and shuffled the cards. I blocked out all thoughts except one. Revenge. Valentina scowled as I fanned seven cards out in front of me.

The first card was the two of cups. A picture of a man and woman, each holding a golden cup. He was reaching out to her.

The second card was of the High Priestess. "Pythia."

Valentina nodded, now intrigued.

Next, the card of Temperance, an angel pouring liquid from one cup to another. Goosebumps covered my flesh. The cups were the same two from the first image.

The three of swords came after. The swords were piercing a beating heart while a storm raged behind it. Three swords, three enemies.

The fifth card was the Hermit. Valentina gasped. Recognition flickered in her eyes. She shuddered and looked away.

Then, the card of Strength, an image of a woman taming a lion. Above her head was a figure eight, the symbol for infinity. A chill ran through me. The Consilium wore this symbol like a coat of arms.

Finally, the last card, the Tower. My stomach turned. The tower burned while figures fell out of it and the sky rained down fire.

I held her gaze. I knew what I had to do. "I have to awaken my magic. Then you and I can link, and we'll be as strong as they are."

Valentina crinkled her brow. "I don't know, Gray. Do we *want* to be like them? To become hybrids?"

My heart raced. "Yes. It's clear from the cards. The cups pouring into one another is a symbol of the linking ceremony. Tame the lion, burn the tower. We *have* to. It's the one thing they won't see coming."

Minutes turned into hours while Valentina weighed my words. I could almost see the wheels spinning inside her head. She let out a deep breath. "Okay. I'm in. I guess this means we have to go back to the bayou."

I clapped my hands, delighted. Yes, we would have to go back to the bayou. Only a Witch could awaken another Witch's magic. Currently, Josephine was the only Witch we knew.

We waited till morning to venture out. The Wolf and Crescent wasn't as lively in the light of day. After our cold welcome, I must have been mad to return, but after four hundred years of chasing ghosts, I had nothing left to lose except my patience.

The air was calm and quiet as we approached. No traces of last night's debauchery. No drunken humans strewn about. It was as if the party had never taken place. We crept into the bar with weapons drawn.

Keeping my eyes peeled for Samuel, I scanned the room for any sign of movement. Nothing. The place was empty. Not that Josephine needed protection, but I assumed someone would be standing guard.

Making my way over to the stairs, the hairs on the back of my neck stood up. A deep snarl filled the room. We both froze. The white wolf glared down at us from the top of the stairs, dripping saliva all over the floorboards.

Valentina leaned in and whispered. "Shit. He doesn't look like he's in a good mood."

I stiffened. "Don't move. He thinks we're trespassing."

Valentina's eyes widened. "Uh, we kind of are."

The wolf's ears snapped back and his snarl turned into a low, guttural growl. His eyes glowed, gold like the sun. Watching him watching us, it hit me.

I cleared my throat and sheathed my sword. "We just need to speak with her."

Valentina gasped. "Gray, have you lost your mind? It can't understand you. You're going to get us killed."

I couldn't believe I hadn't figured it out before. "Relax. He's a shape shifter. Half man, half wolf. A *Lupi*."

She gripped my arm. "He just looks hungry to me."

I swallowed hard, hoping she was wrong. "An ordinary wolf would have attacked us by now. Trust me, he understood every word I said."

The door to the study opened. Josephine emerged and placed a hand on the wolf's head, subduing him instantly. Valentina let out a sigh of relief.

Josephine chuckled. "You're very brave to come back here. Did I not answer all your questions last night?"

I let out a deep breath. "I need you to awaken my magic."

Josephine's eyes lit up like fireflies. "How interesting. Magic comes with a price, Gray. For you and for me."

I swallowed hard. I should have known there would be strings attached. "What do you want in return?"

Her eyes darkened as she mulled it over. "A favor. To be determined...later." Her words lingered in the air like smoke billowing between us.

Valentina shook her head. "I have a bad feeling about this."

"We're running out of options. This is the only way." I looked back at Josephine, who was stroking the Lupi like a pet. "We have a deal."

Her eyes flickered. "Wait outside. I'll join you when I have everything I need for the ceremony."

Valentina paced back and forth in front of the Wolf and Crescent, making me even more anxious. What if she was right?

This could be a very bad idea. I didn't know Josephine at all, and her connection to Jane made me uneasy.

It was dusk when she emerged. She had changed into a plain, white dress that flowed down to her bare feet. Around her neck was a crescent moon necklace, a source of power that held a Witch's connection to the earth. She tossed a burlap sack over her shoulder and motioned for us to follow her into the swamps.

It was dark out there, even in daylight. The paths were hard to discern, despite being lined with black gum trees and swamp maples. Dripping in Spanish moss, each tree ran into the next. There were swamps as far as the eye could see. The water was murky, yet decorated with delicate lily pads and marsh grass. Alligators lurked just below the surface.

Valentina was not fond of the bayou. She shivered and gasped at every twig that snapped underneath her feet. She wasn't afraid of much, but this place was getting to her. It was getting to me too. Ashen trees swayed in the southern breeze, mocking us as we passed.

A mile in, we stopped at a clearing. A flat, wide-open field surrounded by brush and walls of branches. On the ground was a perfect circle of stones.

Josephine emptied out the contents of her sack. She placed seven tea light candles along the inside of the circle. She worked meticulously as she laid out a chalice and a dagger, both engraved with a crescent moon. Next, she set down a canister containing a mixture of bark and bay leaves.

"Gray, step into the circle." Josephine followed me in. She lit the candles and turned to face me while crushing the bark and bay leaves into the chalice. Valentina watched with intent.

I shivered. A cool breeze tickled my skin.

She grabbed my wrist, made a tiny incision with the dagger, and squeezed. My blood dripped into the chalice. I winced as it stung and pinched my flesh. Within seconds the wound began to heal.

Josephine raised the chalice to the sky. "I offer to Diana bark from a sacred oak tree and bay leaves blessed with the blood wishes from one of our own." Chanting in Latin, she swayed back and forth as the wind howled and picked up speed.

My hair whipped around me with the force of a hurricane. I locked my knees as the ground shook. Her magic pulled at every fiber of my being. It pounded at me, like invisible hands reaching into my head and shaking my brain. The world blurred around me.

My lungs tightened, gasping for air. Her words rang out, distorting in my ears. The world went black. Panic, rose in my chest.

Josephine screamed. "Exitare...exitare...exitare." *Awaken*.

The candles blew out. The wind vanished. Everything was still. Silent.

I collapsed on my knees. Valentina rushed over to me and dragged me out of the circle.

"Gray, are you okay?"

Breathless and dizzy, I stumbled onto my feet. My teeth chattered. The wind was still in my bones. "Did it work?"

Josephine recoiled in horror. Her hands shook, holding the remnants of the chalice.

Valentina's eyes turned red. "What did you do to her?"

Josephine shook her head, burying it into her hands. "Nothing... absolutely nothing."

My heart raced. "I don't understand. What just happened?"

Her lips quivered. "You don't have any magic to awaken."

Like a punch to the gut, knocking the air out of me, I keeled over. No magic to awaken? *Impossible*. It was my birthright. The one thing about my life I knew to be true. Since the beginning of time, Witches passed down their magic through blood.

They stood, speechless, staring at me like I was a wounded animal. Pity spread across their faces. No one wanted to say it out loud. I felt like an orphan all over again. If I didn't have any magic to awaken, then Jane could not be my mother.

"It seems she didn't share all her secrets with you," I snapped. Bitterness tinged my tongue like rotten fruit.

The color drained from Josephine's face. "I...I don't understand. I saw you as a baby in her visions. She let me believe you were hers."

I snapped, "That's because she's a liar. Now do you understand why I despise her?" My blood was boiling.

Jane let me think I was like her. That I had magic in my veins. I didn't know what I was anymore.

Josephine darted around, cleaning up what was left of the ceremony and avoiding my gaze. "I better get back before my coven sends out a search party." Her voice shook with unease.

Something was troubling her, and it wasn't the revelation of my parentage. "What else did you see...inside me?"

Josephine shuddered, hesitating before looking me in the eye. "Darkness. Faint, but it grows in you... I really must be getting back."

She gathered the rest of her supplies and sprinted back toward the Wolf and Crescent, leaving us alone in the bayou without a glance back.

The trek back to the Quarter was a quiet one. Valentina watched me like a hawk. Exhausted and covered in filth, I avoided eye contact. With twigs in my hair and dirt on my cheeks, I headed straight for the shower, standing under the hot water until it ran cold. I wanted to block out everything. The swamp. The ceremony. *Jane.*

I dried off, taking my time. The mundane act of putting on clothes somewhat eased my nerves. The repetition was calming. After stashing two daggers inside my boots and two more in my belt, I pulled on a black fitted sweater and marched downstairs.

Valentina had freshened up as well. Wearing black leather pants and a tight green tank top, she looked like a fashion model. I drew in a sharp breath at the sight of her. Her hair was piled up on top of her head in a mass of crimson curls and her skin glowed with an iridescent sheen. Her brightness was a stark contrast to the dark shadows that lingered under *my* eyes.

Her brow furrowed. "We should talk about what happened in the bayou. Maybe Josephine was wrong."

I shook my head. "No. It all makes sense. She abandoned me

because I'm not her child. She never loved me. At least I know the truth now. Josephine did me a favor."

"Gray, don't say that. There has to be a good explanation for this." Her voice cracked in desperation.

My heart ached. I had been angry with Jane, but a part of me had imagined forgiving her someday. That fantasy was gone. I knew Valentina was trying to make me feel better, but I wasn't in the mood for sympathy.

I shook my head. "I don't want to talk about it, Val. I'm going for a walk. I need to clear my head."

I headed toward the front door with Valentina at my heels. I spun around. "*Alone.*"

She nodded and backed away. Her face twisted in agony. I didn't care. I should have stayed in that coma. At least in there, I was oblivious. With my eyes wide open, there was nothing but darkness ahead of me.

Stepping out into the street, I took a deep breath and swallowed a fragrant gulp of Louisiana air. I needed a distraction. Turning away from our house and toward the Quarter, my spine tingled.

Let's see what kind of trouble I can get into tonight.

FOUR

THE AIR WAS WARM AND STICKY. SCENTS OF SUGAR AND BOURBON wafted past my nose. Nights like these made it hard to remember what an English winter felt like. I was happy to forget.

I found myself on Pirate's Alley, in search of a stiff drink. A busy street lined with trinket shops, cafés, and bars, it bustled with Witches and humans alike. They poured out from every corner, stumbling and laughing amongst each other. A pang of envy twisted in my gut. The weight of our existence was on my shoulders, but they didn't have a care in the world.

Voices echoed from miles away. I heard everything. Not just train whistles and car engines, but conversations. Heartbeats. Whispers. A blessing and a curse. I could switch it on and off whenever I wanted, but tonight I let it roar. I welcomed any noise that could drown out my own thoughts.

Time escaped me as I wandered, exploring the Quarter. The night grew more desolate the further I walked. Shopkeepers pulled in their wares and cafés piled chairs on top of tables. The voices were becoming more and more distant.

It was hopeless. The night was over, and I felt worse than I had when I first ventured out. There was nothing here for me. I let out a sigh and turned around toward home.

My ears prickled. Voices again, muffled as they filtered in and out over an arrangement of music.

I followed the sound to a building, completely dark with boarded up windows. An out-of-service laundromat. A "closed" sign hung on the door. *I could swear the music was coming from inside, though.* I reached for the door just as it swung open.

Music blasted out like a symphony. A young couple, deep in conversation, lingered in the doorway. I cleared my throat. The man looked up, startled.

"Pardon me, ma'am. Didn't see ya there." He and his female companion smiled and moved to the side to let me pass.

I paused. Noticing the puzzled look on my face, the woman chuckled. "You goin' in? The Green Fairy is playin' tonight."

My ears buzzed. *There was magic here.*

"Yes, I think I am."

The couple giggled, staggering off down the street holding hands and whispering. That familiar pang of envy returned.

Stepping inside, my mouth fell to the floor. I was standing in a bar, fully packed with people. Plush velvet couches and mahogany tables were scattered around the room. The lighting was muted, casting a glow of rose gold across the cream-colored walls.

The bar itself was twelve feet long and carved from antique wood. On the wall behind it hung a sign that read "Three Blind Mice est. 1920." That was the year prohibition began. Excitement tingled through me. This was a speakeasy, a secret bar originating back to when alcohol was illegal. If only these walls *could* talk.

A pretty blond bartender approached. "What can I get ya, darlin'?" Her charm was as thick as her drawl.

"Whiskey, neat."

She winked. "You got it, doll face."

Scanning the room, I noticed several pairs of male eyes on me, leering and licking their lips. I chuckled. I wondered how fast they would run if they knew what I was.

The bartender returned minutes later with my drink. "This one's on the house tonight, darlin'."

I cocked my head to the side, puzzled. "Thanks, but...why?"

She batted her lashes. "Owner's rules. One free drink a night to whomever strikes my fancy."

It took me a minute to get it. "Oh...ohh. Well, I'll drink to that." This was turning into a lovely evening after all. Just the distraction I needed.

I learned that the bartender's name was Jenna. She was quite chatty and knew a lot about the city. I enjoyed listening to her go on and on about its history and legends. We chatted about the Three Blind Mice and how it was the oldest speakeasy in New Orleans. Her grandfather bartended here when it opened in 1920. Every detail captivated me.

"Tell me, Jenna, who owns the bar now?" I was warm from my third whiskey and enchanted by her stories.

Jenna lit up. Her face was animated as she spoke. "It's been passed down through the generations. The owners were bootleggers. Aldric is their grandson. He's kept it just as they left it."

"What's Aldric like? I bet he has some great stories." I was fascinated.

Jenna smirked. "Aldric is cool. He's a ladies' man. Good lookin', rich, the king of southern charm." We both giggled.

I raised my glass. "I'll drink to that. Cheers to the King of New Orleans."

Jenna giggled again, pouring herself a shot. "Hear, hear. All hail Aldric Bannister."

My stomach dropped as I choked on my whiskey. "Did you just say...Bannister?"

Jenna crinkled her brow. "You okay, darlin'? You look like you just seen a ghost."

I couldn't breathe. I closed my eyes. The room spun. Images of flames flashed in my head.

Jenna put a glass of water down in front of me. "You know him or somethin'?"

Ignoring the water, I downed the rest of my whiskey. "I knew his uncle. A long time ago."

Jenna stared at me, blank. "Huh. He's never mentioned him before. Must not like him all that much."

I shuddered. "I never liked him much either."

Seeing me press my hands to my temples, Jenna insisted I drink the water. "Aldric will be here soon. I can introduce you."

My head pounded. This was too much, too soon. I wasn't prepared. "No, I need to go. Maybe next time." I stood up too quickly and leaned against the bar to steady myself.

Jenna frowned. "Well, it's been...interesting."

I nodded, forcing a smile. "Thanks for the drink."

A warm draft pulled Jenna's attention toward the door. She smirked. "Well, darlin', looks like it was meant to be. That's Aldric."

I spun around, knees trembling. Good looking was an understatement. He was gorgeous. His pale blond hair was loosely slicked back, half-tucked behind his ears. Standing tall with broad shoulders, he wore a white button-down shirt and black slacks. Simple, but elegant.

His top button was undone, exposing the pulsing vein in his throat. The scent of his blood filled the room. I licked my lips, wondering what it would taste like.

His eyes were a cool shade of blue, aquamarine with flecks of violet. My head throbbed. It was as if I was in my body and out of it at the same time. I couldn't move or look away.

My cheeks flamed as I imagined wrapping my lips around his throat. His soft flesh against my teeth. *What was happening to me?* I must have had too much whiskey.

Aldric never broke eye contact as he made his way over to me. "Pardon me, but have we met before?" His voice was warm, but deep, like smoke and honey.

I couldn't speak. My entire body was on fire. I had to get away from him. Pushing past him, I bolted out the front door. As I sprinted down the alley, I could still feel his eyes, staring after me.

I ran the entire way home. Throwing open the door, I rushed

inside and collapsed on my knees. I was broken. Every emotion flooded out like a storm. I couldn't hold back the tears anymore.

Valentina darted over, throwing her arms around me. I shook and trembled till I was nothing more than a heap of bones on the floor. She didn't let go. We stayed like that for the rest of the night.

Morning light poured through the window, warm but blinding. Valentina sprang up. "You need to feed." She started for the basement to fetch me a blood bag.

"I saw him." My tongue scratched against my throat.

Valentina spun around, eyes wide. "You saw who?"

I pushed myself up off the floor. "Elemi's human. Aldric Bannister. I saw him."

Her mouth dropped open. "Where? What happened?"

"On Pirate's Alley. I found a speakeasy called the Three Blind Mice. The Bannisters own it. I should have known right away. It was cloaked in magic."

Valentina listened intently while I recalled all the details of last night's events. How I almost lost control around him. She grinned from ear to ear. "You *want* him."

My cheeks burned. I shook it off. I couldn't let myself be seduced by him. He had magic running through his veins. *Ancient magic*. And I needed it.

"*No*. I want to link with him. That's all."

She smirked. "Sure. Keep telling yourself that. So, what's the plan now?"

I didn't really have one. "Well, I can't just march in there and tell him I'm a four-hundred-year-old Dhampir who needs help destroying an ancient coven that he is a descendant of."

Valentina giggled. "He'll think you're crazy."

I paced around the parlor. "I have to be patient. Follow him, get to know his routine, and wait for an opportunity."

Valentina huffed. "Gray, there's never going to be a right time to tell him that his whole life is a lie."

My heart raced. "Look, I know what he's about to go through. My life was ripped away from me without warning. No one deserves that. I just need time to find the right words to say to him."

Tears welled up in my eyes. Old wounds were reopening. I wasn't sure I was ready for it.

Today marked two weeks in a row of following Aldric around the city. I wanted to figure him out, but I was also stalling. Either way, he fascinated me. Everything about him was fluid and effortless. The way he walked, spoke, even the way he stirred his coffee was light and rhythmic.

Every morning, at eight a.m. sharp, he strolled into the Honey Butter Café. He would come out minutes later with a steaming cup of black coffee and a flaky croissant. He'd polish both off as he walked through the Quarter, smiling and savoring every bite. Keeping to himself mostly, he would stop to chat with a local merchant or street performer on occasion.

At night, he was at the Three Blind Mice. I discovered he lived in the loft directly above it. Like clockwork, he would leave for the night with a beautiful woman on his arm. A *different* woman.

He had each one of them wrapped around his finger with his infectious charm. The women would giggle and bat their lashes as he walked them home. He would escort them inside and stay a while, but always left before morning. He slept with them, but he didn't *sleep* with them.

Before heading back to the loft, he would walk down to the river front. That's when his face would change. His eyes would darken as he stared, vacant, out into the water. For hours on some nights.

Tonight, I had to fight the urge to touch him. Looking up at the sky, his brow furrowed harder than usual. It took everything in me to remain hidden. I wanted to wrap my arms around him, shielding him from the world. What was torturing him? What kept him up at night?

Valentina was right. I wanted him. Body and soul. I wanted to know him. Be with him. My heart ached because the minute I touched him, his life would no longer be the same. It would cease to be normal. But I couldn't take my eyes off him.

Like a drug, the pull to him was intoxicating. I wanted more. I imagined his mouth over mine, his body pressed up against me. My entire body tingled at the thought. I whimpered softly, my breath quickening.

Aldric spun around, straining his eyes in my direction. *Damn.* Did he hear me? I backed up, further into the shadows.

He froze, his eyes darting around like a mad man. "Is someone there?"

I held my breath. I could have kicked myself for being so careless.

Aldric called out again. "Hello? Anyone out there?"

I stood as still as I could. Beads of sweat dripped down my temples.

He took a couple steps back, convinced something was lurking in the dark. He moved backward toward the city before turning on his heel and sprinting down the alley.

I let out a sigh of relief and fell to my knees, bracing my trembling hands on the pavement. Darkness crept into my mind. I sickened myself. *You have no right to him. You're nothing but a demon. A monster.*

What sickened me more was that I knew what I had to do next. I had to turn him so we could link. I had no other choice. He was a Bannister Witch. His magic was stronger than the others'. I needed that power in my veins. Tears streamed down my cheeks, falling harder with each step I took.

Longing for my humanity, I mourned his. I said a silent prayer to the gods. *Forgive me for what I am about to do.*

FIVE

As I followed Aldric's scent, the back of my neck tingled. A subtle breeze fluttered past me. My heart pounded. *I was not alone.* Something was lurking behind me. Picking up my pace, I turned down a side street away from Aldric.

The fluttering continued. It darted back and forth like a firefly, just out of my line of sight, but teasing my peripheral. The shadow fragmented like shards of glass, staying with me as I turned down another street. There was only one thing that could move this way. *Dhampir.*

I picked up speed as it gained on me, sprinting around corners and twisting in and out of the shadows. I clenched my fists, my anger rising as I led it away from the city. The fluttering turned to footsteps. It shook the ground with each stride. It was getting closer. *Good.* My lips curled into a half-snarl, half-smirk as my eyes shaded to black. I gripped my daggers tight.

Closing in, its breath tickled my neck. I took a deep breath and braced myself. *Now.* Spinning around, I crouched down, daggers out in front of me. The shadow materialized, taking on a solid shape. A female. I lunged forward.

Her eyes widened, throwing up her hands to block my attack. A gust of wind pushed toward me, whipping my hair into my eyes. My daggers were ripped from my hands. Blood rushed to my head. *Magic.*

I threw my hands up, willing my body forward. I cried out, channeling every ounce of anger and rage. My mind raced to Aldric. Did I just lead them to him? I pushed forward, overcome with a need to protect him.

The wind howled, piercing my ear drums with the force of a banshee. Blood spilled out of my eyes, obscuring my vision. A pressure filled my head, threatening to burst it. I collapsed, dry heaving on the way down.

The wind stopped. I blinked the last drops of blood from eyes. With my heart pounding out of my chest, I raised my head toward my attacker. A chill passed through me. It was Elemi Bannister.

She stood over me, a raven-haired beauty, trembling with fury. The moonlight cast a glow across her face, illuminating her like a dark angel. Her pale skin was smooth, but her eyes gave away her age. She was much older than I.

The infinity necklace draped around her neck confirmed my suspicions. She was still with the Consilium. Why did she show me restraint? And why was she following me?

"Elemi." Her name rolled off my tongue like sour milk.

Her eyes were full of ice, cold and unflinching. "What do you want with my nephew?"

I returned her icy glare. "I mean him no harm. I can promise you that."

Elemi took a careful step forward. "You despise us for what we did to you, don't you?"

Flames flickered and flashed in my head. Memories of a long time ago. Being ripped from my bed and tied to a stake. Being set on fire. Despise is not the word I would use.

My eyes narrowed. "Ah yes, the night you created a monster. You should've seen the look on your brother's face when my flesh didn't burn. Why weren't *you* there? And Tobias, your demon king...no sign of him either. I guess you both just let Nicholas do your dirty work."

Elemi's mouth fell open. "Just to be clear, I had nothing to do with what happened to you that night. Nicholas had his own agenda. You have every right to be angry, but I will not let you punish Aldric for our mistakes."

I snapped, "Angry? That doesn't even begin to cover it."

Elemi lowered her eyes, her voice a pleading whisper. "Aldric is innocent. *Please*."

I wanted to stab her. "I was innocent too once. Just a young girl who was never given a choice. Funny, no one came forth on my behalf." I pursed my lips in disgust.

Elemi kept her head down. "There is so much you don't know. So much." Her eyes welled with tears.

I sighed. "Relax. As I said, I have no intentions of harming Aldric."

She looked up, puzzled. "Then why are you following him? What do you want?"

I took a deep breath and looked her dead in the eye. "I'm going to turn him and link with him."

She blinked rapidly, pondering my words. She swayed from side to side, as if lost in a dream. "It makes sense that you would find him. All these years, I've cloaked him with magic. But magic doesn't seem to affect you the way it does others."

I shrugged it off. "Nonsense. I didn't track him. I found him by accident."

Elemi's eyes drifted off, trancelike. "There are no accidents in our world. I don't want Aldric in Tobias's hands. He's not the same man I believed in hundreds of years ago. Darkness consumes him. Aldric is safer with you."

I was stunned. Dumfounded. My head was pounding. "I don't understand. You're with the Consilium. Why would you think he's safer with me?"

She looked away. "This world will suffer at their...our hands. It's too late for me, but Aldric still has a chance at freedom. Once the two of you link, I won't be able to cloak him anymore. It will be up to you to protect him. Don't make me regret this." Elemi's face twisted in pain.

I understood the sacrifice she was making. Committing an act of betrayal against her demon family to protect her human one.

I let out a deep breath. "In four hundred years, I've never been able to piece together what happened to me that night. I've been chasing ghosts. But Aldric has given me hope. I will get my answers, and then I will destroy every last one of them."

I had to get to Aldric. I started toward the Quarter when Elemi called out.

"You should start with Jane. She might be able to help you get some of those answers." Her tone was firm.

The sound of my mother's name turned my blood to venom, but I swallowed my rage. Without looking back, I sprinted forward, leaving Elemi alone at the edge of the river bank.

Dear Aldric,

Dhampirs are real. We are not what you expect us to be. You cannot hide behind your crosses or braids of garlic. Sunlight cannot harm us. You will not be able to recognize one on the street. Not yet. I was like you once. Human. I believed that all creatures were inherently good. That was another lifetime. There is a war going on behind the veil. A war between monsters and demons. That veil is about to come down. Only you can help me stop that from happening. If we fail, blood will spill into the streets and there won't be anything human left. I will reveal all that has been hidden from you. Get ready. I am already on my way.

- Gray

I tucked the letter into my coat and headed out the door. Sneaking into the Three Blind Mice would not be difficult. It was what came after that terrified me. Rehearsing what I would say to Aldric, butterflies danced in my stomach. No matter how I arranged the words, it sounded ridiculous.

Slipping into the bar, the usual crowd of twenty-somethings swayed to the old jazz melodies. Familiar songs from distant pasts that clung to them like lovers. Darting past the band, I charged up the stairs to Aldric's loft and picked the lock with one of Valentina's hair pins.

Just past ten p.m., the loft was empty, as I suspected it would be. I wondered which beauty had the pleasure of his charms tonight. None of that would matter in the morning. I shut the door behind me and flicked on the lights.

The room was wide open with no dividers. A brown leather couch stood in the center amidst small piles of books and album covers. Across from it was a wood coffee table with an empty bottle of bourbon and a half-smoked cigar, propped delicately inside a marble ashtray. Traces of honey and tobacco still lingered. A king size bed stuck out a few feet away, its blankets tucked in tight and unruffled. *Did he ever sleep here?*

Placing my letter against the empty bottle on the table, an alarm went off inside my head. I froze. Footsteps. *Damn.* Why was he back so soon? As I paced around the room in a frenzy, the footsteps got louder. I should have made sure he had plans for the night. Just my luck, this was the one night he didn't.

I spun around, panicked. Nothing but a closet to hide in. *Great.* He was almost to the door. My heart beat loud and fast in my chest. With palms sweating, I threw myself inside the closet just as the front door opened.

Aldric stumbled inside, stinking of liquor and cheap perfume. He cried out, banging himself into the coffee table. A glass shattered. Keys crashed to the floor. He was drunker than usual. I held my breath, waiting for him to pass out.

Two hours went by in that small, dark closet. My skin burned and itched from the wool sweater I was shoved up against.

Every time he poured himself another drink, the bottle hit the table a little harder. He cycled through a raw range of emotions that bordered on hysteria. Going back and forth between sighing, laughing, and talking out loud. He mumbled with a slurred incoherence that was undecipherable.

Silence. *Finally*. It was short-lived. He ruffled a piece of paper. My breath quickened. *The letter*. I'd been so consumed with being trapped in his closet that I had almost forgotten why I came here to begin with.

The sound of his voice reading it aloud made my stomach turn. Drunk and chaotic, he burst out laughing. He read it again. And again. Now, on his third read through, his voice changed. It was hoarse, raspy, choking on the words. A twinge of guilt stabbed at me. *I shouldn't be here*.

His mumbling turned to snoring. I breathed a sigh of relief. Pushing the door open, I peeked out, still terrified that he would see me. My fingers unclenched. He was asleep sitting up, with his head cocked back against the couch, the letter still in his hands.

His face was calm and serene. I laid a blanket over him and brushed a strand of hair back from his forehead. I couldn't resist. Seeing him in this state, drunk and tortured, pulled at my heart like quicksand. I couldn't bring myself to leave.

I had to face this. It wasn't fair to leave him with that letter and no explanation. I took a seat at the other end of the couch and waited. I watched his chest rise and fall, all the way into the morning.

SIX

MORNING LIGHT SPILLED INTO THE LOFT. THE STAINED GLASS windows cast a kaleidoscope of color onto the walls. I sat there, mesmerized by the reflections they created on his hardwood floors. Reds, golds, and deep blues swirled together like spilled paint.

Aldric let out a groan and grabbed his head. My heart skipped, snapping me out of my reverie. With my stomach in knots, I fought the urge to run away. He yawned, struggling to open his eyes. I didn't move a muscle.

A few minutes passed before he noticed me. He blinked a few times and cleared his throat. "Uh, hello." It was more of a question than a greeting.

I stiffened. "Hello."

His eyes lit up in recognition. "I've seen you before. Downstairs, at the bar the other night."

I racked my brain for words, but my voice betrayed me.

He leaned forward. "Did we...you know? I mean...you *are* stunning."

My cheeks burned. "*We did not.* Do you remember anything about last night?"

Aldric shook his head. "Not much. Had some crazy dreams,

though. Like, really weird shit." He chuckled and reached for the bottle of bourbon.

I jumped up, snatching it away before he could get to it. "You need to pull it together. Take a shower. Eat some breakfast. *Change your clothes.*"

He chuckled again. "In that order?"

He started to stand up, but his legs buckled. His eyes landed on the letter. Picking it up and reading it again, his face paled. The realization that last night was not a dream began to sink in.

His brow crinkled. Beads of sweat formed. "Did you write this?"

I nodded, holding my breath. The awkwardness of the situation was sinking in.

He stood up, bracing himself against the back of the couch. "Just my luck. All the pretty ones are bat-shit crazy. I'm going to need you to leave darlin'."

Aldric tensed as I stood up without warning. "I'm not crazy. If you'll just let me explain..."

His eyes shifted toward the front door as he gripped the back of the couch, his heart rate beating through the roof.

I sat back down, in hopes of appearing less threatening. "If you really want me to leave, I will, but I need you to hear me out first. Please."

Still clutching my letter, Aldric's eyes continued to dart back and forth between me and the door. He swallowed hard. "Alright, I'll humor you. But then, you really need to get going."

Relief swept through me, but also, fear. *Would I be able to convince him?*

I cleared my throat, my lips quivering. "My name is Gray, which you already know from the letter. I'm not sure how to say this. It sounds absurd when I say it out loud. Well, it sounds crazy just thinking it too. So, I'm just going to come out and say it. I'm an immortal who feasts on human blood. A Dhampir. I've been one for over four hundred years. I didn't choose it. I've been hunting the ones who made me. The Consilium. I'm here because I need your help."

Aldric's eyes narrowed, then widened. "Are you on medication? Is there someone I can call for you?"

He spoke as if I were a mental patient. I couldn't blame him. To humans, my world only existed in fairytales and nightmares. We were campfire stories told in the middle of the night to strike fear into children. How could he even begin to fathom that these tales might be true?

"I know it sounds unbelievable, but the Consilium have discovered a way to link Witches and Dhampirs using blood magic. They're creating a new breed, an army of them, turning humans against their will. If they get their way, they will take over your world. I need your blood to help me stop them." My hands trembled.

Aldric took a deep breath, running a hand through his blond hair. "Look, I can see that *you believe* what you are telling me, but that doesn't make it true darlin'. Now, why don't we go downstairs and make some calls. Try to find some help for you."

Desperation clawed at me. I sprang to my feet. "For the last time, I am *not* crazy. Haven't you ever wondered why you felt different? Or why your Aunt Elemi never looks any older?"

Aldric's face flushed bright red. "How do you know about my aunt? Have you been following me?" His hand tightened on the chain around his neck.

"Your aunt is a Bannister Witch. That magic runs through your blood. You're even wearing a crescent moon necklace. I bet she gave that to you, didn't she?"

His skin was pale, clammy. He shook his head. "This is insane. We don't live in a world where any of that is possible."

"*Yes, we do.* You just didn't know it existed."

I stood still and silent, waiting for Aldric to respond. Would he make a run for it? Run out screaming into the streets like a madman? I would.

He sat down and poured himself a drink. "A part of me wants to believe you. *That's* what's crazy." He stared into the glass before knocking it back.

My heart fluttered. "I can prove everything. Give me a chance to show you. What have you got to lose?"

Aldric chuckled. "My sanity." His shoulders relaxed slightly.

I let out a sigh of relief. There was a mischievous gleam in his eyes I hadn't noticed before.

"So, how are you going to prove it? You're not going to bite me, are you?"

I rolled my eyes. "I didn't come here to attack you, Aldric. We can go to the Wolf and Crescent. It's in the bayou. The other Witches are there. They'll show you who you are."

Aldric took a swig from the bottle. "I've been to the bayou a hundred times. I've never seen or heard of this place."

I chuckled. *That's the point*, I thought. "The Wolf and Crescent is cloaked from humans. Your magic hasn't been awakened yet, so you wouldn't be able to see it. If you don't believe me, call Elemi. Although, doing so could put her in danger."

He raised an eyebrow, alarmed. "I don't understand. Why would *she* be in danger?"

There was so much he didn't know. "She has gone to great lengths to keep you hidden from the Consilium. You're the last human descendant of the Bannisters. Let's just say, they wouldn't be pleased with her for keeping you from them."

His apprehension hovered in the space between us. He sighed. "I still think this is nuts, but I'll play along."

Now, I just had to convince the Witches to awaken his magic. They weren't too pleased with me the last time I showed up.

Rummaging through his closet, I found a pair of sneakers and tossed them to him. "Put these on. It's a long walk."

He shook his head but did as I asked.

Aldric watched me like a hawk as we made our way through the marsh. I hadn't been this close to a human in a long time. He fascinated me. His body was strong, yet fragile at the same time. He stiffened every time I made the slightest gesture. I couldn't help but chuckle.

He stopped, throwing his hands up. "What's so funny? Oh wait, never mind. I almost forgot, you're a crazy person."

I burst out laughing as we exchanged a playful look. He was lovely to look at. He couldn't help but be charming. It was in his nature.

"To answer your question, I've never had a man fear me for *not* being a Dhampir. I find that *very* funny."

That mischievous gleam in his eye returned. He shook his head, unable to keep the smirk from forming. There was an ease about him I enjoyed. I couldn't remove the grin from my face as we walked.

As we moved closer to the Wolf and Crescent, the scent of smoke hit my nose. Faint at first, but sharper and more pungent as we neared. Uneasiness formed in the pit of my stomach. Something wasn't right.

I spotted flames leaping out from behind the trees. I broke into a sprint. Aldric called out behind me. Smoke poured out in every direction, filling my lungs. *The Wolf and Crescent was on fire.*

Aldric caught up as I sank to my knees, shaking. He pulled up the edge of his shirt, covering his mouth and nose with it. "Gray, we need to get help."

I couldn't hear a single heartbeat but his. Fear rattled through me. "Trust me, there is no life inside."

Plopping down next to me, we sat in silence and watched it burn.

Night fell upon us. The flames began to smolder out. The dampness of the swamps kept the fire from spreading, but the Wolf and Crescent was no more than sticks and a frame.

I moved toward it to get a closer look. Aldric followed, tugging at my arm. "Be careful. This structure isn't safe."

I nodded. His chivalry sent a warm rush through my veins, but only for a moment. He still had no idea what I was capable of. That I couldn't be harmed the way he could be.

Creeping along the base boards, I scanned the wreckage. I wasn't sure what I was more afraid of—finding the Witches dead...or alive. To my relief, it was neither. I let out a sigh. "They got away."

Aldric crinkled his brow. "I don't get it. Why wouldn't they come back with help? What would make them just desert their home?"

I shivered. "Not what, but *who* is the real question. I have a pretty good idea."

We sifted through the rubble, searching for anything that could tell us what happened. There wasn't much left, just ash and dust. Picking through piles of burnt wood, something caught Aldric's eye. He fixated on it. With trembling hands, he bent down and picked something up, drawing in a sharp breath. It was a crescent moon hanging from a silver chain, identical to the one he was wearing.

I touched his arm. "Do you believe me, now?"

Aldric shook his head in disbelief. With white knuckles, he clasped the necklace in the palm of his hand. "This isn't happening. This...can't be real." His eyes scanned the room, darting back and forth between me and the floor.

"Aldric, breathe. You're as pale as a ghost." He was in shock.

"Ghost? Do those exist too?" His knees wobbled. I feared he might pass out.

"No. I don't think so. I mean...I don't know. Look, we have to go. Whoever did this will be back. And if they're working for the Consilium, then we'll be outnumbered. It's not safe here anymore."

Aldric was disheveled. His icy blond hair matted against his forehead. His eyes were cracked, dry, and red from the smoke. He flinched as I reached for his hand.

I sighed. "You have to start trusting me. I'm not going to hurt you."

He nodded, unsure, staring off into the distance. There was a battle raging within him. A struggle to grasp this new reality. I backed away, giving him a moment to collect himself.

The smoke and ash fell over us, coating our skin and hair. Aldric wiped his face with his shirt. "I need a drink. I feel like my head is going to explode."

I licked my lips. "You and me both. First, I need you to take a deep breath and close your eyes."

He stepped back. "What are you going to do? Drink from me?" His chest tightened, pulse racing.

I chuckled. "Not that kind of drink, Aldric. I meant, I need a real drink. *Whiskey*."

His heart pounded like a drum beneath his chest. I had never traveled with a human before. Not the way *we* travel. The force and speed could tear them apart. But Aldric was different. He was a Bannister. Human or not, Bannisters were not easily destroyed.

"Relax. I'm going to get us out of here. Just don't resist and *don't* let go of my hand."

Aldric grumbled, rubbing his temples. "Fine. Nothing to lose, right?" His tone was sharp. Annoyed, he grabbed my hand, hard.

A spark shot up my spine. His eyes widened. He felt it too. The energy between us cracked and sizzled. His pulse quickened. He grazed the back of my hand as our fingers touched and interlocked. I felt light and tingly.

I pulled him close. "Close your eyes."

He nodded but his eyes lingered on my lips. His breath was warm and heavy.

I reached up and pushed down his eyelids, gentle and soft, letting my fingers trace the line of his jaw. His heart beat faster as I guided his arms around my waist. His body leaned into mine as he exhaled, shoulders dropping. It was now or never.

I tightened my grip. "Hold on tight. This is going to hurt."

SEVEN

THE DAWN WAS BREAKING OVER THE HORIZON AS WE SKIDDED TO A stop outside of Lafayette Cemetery. I spun around, bracing Aldric as the world snapped back into focus.

The first time I used my demon speed was back home, in England. I was hunting for food in Pendle Forest. In the beginning, I had panicked when I found myself surrounded by a vicious pack of wolves.

I could have ripped them apart with my bare hands, but unaware of my strength, I ran. Afterward, I was disoriented for hours. Like being drunk and hungover at the same time. It took me decades to master the laws of my own equilibrium.

Aldric fell to his knees. His hands shot out in front of him and slammed onto the ground. I grabbed his shoulders to steady him. Dry heaving, he struggled to catch his breath.

"My head. It won't stop spinning."

I stroked his hair. "Deep breaths. In and out. There, that's it. Open your eyes. Let them adjust."

The effects of the run were amplified by a thousand for a human. I felt horrible, but I was relieved that he was in one piece.

His breathing steadied, his heartbeat returning to normal. I wiped the sweat from my brow and sank down beside him.

He looked at me wide-eyed. "How did you do that?"

I shrugged. "It's just something that I can do. We all can."

He shook his head, amazement in his eyes. He chuckled. "Incredible. I hope I wasn't the first person to almost pass out on you."

I looked down. A pang of guilt shot through me. "No. You were just...the first."

Aldric's eyes widened. "You've never done that with anyone before? How did you know it wouldn't kill me?"

My cheeks were hot. Nausea crept up. "I didn't."

He burst out laughing. "Thanks for not killing me. See, you are crazy." He nudged me playfully.

My cheeks got hotter. "I'm sorry. I should have warned you. Sometimes I just do things..."

Aldric touched my arm. "Hey, I'm good. Still in one piece. Don't beat yourself up about it." He waved his hands around, wiggling his fingers to show me they were all still there.

I forced myself to meet his gaze. It flickered with a thirst for adventure, infectious and sparking something in me that had long since been put out.

I pulled him gently to his feet. "We should head back to your place."

We were exposed, out in the open. Anyone could have been watching.

Racing down Pirate's Alley, toward the Three Blind Mice, my thoughts drifted to the Wolf and Crescent. *Where had all the Witches gone?*

Approaching Aldric's bar, a figure lurked outside, petite with a mass of ruby red hair. *Valentina.* She paced back and forth, nostrils flared. Her eyes matched the color of her hair.

"Val, what's wrong?"

She sucked in a sharp breath. "After you left last night, I went for a walk. I wandered into the Quarter. I was so caught up in the festivities, it took me a while to notice I was being followed. At first, I thought it was one of the Witches, but then I smelled blood."

Dhampir. My fists clenched, sweat forming between my fingers. "Who was it?"

She shook her head. "I don't know. I was able to lose him eventually. I thought I covered my tracks, but when I got back to the house, it was on fire."

My stomach dropped, knocking out my breath. First the Wolf and Crescent and now our house. The Consilium was sending us a message.

A faint prickle traveled up my back. "We have to get off the street."

Once inside Aldric's loft, I went straight for the whiskey. It soothed me and coated my throat like medicine, but my hand still trembled with each sip I took. *Were we even safe here?*

Aldric, who had been quiet since we arrived, broke the silence. "Why are these people...I mean, Dhampirs after you?"

Valentina and I exchanged a loaded look. A look that held centuries of secrets between us. I took a deep breath before knocking back the rest of my drink.

"It's complicated. The Consilium made us this way against our will. Well, technically, my mother made me. She was working for them. Now they think we belong to them." My voice trailed off, overcome with anger and sadness.

Valentina squeezed my hand. "They have my brother, Dragos. He's on their side. They've taken everything from us. So we're going to take everything from them. Or die trying."

Dragos. I longed for the day that I would get to wrap my hands around his neck. I gripped the arm of my chair, the leather cracking under my fingertips.

Aldric fixated on my hands, his voice unsteady. "Where do I fit into all of this?"

Seeing his beautiful face, pained and twisted in agony, my heart sank. He was an innocent in all of this, but part of it, nonetheless.

I cleared my throat. "Centuries ago, Dhampirs hid in the

shadows. Outcasts, feeding on animals and fresh corpses. They feared humans. Saw the destruction they caused. One day, a Dhampir discovered it was humans who were the weak ones. Tasting fresh blood, power surged through him, making him stronger."

Aldric leaned forward and rested his elbows on his knees, giving me his full attention. I poured myself another drink and continued.

"The Dhampir's name was Tobias Wynter. He showed his new strength to the others and they worshipped him. But it wasn't enough. He wanted more. He wanted to live outside of the shadows."

Valentina chimed in, rubbing her temples. "He stole an ancient spell book, the *Sang Magi*. In it was a spell linking Dhampirs and Witches with blood magic. He found a Witch to link to and created the Consilium. So now we no longer hide in the shadows from humans. We just hide from each other."

Aldric crinkled his brow and scratched his head. "I still don't understand what this has to do with me."

A lump formed in my throat. "The Witch that Tobias linked with, the one who helped him form the Consilium...his name was Nicholas Bannister."

Aldric's mouth dropped open. His eyes burned into mine. The weight of my words hung over him like a dark cloud.

I pressed on. "You see, I need *your* blood, Aldric. That, along with recovering the *Sang Magi* spell book, will give us the power to go up against them."

Sitting in a room with not one but two Dhampirs, the realization of his new reality was beginning to sink in. He was the missing piece of the puzzle. The key to defeating the Consilium.

My heart thumped, pulse racing. *What if he didn't have it in him?* They were still his family, regardless of what they had done. And he was still human, with all the emotions and sentiments that go along with that.

Valentina pulled me away. She lowered her voice. "There are few who can decipher and interpret the *Sang Magi*. Only those few can seal the link between Witch and Dhampir." Her tone was cryptic, but I knew what she was getting at.

A chill passed through me. Pythia was in possession of the *Sang Magi*, and she knew how to use it. She was a vile creature. The thought of the sacred text in her hands made my blood curdle. She was known as *Tenebris Sacerdos*. The Dark Priestess. She came from a long line of Oracles, Witches who glimpsed visions of the future. Her ancestors were used as a tool by Apollo, and he treated them poorly. They were stripped of free will and bound to him by blood magic. They grew to despise Dhampirs.

Pythia had an extra disdain for me for some reason. We had crossed paths a few times, but never had much to say to each other.

I shook my head. "It will be impossible to take back the *Sang Magi* from Pythia. Even if it were, who else could perform the link?"

Valentina's eyes lit up. "*The Keeper*. We won't have to take the *Sang Magi*. Not yet, anyway. He has it memorized, cover to cover."

My heart was pounding. The Keeper was the guardian of all things that were a part of our world. He protected our books, talismans, and scrolls. He kept our history, our records, and our secrets. He had been guarding the *Sang Magi* until it had been stolen from him centuries ago.

There was only one problem. He was hidden by *Dissimulare*. A cloaking spell. No one had seen or spoken to him since the text was taken. "Val, *we* don't have the power to locate him."

Valentina licked her lips, curling them into a smile. "We will. An old friend owes me a favor. His name is Seven. He can get us there."

Another old friend. I hoped this one wasn't as creepy as the last. "I've never heard of him."

Valentina's eyes sparked like a flame. "No one has. That's why he's perfect."

I hoped she was right. Trust was not something I was fond of. Few creatures had mine. But if this Seven character could take us to The Keeper, it might be worth the risk.

Aldric was glued to the window, his thoughts a million miles away. He stared out, listless, peering through the colored glass. His skin perspired with each scattered breath he took. I approached with caution.

He flinched, closing his eyes and folding his arms into his chest. "Everything has been a lie. My entire life. I have no idea who I really am. Elemi has kept all of this from me...these secrets."

I wanted to comfort him, but I froze. I couldn't move a muscle. Nothing would make him feel better now. No one could have comforted me amidst my own family's secrets and betrayals. I had to move through the dark on my own. And even now, centuries later, I was *still* dealing with it. For Aldric, these were fresh wounds. Yet, I understood why he was kept in the dark. Whereas I was plunged into it.

"Elemi was protecting you. She was keeping you safe. That was not the case with my family. You have a right to be angry, but at least you know her intentions were good."

Aldric whipped around to face me. "Safe from who? From my own family? From you? A lot of good it did. Here I am in a room with two Dhampirs who believe I am a direct descendant of a Witch that destroyed both their lives. I'm a human. I have no power. She hasn't kept me safe. She's kept me weak and ignorant."

We had more in common than I had imagined. We had different weaknesses and vulnerabilities, but the outcome was the same. Abandonment can take many forms. Betrayal has many paths. His led him to mine for a specific reason. I would not forsake that.

"Aldric, you're safe with *me*. I will never let anything, or anyone, hurt you. I'll never lie to you. I promise."

He leaned in close. With our faces only inches apart, I could feel his breath on my lips. He looked at me with a hunger I had never seen before. His pulse was fast and erratic. I swallowed hard. His lips moved closer to mine, almost touching. His scent consumed me, awakening my senses. *I wanted to taste him*. His hand reached out toward my face.

Valentina cleared her throat. "I need to feed."

She wasn't the only one. I was lightheaded and dizzy. The thirst clawed at me like a vulture. But we were out of blood bags. They had burned, along with everything else we owned. I could control myself around Aldric, but Valentina was unpredictable. She was irritable to begin with, and that would soon lead to delirium, then madness.

Her voice was hoarse. "Go get us more blood bags."

I shook my head. "We can't risk it. No one can know we're here."

Valentina let out a dramatic sigh and draped herself across the couch. "Let's have a little taste of your boyfriend then." Her words slurred like she was in a drunken stupor.

I raised an eyebrow at her. "No, Val. We are not going to *feed* on Aldric. Don't even think about it."

She pouted. "Well, who then? I *have* to feed, Gray."

I did as well. I took no pleasure in feeding off humans, but we didn't have any other options. We would both snap. The thirst would take over and Aldric's blood would be spilled. I promised to keep him safe. That meant even from myself. Lucky for us, there was an entire bar downstairs filled with humans. There was bound to be some unsavory ones lurking about.

Aldric watched me close. His expression was a mixture of fascination and fear. "So, you want me to be your human blood bag now?"

His tone was sharp, reminding me of what I was. It filled me with shame. Having to drink blood to stay alive sickened me. Tears welled up. I swallowed hard to keep the sob from rising in my throat. *Why did I care what he thought of me?*

Aldric's face fell. "I'm sorry. I didn't mean...I know it's not your fault."

I shook my head and wiped the tears from my cheeks. "No. *I'm* sorry. Sorry you got dragged into all of this."

Aldric took my hand in his, soft and comforting. "What do you need me to do?"

I raised my head, forcing myself to look in his eyes. "I need you to bring us someone from downstairs. Someone no one will...miss."

I knew that what I was asking of him was more than he should give. The risks, the consequences, the morality of it all, was too much a burden for him to bear. No, I couldn't let him do this.

Before I could protest, he spun around and charged toward the door. Hesitating only for a moment to look back at me. His eyes darkened and his hands trembled. "Just make it quick."

I nodded, understanding, as he flew out the door.

Valentina sprang up from the couch. "Well, thank Apollo. It's about time."

Thirty minutes passed before Aldric returned. I clasped my hands together to keep them from shaking. Valentina eyed the door like a rabid dog. I stood in front of her as he entered.

Aldric was accompanied by a wiry man with puffy eyes and brown hair that was matted against his shiny forehead. He stank of cheap liquor and cigarettes. The man's lips formed into a smirk as he leered at us.

Aldric shoved him toward us like he was walking the plank. Valentina let out a low, guttural sound as she pounced. I was right behind her.

I clamped down on his neck. His body jolted. My veins were on fire as his blood entered. He cried out. Valentina bit down on his wrist. We drank till there was nothing left. No other thoughts or desires mattered. Only blood. We sucked away his life like quicksand. His breath slowed to a whisper. His body relaxed and then went limp. He was dead.

The fresh blood flowed through me like a river. My thoughts were clear again. My senses renewed. Valentina's eyes glowed bright, like a pair of fireflies. We embraced in a sea of relief.

Aldric backed up against the wall, his eyes and mouth wide open. His face frozen in a state of terror.

Valentina paid no attention. "We have to burn the body. He'll start to decompose soon, and the stench is rather unpleasant."

I drew in a sharp breath. Annoyed by her flippancy. "*Val*..."

She threw me a blank stare. "What?"

I nodded toward Aldric.

"Oh, ah. Um...sorry." She bit her lower lip.

He threw his hands up, waving them around like a madman. "*You just...you...just killed someone. In my apartment. You were just supposed to drink a little. But he...he's dead."*

I took a step toward him. "Please sit down before you fall over."

He jumped back. "Don't come any closer."

"Aldric, I'm not going to hurt you."

He was on the verge of hysteria. "No. This is crazy. There is a dead body in my living room."

My heart sank. He saw a monster in front of him. I shouldn't have let him see this. I should have told him to leave the room. It was too late for that now.

I sighed. "This is who we are. This is what we do. We drink blood to survive. I told you this."

Aldric sank to his knees. "I know. But...seeing it. It's just too much. I don't think I can do this."

The realization hit me like a ton of bricks. Aldric didn't believe we were actual Dhampirs until he watched us drink that man's blood. He thought he did, but it wasn't real in his head. Now it was, and it horrified him. He'd never forget what he saw me do, and it would haunt him for the rest of his human life. I had to fix this.

"Aldric, you're a part of this, whether you want to be or not. This life, our world, it's in your blood. It's where you belong. Don't run from it. It will just keep chasing you till there's nothing left. Believe me, I know."

Aldric's eyes locked with mine in fear and desperation. He swallowed hard, his body trembling. "I'm sorry. I *can't* do this."

I bit my lip to keep the tears from falling. Everything ached. I barely knew him, but a hole was already starting to form at the thought of his absence. He was losing his mind. His sanity. And it was all my fault.

I shivered, my thoughts darkening. "I'm not going to do to you what they did to me."

His eyes darted back and forth between me and Valentina. She stayed quiet, still. He wouldn't budge. His mind was made up. It was time to go.

I lowered my head. "I understand. We'll let you get back to your normal life."

Valentina was already out the door before I could finish. I did my best to smile even though my heart was aching. I wanted warmth to be the last thing he remembered about me, not bloodshed.

Aldric ran a shaky hand through his wet hair. "Gray...I—"

"Take care of yourself, Aldric. They *will* come for you. It's only a matter of time. Keep your eyes open and watch your back."

I sprinted out the front door without looking back.

Outside, the air was damp and sticky. It only added to my uneasiness. We had nowhere to go and no one we could trust. The Consilium could have been anywhere, watching us at that very moment. Despair filled me like a disease. I slumped down on the sidewalk and buried my face in my hands.

Valentina draped an arm across my shoulders. "I've sent word to Seven. He'll meet us at the port in two days."

I shuddered. "And then what? Without Aldric, I have no one to link with. I'm so tired of losing. Maybe I'm not supposed to win."

Every time I thought I had my head above water, the tide would drag me further down. It was hopeless.

Valentina pulled me up off the ground to face her. "You need to pull it together. We'll find another way. Another Witch. We're so close. *I can feel it*. They wouldn't have burned our house to the ground if we weren't."

She was right. We *were* a threat to the Consilium. Losing Aldric was a major setback, but I had to keep moving forward. We'd come too far for me to fall apart now.

"Sorry. Thanks for snapping me out of my pity party."

Valentina nodded. "That's what I'm here for. We need to lay low until Seven arrives."

We made our way to the bayou just as the rain came down upon us for the first time since we'd set foot in the city. My breath was heavy, like my heart, as I prayed that we would make it through the next two nights.

EIGHT

IT WAS A LONG WALK TO THE PORT. WE TOOK CARE WITH OUR steps and kept to the outskirts. The moon was full and bright, illuminating our path. We darted between the fragments of its light. With my nerves on edge, I flinched at every twig that snapped and every bird that crowed. At times, it was almost too quiet. I imagined monsters, greater than us, lurking behind every corner. I shivered with every step I took.

Valentina appeared calm, but every few feet, her nose would crinkle in different directions, a nervous tick she developed years ago. We stayed quiet as we forged ahead. The silence drew me to my own thoughts. To Aldric and that look in his eyes. What was he doing at this moment? Did he flee the city? Or was he still paralyzed with fear? I wished that he could escape this life, but it wasn't possible. There was no running, only hiding. The demons always caught up.

The docks were in sight. I spotted a cluster of ships huddled together in the harbor. *We made it*. My heart fluttered with excitement. Valentina shot me a relieved look. We were almost to the ships when a wave of magic rippled through me. It stopped us both dead in our tracks. A chill shot down my spine.

There were five, maybe six—no, ten figures in the distance, blocking our path to the docks. They moved toward us. Valentina crouched down and let out a deep snarl. I whipped out my daggers and planted my feet. The ground shook underneath me. The figures swarmed us. We pressed our backs together as they circled. My stomach dropped. It was the Crescent Witches.

The Witches hissed and spat at us. They chanted and spoke in strange tongues. I scanned the mob for Josephine, but she was nowhere in sight. My muscles tightened. I spotted the Harpy. She narrowed her eyes at Valentina. They were not here to give us a warm send off.

My mind raced. We could take out a handful of them in a heartbeat, but not before the other half would rain spells down upon us. We had nothing to shield us. Without magic, we were as good as dead. As if reading my mind, the Harpy stepped forward.

"You demons brought your curse down upon our house. We have lived in peace with the Consilium for hundreds of years. Now we are being hunted. Because of *you*."

She was right, but she was also wrong. I addressed the angry mob. "There is only peace when you obey them. They burned your house down for helping us. Is that how you want to live? That's not peace, that's servitude. I'm sure your ancestors had higher hopes for your kind."

The crowd gasped as if my words were daggers, piercing through the air. The hissing continued. A few of them lifted their hands toward the sky to conjure the elements. Others shrieked and waved their talismans. It was chaos. Where was Josephine? Samuel?

Valentina pulled out her sword and held it out in front of her. I lowered my voice for her ears only. "They are going to attack us. We need to create a distraction so we can make a run for it."

My heart beat out of control. There were only a few steps between them, and our safety. We were so close.

Valentina huffed. "I am going to rip open every single one of them."

"We can't fight them all. Not today. There's too many."

After a long pause, she sighed but nodded her head in agreement. We would have to be fast. We only had one shot at this. "When I say go, throw your sword at the Harpy as quick as you can. They will rush to protect her. Don't stop running until we reach the ship."

A smirk spread across Valentina's face as she eyed the Harpy. A look of sadistic pleasure passed over her.

I took a deep breath and said a silent prayer to Apollo. My breath became a whisper. "Okay. Get ready...now. Go."

Valentina raised her sword high above her head. I clenched my fists and braced for impact. She started forward, then stopped.

The Witches erupted into shrieks and gasps. They ran around in a frenzy. We both froze, but they weren't looking at us anymore. They scurried around us like we weren't even there.

Valentina shook her head, confused. "What's happening? Are they drunk?"

My adrenaline raced, and I was bordering on delirium. "It's like we're invisible."

The Witches flailed around in a fit of hysteria. This was our opening. I nodded at Valentina. She understood. It was time to make a run for it. That's when I saw him.

Aldric. Just a few feet away. He was with Elemi. Her arms extended out and her eyes were rolled back into her head. *She was cloaking us.* Aldric was helping her. My heart skipped.

Valentina let out a sigh of relief. "Good timing. I take back everything bad I ever said about him." We both chuckled as the Witches fled in horror.

Elemi strutted toward us with the air of an aristocrat. Every step was poised and polished. Calculated. Aldric followed behind her. My heartbeat quickened when we locked eyes.

"It looks like we showed up just in time." Aldric flashed me a nervous grin.

Elemi gazed at him like a proud parent. "I knew the day would come when Aldric would become like us. I tried to prolong it for as long as I could. But it is too dangerous to keep him in the dark. I have told him everything."

Aldric gave Elemi's hand a gentle squeeze. His eyes were bloodshot, and his forehead creased.

I smiled. "Thank you for coming to our aid. I won't forget this."

Elemi tipped her hat in gratitude and gave a slight bow. "Just keep him safe, Gray."

I swallowed hard. "I will protect him with my life."

Valentina squeezed my arm. "It's time to go. Seven is here."

Aldric stiffened, looking out toward the sea, wide-eyed.

Seven's ship stood tall in the harbor, a magnificent spectacle. The word *Resistance* was scrawled across it in black. Its magic radiated out like sun beams. Like something not of this world.

Valentina had filled me in on what she knew of him, but Seven was still a bit of a mystery. A Dhampir-pirate, he ruled the seas like a thief in the night. He was believed to be a direct descendant of the goddess Inanna, a Sumerian known for her short temper and most famous for her descent into the Underworld. Inanna also controlled the stars and the tides.

Some believed that it was because of her that Seven was given the gift of fast travel. He could bend time and space to his will. Not a time traveler by any means but, rather, he could travel above it.

We bade farewell to Elemi and made our way toward the ship. Valentina was giddied with excitement. "There he is."

Seven emerged like a giant at the head of the ship's bow. He was barbaric, with arms thicker than most men's thighs. But he was not like most men. He was not a man at all. He was a warrior.

Seven came down to greet us. His long black hair blew wild in the warm Louisiana wind. His skin was sun soaked and glistened underneath a hint of stubble. His eyes lit up like two gemstones reflecting the light of the sun, full of honey and amber. Even aboard this massive ship, he resembled a god.

There was a crew of about thirty on board. Some Dhampir, some human, but all of them intent on their duties. They moved around the ship like an orchestrated dance, preparing us for departure.

Once on deck, we were encased in magic. It cracked and sizzled like a lightning storm, yet soft and quiet like a slow breeze. It took a few moments to adjust my vision and my senses.

Seven's height was greater up close. He towered over us as Valentina squealed with delight. She batted her eyelashes at him. "Seven, you are looking *rather* well."

He picked her up and spun her around. "You are a sight for sore eyes. The gods would leave the sky if they could to come down and ravage you." Valentina giggled as he set her down.

His golden eyes turned toward me. "You must be Gray." I nodded while he looked me over. He gave me a slight bow. "I am humbled and enchanted." He spoke like a nobleman, but that was the extent of his refinement.

Aldric was not impressed. He raised his chin to look him square in the eye. "Nice ship, but I've seen better."

Seven chuckled. "And you are?"

"Aldric Bannister."

Seven stiffened and narrowed his eyes at Valentina.

Aldric scoffed. "Is there a problem?"

The uneasy look on Seven's face left as quick as it came. He flashed a smile at Aldric. If it was insincere, I couldn't tell. "No problem, my friend. We can't all be perfect."

The tension was as thick as it was deafening. *Aldric was going to have to stop telling people his last name.*

I broke the silence. "Thank you for letting us aboard your ship. I owe you a debt of gratitude."

Seven's face softened. "Yes, of course. Welcome. Come, let us have a drink."

The whiskey was warm and didn't last long in my glass. With Valentina and Seven catching up below deck, Aldric and I were alone at last. I needed to know what he was thinking. One minute he wanted nothing to do with me, but then there he was on the docks protecting me from the Witches.

"What made you change your mind?"

Aldric stared out at the sea. He ran a hand through his damp hair. "I sat in my apartment for hours, next to the corpse on my floor. As horrified as I was, I couldn't get you out of my head. I kept replaying everything over and over again. Everything you said, I knew it was true. Then Elemi walked in. She took one look at me and made the decision. She couldn't lie to me anymore."

The thought of Aldric stuck in that room with a dead body made my stomach turn. I should have done things differently.

He continued. "So she turned on my magic. As soon as the first spark pulsed through me, I understood."

Aldric *was* different. His words were more direct, intentional. His voice smokier. But the biggest change was his eyes. They were still blue, but now filled with a far-away sorrow. The burdens of our kind weighed upon him. It crushed me.

"I'm sorry, Aldric. I brought all this upon you." I couldn't look him in the eye.

He lifted my chin up. "No, you were right. I *am* a part of this. I shouldn't have let you leave that night. I promise you, it will never happen again."

"But this is all my fault. If I hadn't gone to New Orleans, the Consilium would have never known about you."

He shook his head. "Don't blame yourself. You and I both know they would have found me either way. I'm just happy you found me first."

My heart skipped. I was drawn to him like a moth to a flame. I wanted him in every way. My eyes couldn't hide this.

Aldric leaned in close. His fingers traced the collar of my shirt. I drew in a sharp breath as he pulled me to him, his grip tight on my waist. In that instant, his lips came down, hard upon mine. My hands were in his hair as we clawed at each other like wild animals.

His breath was hot as his tongue plunged deeper into my mouth. The scent of his blood filled my nose as I kissed his neck. I wanted to taste him more than I had ever wanted anything else. He pressed me up against the rail. All rational thoughts faded away. I forgot who I was. Who he was.

The salty air was refreshing against my skin, still warm from

Aldric's touch. We stood side by side, breathless. I wasn't myself with him. Or maybe I was never myself before.

I strained my eyes to catch a glimpse of land. There was nothing but water in every direction. We were traveling on another plane of existence. Above time, as Seven explained it. The world whipped by us in a blur of fog and particles, even as we stood still on the ship.

The human crew went below deck to sleep. As midnight approached, the Dhampir crew stood watch. Valentina and Seven huddled together at the stern, deep in conversation.

There was an ease between them. They laughed and reminisced about wars and conquests from another time, long ago but not forgotten. This wasn't their first adventure. I had a feeling it wouldn't be their last.

It was hard to keep track of time on the ship. It was as if it was its own clock. We had been traveling for hours in total darkness. When night lifted, the morning star shined down upon us like a beacon of light.

A chunk of land became visible. An island, floating just a few yards ahead of us. It wasn't there, and then it was. At its highest point stood a lighthouse made of stone and glass. Just below that was a sprawling villa, milky white and drenched in ivy. It was spectacular.

My mouth dropped open. "Where are we?"

Seven's eyes lit up. "In the Sea of Magia. And *that* is the sacred Hall of Secrets."

I wasn't sure what I was more in awe of, the richness and beauty of this angelic island or the fact that Seven's ship managed to get us here and past its cloaking spell.

My skin tingled as its magic glided over me. A new energy shot through me as I wondered what strange and unusual secrets we would find. Before my mind could wander any further, a figure emerged on shore like an apparition.

Seven sucked in a sharp breath. "The Keeper."

I was expecting an old man. I imagined he would've had the appearance of a monk or a priest. Instead, he had a youthful face.

His brown hair was cut short, revealing scalp. He was slender, but with broad shoulders and a square jaw.

Dressed in all black, his rolled-up sleeves and open collar revealed he was covered in tattoos. I tried to decipher their meaning, but the symbols and markings were unfamiliar. His eyes were clear and bright. He was neither young nor old. He just was.

The Keeper didn't speak as he motioned for us to follow him. The villa sprawled across the hills in the distance. The island it was on was massive. It was hard to believe he lived here by himself. A burden or a blessing? In loneliness, you have no attachments. No one to cling to, but also no one to lose.

We followed him through several gardens filled with foliage I had never seen before. The colors were so bright and vivid, they didn't look real. He took us down paths lined with fully grown trees that were smaller than the palm of my hand. Emerald leaves covered the ground like a blanket. They didn't crunch underneath our feet but were soft and spongy.

We also passed larger trees that stood over ten feet tall. Red and purple flowers hung from their branches like wind chimes. Each gentle gust of wind exuded scents of jasmine and honeysuckle, dark chocolate, black pepper, and lemon meringue pie.

We crossed over a dozen stone bridges as we made our way higher up the hill. The temperature changed with each step. The air became cooler, icier, as we climbed in elevation. The ground was covered in snow and slush. Skeleton trees lined the path before us. All those rich colors were gone without a trace.

Approaching the gates of the villa, the snow liquified and the sun shone down on us once again, melting the ice crystals from our hair and clothes. I was dumbfounded. The Keeper regarded my confusion.

"Elemental magic." His voice was low and wistful.

I still didn't understand. "Forgive me, but I thought only Witches could do magic."

The Keeper smiled. "Magic needs only a vessel, and not all vessels are called Witch."

His words lingered as I struggled to find the meaning behind them.

Seven stopped us at the gates. "This is as far as I go, my friends. Valentina, my lovely, until we meet again." They embraced, and he gave her a soft peck on the forehead.

"Gray, it was a pleasure." Seven looked me up and down, much to Aldric's annoyance. "Aldric, you are a lucky man." Seven chuckled as he made his way back down the hill.

Aldric rolled his eyes and began to mutter something under his breath.

The Keeper raised his hands. "Come, we have work to do."

NINE

THE HALL OF SECRETS WAS MUCH MORE THAN A HALL. THE Keeper walked us through endless hallways, secret passageways, and spacious libraries holding books from floor to ceiling. There were hidden doors and staircases that went in every direction. He even took us down to the underground catacombs. They were damp, musty, and a bit unnerving.

The Keeper gave us a brief history as we walked. He explained how the Hall was built on sacred ground. That it contained everything from history books, potions, talismans, and ancient scrolls. This was the center of all things that belonged to our world. It was his duty to protect it, just as The Keepers did before him.

We ended our tour at a small room near the entrance. It was warm and inviting. A green couch sat in front of a stone fireplace, next to a couple of brown leather chairs. Their arms had begun to crack and wear from being gripped. A dark wood coffee table stood in the center.

The Keeper motioned for us to take a seat. His eyes glowed from the firelight as he spoke. "First, to move forward, you must come to terms with your own secrets. *All of you*." His eyes burned into mine. "There is much at stake. You must be willing to sacrifice your own desires for the greater good. The *Sang Magi* is our most sacred text. It was taken from me." His face twisted in agony.

Valentina nodded. "We know the Consilium has it, but how?"

His eyes darkened. "Pythia. She spent some time here. I didn't know...she was already working for Tobias."

My stomach turned. "I *will* get it back for you. I promise."

His expression softened. "I have no doubt, but you are not ready. Not yet."

The Keeper turned to Aldric for the first time since we had arrived. "You are a Bannister Witch. Just awakened, but I can sense your power. I know you wish to link with Gray. For you, becoming a Dhampir will not be difficult. Painful, but not difficult. Be sure it's what you truly want. There is no undoing it."

Aldric's eyes darted around the room as he shifted in his seat. It never occurred to me that he could be having second thoughts again. His face was pale and clammy.

Sensing the uneasiness, The Keeper showed us to our rooms. We followed him down another hallway on the opposite side of the Hall. He brought us into an alcove with three doors.

"Get some rest. We'll begin your training in the morning." With that, he disappeared around the corner.

Valentina stumbled into one of the rooms as she mumbled something that sounded like "goodnight." Aldric lingered in front of the second door. Butterflies swam in my stomach. I was nervous. He had remained quiet all night. It worried me.

His fingers fumbled nervously as he ran a hand through his hair. The awkward tension was palpable. I swallowed hard. "So, um, do you—"

"Goodnight, Gray."

My heart sank. *Why was he being distant?* I was too tired to persist, though. All I could muster was a nod. Closing the door behind me, I couldn't help but wonder if he *was* ready for all this. Tomorrow couldn't come fast enough.

The morning light came in sharper than I had anticipated. The sun was brighter here. *Elemental magic.* I still didn't understand how it worked. Maybe I wasn't supposed to. A knock at the door broke my train of thought. My heart leaped, then sank.

Valentina's voice was hoarse and unsteady. "Gray, can I come in?"

I sighed, disappointed, but waved her in. She poked her head through the door, her red curls sprawling across her shoulders like ribbons. There was something about the way she crept in, with her back hunched and head lowered. It was a stark contrast to her usual perfect posture.

A familiar prickle traveled up my spine. "Val, what's wrong?"

Her eyes darted around the room. "I spent all night thinking about what The Keeper said. About secrets. We all have them, but mine might be the worst. We need to talk about that night, Gray. The night you woke up."

A wave of nausea hit me. That was the last memory I wanted to revisit. "There's nothing to talk about. Dragos helped Pythia put me in a coma for three years. You protected me until I woke up. End of story."

Valentina's face tensed, tightening her cheeks and jaw. "Well...I may have left out a few details."

My stomach turned. I didn't want to know the details. I didn't want to hear about Dragos anymore. "It doesn't matter now. Can we please move past this?"

"No. You need to know *how* you woke up. I'm sorry, but I lied. You didn't wake up on your own. There was a Witch who broke the spell. She *wanted* to help. Please, don't be mad at me."

A sharp knife twisted in my gut. "Who was the Witch?"

She took a deep breath and closed her eyes. Her words floated out, just above a whisper. "It was Jane. Your mother broke the spell."

The room spun around me. My knees trembled as I struggled to remain upright. With fists clenched, I paced around the room like a lunatic. I wanted to throw her against a wall. Valentina eyed me like a hawk. I was on the verge of losing it.

"Why Jane? Knowing what she did to me, how could you call *her*?"

Valentina drew in a sharp breath. "I was desperate. There were other Witches that tried, but the spell was too strong. I *needed* you to wake up. I didn't want to be alone anymore."

Her voice trailed off into sobs. Throughout four centuries, I had never seen her like this before.

My heart ached, but my anger subsided. "How did you know she would come? That she wouldn't betray us?"

Valentina sniffled and plopped down on my bed. "I didn't. But I was out of options. She came right when I called her, and she left just as quick. She begged me not to tell you. She said it was best if you didn't know."

Valentina was terrible at keeping secrets. The fact that she kept this from me for this long proved to me just how manipulative *Jane* really was. I couldn't blame Valentina for this.

"Thank you for finally telling me. I know how hard that was for you."

Valentina wiped the tears from her cheeks. "So, you forgive me?"

I sighed. "Of course. But don't ever keep something like that from me again. Especially when it comes to Jane. She can't be trusted."

She threw her arms around me in a fit of relief. "I promise. Never again."

I wanted to believe her, but I knew that promises were hard to keep in this world.

The Keeper waited for me in the study. He relaxed in a chair by the fire. "Cup of tea?" Aromas of sage and lavender wafted from his cup. It reminded me of England. I was a long way from there now.

I shook my head. "I need something stronger."

The Keeper nodded and left the room. He came back moments later with a carafe of blood.

I licked my lips as the dark red liquid slid down my throat.

By the way he watched me in quiet contemplation, I could tell this wasn't the first time he had catered to my kind. His eyes held many secrets. Flickers of magic, and something even more ancient than that.

He smiled as if he could read my thoughts. "Let us begin."

TEN

THERE WERE MANY THINGS I NEEDED TO COME TO TERMS WITH. Things I needed to confront. I have laughed in the face of chaos and found fleeting moments of joy, but the anger was always bubbling right below the surface. It threatened to destroy every shard of light.

The Keeper took me on an extended tour of the libraries, describing in detail the history of our kind. Some of it was familiar and some was not. I knew that we were created by Apollo, and that the Witches came from his twin sister, Diana. I also knew that our two races were connected because of them. What I didn't know was that Tobias believed that linking us with blood magic was the only way we could attain salvation. The only way we could ascend and return home to the gods.

Tobias's intentions might be noble, but his methods were insane, and I doubted the gods would welcome him with open arms. Turning people against their will and forcing them to link, where was the salvation in that? The irony was that we would have to do just that to beat him at his own game.

The Keeper came to a halt outside an ornate wooden door. "The ceremony room. This is where you will link with Aldric."

I stepped inside and let out a gasp. A large oak tree grew in the center of the room. Its branches twisted up through the ceiling. The ground was submerged in water, with only narrow bridges to navigate around. They were built in a star shaped pattern surrounding the oak tree.

The only light in the room came from hundreds of torches that ran across every wall. It took my breath away. The magic was heavy. It was as if the room had its own heartbeat.

"This room is sacred. It has been blessed by Diana and it contains all four elements we need to channel the power of the *Sang Magi*. I must warn you, however, that only *light* magic can be accessed here. Your intentions must be pure or the spell will not work."

I let his words sink in as we walked back to the study. *Were my intentions pure?* I intended to destroy the Consilium. *To kill them.* I intended to link with Aldric. His blood would give me a fighting chance.

In the beginning, Aldric had been a means to an end, but things were different now. I felt connected to him. In such a short time, he had become much more than a pawn to me. He *was* the light. I just hoped he had enough light for the both of us.

Aldric was waiting for us in the study. Our eyes locked. A surge of electricity shot up my spine. His skin glowed, smelling of sea salt and sandalwood. I wanted to bury my head in his neck and breathe in nothing else. I was so intoxicated, I didn't notice what was in his hand.

The Keeper took the carafe of blood from Aldric. "There are decisions that need to be made."

Aldric gazed into the fire, his eyes a million miles away.

The Keeper hovered next to him. "Aldric, your family is the oldest coven. Direct descendants of the gods. With that comes great power, but also a great burden. The Consilium have abused that power. Family or not, they must be stopped. Otherwise, you too will pay the price your parents did."

Aldric jolted out of his chair. "My parents? What do they have to do with this? They died in a fire when I was a baby."

The Keeper sighed. "Ah yes, a fire. Like the one at Gray's villa? Or at the Wolf and Crescent? Maybe it was just a coincidence. Or maybe not. Elemi only had time to save one of you. Your parents begged her to choose you. She has been protecting you ever since."

The color drained from his face as he ran a trembling hand through his hair. He swallowed hard, grasping for words. "So, they tried to kill me too? When I was just a baby? What threat could I have been to them? I couldn't even crawl yet."

"It is hard to say. They may have thought you would grow up to seek revenge. Perhaps they didn't know you were inside. Either way, the Consilium will stop at nothing to get their way. Even if it means killing their own."

Aldric's eyes watered as he cleared his throat. "I've been living a normal life for twenty-five years. Why now? Why is everything changing?"

The Keeper looked over at me. "Because of her. They tried to stop Gray from finding you, but they failed. The Consilium fears nothing...except...the two of you. Together you will be the first *true* link."

My pulse raced. "The first? But the Consilium has been linking people left and right."

The Keeper's eyes darkened. "Yes, but they've been using dark magic. A true link, the way it was intended, can only be forged with light magic and Diana's blessing. That exists only here. And it has never been done before."

Aldric gazed into the fire. "What if I'm not cut out for this life?"

The Keeper smiled. "You wouldn't be here if you believed that. You're just afraid to let go. You wrestle with your desires. Your demons. The more you resist, the more it hurts. Surrender and let go."

I suddenly felt like I was intruding on a private moment. Aldric was in turmoil. As if he *was* in physical pain. It hit me.

Every Witch inherits a unique ability. When they're human it manifests from time to time, but it's triggered, heightened, when they awaken their magic.

It was so obvious. "He's a sensitive, isn't he?"

The Keeper nodded. "Yes. He feels everything. Love, fear, hate, sadness. All at the same time. It's consuming him."

Aldric sighed and put his head in his hands. This was why he was being so distant. His emotions were amplified, and he didn't know how to control them.

The Keeper placed a gentle hand on his shoulder. "I will teach you how to use this power to your advantage. How to manage it. Turn it on and off. But you must let go."

Aldric nodded. "Tell me what I have to do."

ELEVEN

WHENEVER I WANTED TO FIND VALENTINA, I JUST HAD TO follow the sweet scent of whiskey. As I suspected, she was drowning herself in a bottle down in the catacombs. She sat on the ground, legs crossed, pouting like a child with the bottle half empty. I swiped it from her hand before she could protest.

"They say you should never drink alone." Valentina chuckled as I took a swig.

I sat down across from her. Tension still laced the air between us. I was no longer upset with her, but something still wasn't right.

"Val, are we okay?"

She hugged her arms to her chest and took a deep breath. "I need you to promise me that you won't kill my brother."

My stomach dropped and I nearly choked on a swig of whiskey.

"What would you have me to do with him? He betrayed us. He's probably conspiring against us right now."

Valentina flinched. "I agree he needs to be dealt with, but he is still my brother. I don't want him to die."

There was a time when I would have shared her sentiment. Dragos and I were like two runaway trains heading toward each other, determined to crash and burn. We were on two separate tracks, always missing our destination.

It hadn't occurred to me that she would still feel something for him. Right before his betrayal, we had learned that Dragos was the reason why Valentina was turned. He brought the Consilium into their lives, and they never gave her a choice.

My blood pressure was rising. "I can't believe that after everything he's done, you still want to *save* him?"

Valentina stifled a sob. "Not save him. *Spare* him. There's a difference. I will always love him. And you're lying to yourself if you can't admit that you still love him too. I remember what he meant to you."

"You're wrong. I have no love left for him. He made sure of that. If you want to keep Dragos on a pedestal, that's your business. But don't expect me to do the same."

Valentina's lower lip quivered. "Promise me, Gray. *Please.*"

A knot formed in my chest. Feelings of guilt, anger, and sorrow trickled out like spilled ink. "Fine, but make no mistake, I will put him in chains."

Her eyes blinked back tears

"I'm glad you're making yourself comfortable down here, Val. I suggest you get used to it because this is going to be Dragos's new home."

A whimper escaped her lips as I stormed out.

I'd been sulking in the garden for hours when The Keeper found me. "Aldric isn't the only one who needs to let go. Something is troubling you."

He had no idea. It gnawed at me like an itch that I refused to scratch for fear that I wouldn't ever stop. Love swallows you whole. It consumes you. Like darkness, it can disorient you. I needed my thoughts to be clear right now. Thinking about Dragos was not an option.

The Keeper studied me. "You're different, Gray. You have a purity inside you that the others do not."

"I'm full of vengeance and hate. I fantasize about spilling their blood out into the streets. Decapitation, torture, death. These are the things I dream about. I'm not as pure as you would like to believe." I couldn't hide the bitterness in my voice.

He touched his hand to my cheek. "You have every right to be angry. I know it haunts you night and day. But it won't always be so. Your journey will twist and turn like branches in Diana's Forest. You will feel rage and you will feel joy. In the end, I have faith that you will do what is right. There is nothing purer than that."

Would I, though? When I come face to face with my nightmare, would I do what's right? I feared I was just as monstrous as my enemies. We all had our demons. Even the purest of souls.

"Why do you do this? You are more powerful than all of us. You could leave at any time. Why do you stay here, guarding our secrets?"

His eyes burned into mine, flickering like flames. "It's my duty. We all have a destiny, Gray. I cannot fulfill mine unless I help you fulfill yours."

"What if I can't be helped? I fear that I am already lost." A sinking sensation formed in the pit of my stomach. Despair and desperation wrestled within.

The Keeper smiled. "You will not be lost forever."

His words stung. I wasn't just lost. *I was broken.*

"Have you ever been...lost?"

Something flickered in his eyes. "Once. Many moons ago. But the light brought me back. My path was then clear."

Sadness covered him. A weariness behind the gentle smile. I felt a pang of guilt. I wasn't the only one being haunted by demons. He just kept his further away.

"Tell me, what is your true name?"

The Keeper's eyes lit up. "No one has asked me that in a very long time." His smile was full of warmth and surprise. "I used to be called Gabriel."

"Like the angel."

The Keeper sighed. "I'm no angel. More like a guardian."

I wasn't an angel either. That much I knew. He was right, though. There were many things I needed to face. But tonight, all I wanted to do was forget. I excused myself from the garden in search of the means to do just that.

It was late and I was drunk when I knocked on Aldric's door.

He stood in the doorway, shirtless. The firelight flickered across his chest. My heartbeat quickened. I wanted him more than I wanted blood. I put my hand to his mouth before he could speak, caressing his lips with my fingers. Our eyes locked, and the rest of the world faded away.

Aldric took my face in his hands, pulling me toward him. His hands slid down my shoulders and found the small of my back. I arched toward him, pressing my hips into his. That was all it took. His lips came down hard on mine.

His body was warm and strong as he pressed me up against the wall. We tore at each other's clothes, shredding them to pieces around us. With my legs wrapped around his waist, he lowered me to the ground.

He let out a deep moan as we rocked back and forth. I cried out as we exploded into each other. The ground shook, and we collapsed in each other's arms.

Aldric looked at me. His lips curled into a boyish grin.

My heart raced as he stroked my cheek. "What are you smiling about?"

"*You*. You're...beautiful."

My cheeks flushed. "So are you."

Aldric tilted my chin toward him. "I want to be with you in *every* way."

I sat up and looked hard into his eyes. My heart fluttered. I never knew how bad I wanted it until I heard him say it. "Are you sure? There's no going back, you know."

His eyes lit up. "I'm more than sure. This is what I want. I'm ready."

His arms wrapped around me tight, safe and comforting. I didn't want to leave the warmth of his embrace, but it was time to get back to reality.

We still had a war ahead of us. We had to link, but it was more than that. More than my desire for revenge. I *needed* to link with Aldric. I needed it like blood. And soon, I would no longer have to thirst for either.

TWELVE

THE KEEPER WAS IN HIS CHAIR IN THE STUDY. HIS EYES LIT UP when Aldric and I entered the room. We stood before him, hands clasped.

He nodded and smiled. "I see. I will begin the ceremonial preparations. Gray, you know what you must do next."

Aldric swallowed hard as The Keeper made himself scarce.

His heart beat out of control. I squeezed his hand. "This is going to hurt a little."

Aldric chuckled, but underneath his casual exterior, I sensed his apprehension. "Just make it quick."

Aldric tilted his head, exposing his neck. I moved with caution, apprehensive myself. There was no going back from this. He would never be human again. If one day he regretted this, I would be the one he blamed.

"Gray, it's all right." Sensing my hesitation, his voice was soft and soothing.

Pain shot through my fingers. I had been digging them into my palms so hard, they were covered in blood. Was I doing the right thing? If he hated it, would he ever forgive me?

Aldric moved closer, arching his neck toward my lips. My hunger rose toward the blue vein throbbing inside his flesh, drawing me in. I inched closer. The scent of blood and sandalwood filled my nose.

My head spun. His fingers tangled in my hair, nudging my head further down. His skin was soft and smooth against my lips. Like butter. I closed my eyes, took a deep breath, and sank my teeth in.

Aldric's blood exploded into me like wildfire. It tasted warm and sweet, sticky like molasses. It filled my loins, my veins, and every crevice with urgency. His grip tightened, and his knees shook. I wrapped my arm around his waist and lowered him to the floor.

We both gasped as I pulled up for air. My body tingled. The color was draining from his face. *Focus.* I bit into my wrist and pressed it to his mouth. He flinched, pulling away. I held his head, pressing down harder. His eyes widened, but he gave in and began to drink.

His heartbeat slowed as the venom entered his bloodstream. His body twitched and convulsed. A knot formed in my chest as he writhed around on the ground, his life force leaving him. His eyes rolled back and then forward again. His body went limp. Still. Dead.

I held my breath. Time seemed to stand still. Every second was an eternity. On the brink of madness, panic rose in my chest. I touched his face, my hands trembling. He was ice cold.

"Aldric?" No response. *No.* I had to get help. I had to find The Keeper. No, there wasn't time for that. My eyes darted around the room, searching for something that might help. *Anything.* "Aldric, please."

Without warning, Aldric's lips parted. He shot up and drew in a sharp breath. I threw my arms around him, choking back sobs of relief. He took my face in his hands. *He was beautiful.* The color had returned to his cheeks and his eyes were clear and bright blue.

"How do you feel?"

Aldric smirked. "Better. Stronger. *Alive.*"

I pressed my lips against his. His tongue danced with mine. My body shivered, aching for more. He kissed my neck, my fingers, every inch of my face. His lips caressed the base of my throat.

His voice was low and raspy. "You're mine now, and I'm yours."

I let out a soft moan as the tip of his tongue moved down my chest. *"Always."*

The ceremony room was more magnificent than I remembered. The ceiling was wide open this time to allow the night air in around us. Thousands of fireflies danced around the room, twinkling like the stars above us.

The Keeper stood at the base of the great oak tree, dressed in all white. He beckoned for us to stand in front of him. He reached for our hands and cut a tiny incision into each of our palms with a steel dagger. Clasping our bloodied hands together, he wrapped them tight with muslin cloth that had been soaked in herbs and tinctures. The wound stung as the mixture seeped into my skin. Aromas of sage and lavender wafted through the air.

The Keeper fastened a crescent moon necklace around my neck. It matched the one Aldric wore. He closed his eyes and raised his hands toward the sky, chanting in Latin as the wind howled around us. The water rippled and the ground shook.

My head began to spin. I closed my eyes to steady myself. Bile climbed up my throat. I choked it back. Aldric gripped my hand tight. We leaned into each other to keep our knees from buckling. It was like being caught in a hurricane.

The fireflies swarmed us. They dove in and out, buzzing in my ears and tugging at my clothes. It took everything I had to not swat them away. The chanting grew louder, faster, until the words became a blur. I was close to passing out. Everything came down at once and swirled around us. Rain, wind, hail, dirt, and ash. *Elemental magic.*

A familiar sensation filled me. A warmth radiated below our hands. It was getting hotter by the second. I swallowed hard and opened my eyes. The Keeper held out a branch from the oak tree, underneath our hands. I gasped. *The branch was on fire.*

A wave of panic and nausea rushed through me. *Just breath, Gray.* Aldric tensed and tugged his hand away. I tightened my grip and kept him in it. I imagined all the horrors that must be running through his mind as the flames engulfed us.

The Keeper shouted over the wind, waving his hands around like a symphony conductor. The force whipped through my hair, drowning out the sound of my own heartbeat. The room swelled and rocked. Just when I thought my head would explode, he plunged our hands into the water.

A burst of energy shot through my body. It spread into every vein and muscle, pushing through my blood. Its fibers threaded in and out, etching an invisible shell. Like a shield beneath my skin. Sparks of light flickered behind my closed eyelids.

Everything went dark and still. I was on my knees, our hands still clasped together. I opened my eyes to a very different room.

The wind had stopped, the fireflies were gone, and the oak tree had bent over with the strength and grace of a ballerina. A single golden leaf fluttered to the ground. The ceremony was complete.

THIRTEEN

MAGIC FLOODED MY VEINS LIKE A RIVER. IT PULSED AND VIBRATED like electricity. Tiny fibers with Aldric's imprint rippled through me. They twisted and turned inside me. Every cell in my body arched toward it. My heart swelled to the brink of bursting.

Aldric looked at me, wide-eyed. "I feel so close to you. I can hear your voice in my head. Not the words, but...the intention. I can't explain it."

He didn't have to. I gave his hand a light squeeze. Here in this room we had become something more together than we could ever be apart. We were linked to each other for eternity. An unbreakable bond.

"So...did it work?" Valentina poked her head around the corner. She lingered in the doorway, wringing her hands together.

Aldric flashed her a grin. "Yep. She owns me now."

Valentina chuckled. "Good. We should celebrate."

I had known Valentina long enough to know when she was putting on airs. She was trying her best to be happy, but her resolve was crumbling.

I turned toward Aldric. "Can you give us a minute?"

He was already making his way out of the room before I could finish my sentence. He paused in the doorway to throw me a quick wink.

It was comforting to know that I no longer had to explain my intentions to him, but it would take some getting used to. I had always kept my emotions closely guarded.

Valentina hesitated before she spoke. "I haven't seen that look on your face in a long time. I'm happy for you."

I knew she wanted to be happy for me, but her tone was sad and wistful. Her eyes watered. "You're in love again."

I let out a deep sigh. "It's more than love. I wish there was another word to describe it. It's not like before. This is different."

Valentina bit her lip and lowered her head. "I know. That's what scares me. Everything is different now. You don't need me anymore."

My heart sank. "Don't say that. I will always need you. No matter who else comes into my life."

She shook her head. "Gray, it's all right. You don't have to pretend to make me feel better. Don't make promises you can't keep."

Her despair was killing me. "I wouldn't be here if it weren't for you. When I was under that spell, you never abandoned me. You risked everything to get me back. So I am not going to abandon *you*. We're in this together. Like it or not, you're stuck with me."

A smile returned to her face. "Okay, okay. Don't go getting all soft on me now." We both chuckled, but her eyes still flickered with apprehension.

<hr />

It was almost morning when The Keeper called for the three of us to join him in the Library of Covens. He had changed out of his ceremonial attire into a pair of black slacks and a gray wool sweater.

His crisp appearance startled me every time. His age slipped through my fingers. During the ceremony, he commanded the room like an ancient mage. He seemed a thousand years old. Now, on this new day, he looked relaxed and boyish.

The Keeper regarded each one of us as we stood before him, but he fixated on Valentina. "You are a warrior. Fierce and loyal. But there is a fire that rages within you, and it must be grounded. If not contained, it will burn everything and everyone around you."

Valentina's mouth gaped open. "*Excuse me?*"

The Keeper raised his hand to silence her. "Like Gray, you must link with another. Someone who is the opposite of fire. You will balance each other and be stronger together. You must seek this one out."

With nostrils flared and fists clenched, Valentina snarled at The Keeper. "And where will I find this one who is going to *tame* me?" Her cheeks flushed as red as her hair.

The Keeper smiled but took a step back. "I didn't mean to offend you. I only wish to warn you of your nature and encourage you to channel it into another. Besides, he may need you more than you need him."

The wheels must have been spinning in her head. Her eyes darted back and forth between me and The Keeper at record speed. She searched my face for answers, but I was as confused as she was.

Her temper flared. "Who am I supposed to link with it?"

The Keeper proceeded with caution. "I can't say, but I believe this link to be true. You will feel it when he crosses your path."

Valentina huffed. "Great. Now I'm going to stare at every Witch I meet like I'm a crazy person. *Thanks.*"

I burst out laughing. "How's that any different from how you've looked at anyone before?"

She snorted. "Whatever."

Aldric chuckled.

She shot him a look of contempt. "I see this amuses you. Forgive me if I don't share the sentiment."

Valentina spun on her heel and stomped off. I rolled my eyes and started after her.

The Keeper put his hand on my shoulder. "Let her be." And that's exactly what I did.

Aldric and I lay beside each other in front of the hearth in his room. The warmth from his body and the heat from the flames enveloped me. Beads of sweat dripped down my back. My clothes weighed me down like heavy armor that I needed to shed.

A tingling sensation shot up my thighs with an ache to feel his skin against mine. I sat up to face him and pulled off my shirt. I let my fingers linger on the straps of my bra before peeling that off as well.

He drew in a sharp breath at the sight of my bare breasts. His eyes followed my hand down as I unzipped my pants and pulled them off, revealing nothing but soft flesh.

His breath quickened in anticipation. My hands stroked his chest as I slid his shirt up and over his head. I traced the ridges on his stomach, making my way down. He swallowed hard as I removed his belt. His legs twitched from the weight of my hands as I slid off his pants. I leaned back so my eyes could drink him in. His naked flesh was smooth, and it glistened against the firelight like a god's.

Without hesitation, he pulled me on top of him. My heart raced as his lips met mine, intoxicated and consumed by the taste of him. His tongue danced around mine while he pressed his lips down harder. His hands squeezed and clawed at my flesh with urgency as we slid into each other. My body trembled with each wave. Harder and faster until we both cried out.

I collapsed onto his chest, snug inside his arms.

"I don't ever want to leave this room." I nestled in closer to him as he stroked my hair.

"Who says we have to?" He shot me a mischievous grin and slid on top of me. We rocked back and forth until the dawn broke through our window and the fire turned to ash in the hearth.

It was the first morning in over four hundred years that I didn't have to reach for a blood bag. I was grateful that Aldric would never have to endure that. It was a torture unlike any other. To be hungry —no—*starving* for the one thing you loathed the most. To be a predator hiding in the shadows, threatening to snap at any moment. To be consumed by bloodlust. It was exhausting.

I never thought I would see the day where I would be free of that curse. This morning's light brought me new hope and the possibility of salvation. I no longer needed the taste of blood, and I would never have to harm another human again. This was how it should have always been.

I had to stop the Consilium from making new Dhampirs.

FOURTEEN

WE TRAINED NIGHT AND DAY UNTIL OUR BONES WERE CLOSE TO cracking. The Keeper taught us how to use our magic. How to channel it through each other. We learned how to push energy outward for force attacks, how to shield ourselves, and how to turn simple ingredients into powerful potions. After a week of this, we moved down into the catacombs to practice combat.

Aldric impressed me with how fast he adapted. He was quick and agile. He moved like an ancient. It was that Bannister blood, fierce and persistent in its desire to be superior.

Valentina spent some of the time watching us, and some of the time joining in. She was highly skilled in hand-to-hand combat and proved to be a great sparring partner for Aldric. Relentless in her attacks, I think she enjoyed it a little too much.

We were getting stronger, faster, and smarter. But we weren't the only ones. The Consilium was out there, building an army. I pushed myself harder at this thought. I pushed until my flesh broke open and I could barely breathe.

The Keeper was satisfied with our training. "It is time you return to New Orleans. You will be safe within the Three Blind Mice.

Formulate a plan of attack and seek out those who will aid you. The Consilium is strong. You will need all the help you can get."

Seven's ship glowed like a beacon in the harbor. My chest tightened. The Hall of Secrets had become my sanctuary. My shelter from the storm. Now that we were leaving, panic spread through my veins. We had no idea what would be waiting for us in New Orleans. We left it in a state of chaos.

I rubbed the crescent necklace between my fingers. I thought of our goddess, Diana, and how she created The Order of The Keepers to guard our secrets. How she created the *Sang Magi* to bring her and Apollo's children together again. Reunited by the magic of *Nectunt*. Forever linked.

I thought of all this and realized that Valentina was not the only one with a fire raging inside her. The Keeper was right. We needed a plan. Diana wanted us to be free, but Tobias wanted to turn us into slaves. I couldn't let that happen.

Aldric watched me. His brow furrowed, sensing my uneasiness. I shook it off and forced a smile. I didn't need him worrying about me too.

Seven sauntered down from the ship to greet us. "Darlings, you both look as beautiful as ever. Memory does not serve you justice... *Aldric*." Seven gave him a dismissive nod.

Aldric chuckled and patted him on the back, almost knocking him over. "How's it going, pal?"

Seven looked back and forth between us in disbelief and then burst out laughing. "Aldric, you sly fox. I leave you alone with these vixens for five minutes and you come back as strong as an ox. Well done."

He winked at Aldric and slapped him on the back. Aldric stifled a cough as he stumbled forward. Seven chuckled and whisked Valentina aboard the ship.

Aldric cleared his throat a few times and wiped his brow. "Why does he always have to one up me?"

I smiled and linked my arm through his as we walked onto the ship. "He's a pirate. That's what they do."

The ship came to life as we pulled out of the harbor. I acclimated faster this time. Instead of being suffocated by its power, my magic danced alongside it. Valentina, on the other hand, looked like she was going to be sick

She was deep in her own thoughts when I joined her at the front of the ship. "Do you think The Keeper was right about me losing control? That I need someone to link to?"

I knew this had been weighing on her. "I think we're all on the verge of losing control. It's in our nature. But we can find balance when we have another to anchor to."

Valentina's eyes welled up. "What if I don't find him in time? I could destroy everything." Her hands trembled as they gripped the railing.

I wrapped my arm around her. "Don't worry. Nothing exists for nothing. You will find him, or he will find you. Diana wills it. Of this I'm sure."

She nodded, but her grip remained firm on the rail. Her eyes fixated on the Louisiana coastline as it neared.

New Orleans was intoxicating. There was a quiet chaos that existed underneath its organized fringe. I drew in a deep breath and let the scent of jasmine fill my lungs. My heart raced, falling in with the pulse that ran through the city. It was as if everywhere else was ordinary and *this* was where the magic lived.

We said our goodbyes to Seven and made our way through the Quarter. The Three Blind mice was packed with patrons when we arrived. We moved through the bar with ease, only stopping for Aldric to greet his staff and shake hands with a few regular customers.

We were almost past the dance floor when the hairs on the back of my neck stood up. Aldric's heartbeat quickened above the music. Valentina's nose crinkled as her hands shot toward her daggers.

There was a presence here, and it wasn't human.

I scanned the room, searching for the source. Aldric nodded toward the stairs just as something stirred above us. It was coming from inside his apartment. In one swift motion, the three of us dashed up the stairs.

The presence grew stronger as we crept down the hall. It scurried around Aldric's loft. With weapons drawn, we surrounded the door. The presence stilled. *It knew we were here.*

I took a deep breath and kicked the door in, knocking it off its hinges. The room was dark. The only light came from the street lamps reflecting off the stained glass windows. My skin tingled and my muscles ached.

A figure swished past me, faster than I was ready for. It darted back and forth, making it impossible to predict where it would go next. Valentina crouched down beside me, snarling and ready to pounce.

The shadow moved past me again, trying to knock me over. Aldric sprang on it, taking it to the ground. They wrestled around, taking turns smashing each other into the floorboards. Valentina went into a frenzy, looking for an opening as they tumbled around the loft. The sound was deafening. Snarls, furniture breaking, bones cracking, and flesh being torn. It was madness. *I had to get to Aldric.*

Aldric and the figure crashed into one of the windows, spilling in more light from the street. I rushed in between them.

A cold hand smacked down against my cheek, sending me flying into the wall. I stumbled forward, and then staggered back. My head was spinning. The shadow lunged toward me again and slammed its body into mine. The force knocked the air out of my chest.

It wrapped one hand around my throat while swatting Aldric and Valentina away with the other, pushing them over like paper dolls. *Magic.* His eyes glowed red, inches from my face.

My stomach dropped. *"Nicholas Bannister."*

FIFTEEN

NICHOLAS TIGHTENED HIS GRIP AS I TRIED TO JERK AWAY.

"It's been a long time, Gray."

"Not long enough," I spat.

His eyes shifted from red to black. With lips pursed into a menacing smirk, he ran a scaly hand through his silvery hair. He was just as vile as I remembered.

Aldric and Valentina started toward him. Nicholas's hand shot up. "Not a step closer or I will snap her in two." Aldric grabbed Valentina's arm and pulled her to a stop.

I burst into laughter. "You and I both know that didn't work out so well for you the last time, now did it? Save your empty threats for someone else."

Nicholas's eyes darkened, shadowed with resentment. "You're lucky Tobias wants you alive. Otherwise, I would have killed you a long time ago."

I snickered. "Like I said, empty threats."

Aldric sped forward and moved in between us. "Hello, *Uncle*. I've heard a lot about you."

Nicholas grinned wide, his fangs protruding out from behind his lips. "All good things I hope."

Aldric took another step, fists clenched. "Let's just say I won't be inviting you over for Christmas dinner."

Nicholas wiped his brow with a yellow handkerchief, right before he threw it at me. "Clearly this bitch has poisoned your mind against me. There are two sides to every story, Aldric. It is I who is the victim here. If it were up to me, she would be punished."

Aldric blew up. "Punished for what? For being turned against her will? You disgust me. I can't believe I'm related to you."

I reached for Aldric's hand. "Don't bother. He lives in his own delusions."

Nicholas snapped, "Keep telling yourself that, Gray. I can only rest easy knowing that not every bad deed went unanswered for. It's a shame you didn't get to say goodbye." He looked directly at Aldric.

Aldric stiffened, his rage building. "What is that supposed to mean?"

Nicholas laughed. "Don't be naïve, Aldric. Did you *really* think we would let Elemi get away with what she did? Keeping you from us all these years. She committed treason. You are family and belong with us. It was not her place to hide you away. Don't worry, I made sure it was quick."

Aldric's knees buckled, his breath escaping him.

I lunged at Nicholas. "Elemi was your *sister*. How can you be that heartless?" I was beside myself as Aldric gasped for air.

Nicholas's eyes shifted back to red as he raised his voice. "She disobeyed a direct order. Trust me, if she hadn't been my sister, her death would have been slower and much more painful."

I spat at him, "You're a monster."

He erupted into laughter. Valentina flew and landed on his back. He flung her off, knocking her to the other side of the room. She hit the ground whimpering. Aldric leaped at him, but he deflected, sending Aldric crashing into the fireplace. He hunched over and cried out in pain.

Nicholas started toward Valentina. I darted in front of him, blocking his path. "*Enough.* What is it that you want?"

Nicholas looked me up and down. "It's not what I want that

matters. I came as a warning. From Tobias. Stay out of our way, or there will be consequences. And they will be far worse than you could ever imagine. Next time, it will not be a polite request."

My heart was beating out of control. Aldric staggered to his feet, coughing up blood. He limped forward—injured, but still intact. Looking at Nicholas, his eyes darkened. "I'm going to kill you. I'm going to rip out your throat, and the only thing you'll be *requesting* from me is mercy."

Nicholas smirked. "Ah, spoken like a true Bannister." Before Aldric could respond, Nicholas dashed out of the room like a bolt of lightning.

Dhampirs don't sleep. We brood and we dwell. We sit for hours in silent contemplation, retreating within ourselves to block out the noise. That is what the three of us did for the remainder of the night.

The air was bitter and thick with uncertainty. Quiet, except for Valentina slurping blood bags in the corner. Our physical wounds would heal quickly, but the other damage, not so much. *I couldn't wait to return the favor.*

The light was blinding as it bounced off the broken shards of stained glass. A kaleidoscope of pinks, blues, and yellows colored the floor around us. I fixated on it, unable to move. With old wounds reopened, I was filled with despair.

Aldric stood and helped me to my feet. He pulled me in close and wrapped his arms around me. The warmth from his body was soothing. I buried my head in his neck, breathing in a mixture of salt and sandalwood. He ran his hands through my hair, kissing my forehead.

Valentina staggered over to us. Her hair sprang out in every direction and her lips were smeared with dried blood. It was the most unkempt I had ever seen her. Her voice cracked as she spoke. "I'm sorry about Elemi."

Aldric choked back a sob. "She raised me. Risked her life for me. She didn't deserve this."

My heart ached. I felt every emotion that passed through his body. It was agony. Waves of anger, pain, sadness, guilt. Everything was amplified and on constant repeat.

He bent down and picked up a piece of broken glass. "I meant what I said, Gray. I'm going to kill him."

I nodded, looking over at Valentina. "We will kill them all."

The Three Blind Mice was no longer safe for us. With Elemi gone, Nicholas and the rest of them could now enter. Her magic had vanished along with her protection spells. Every Witch in the Quarter would soon sense this.

We cleaned ourselves up and headed downstairs. The bar was empty. Aldric poured us each a glass of whiskey and took the rest of the bottle for himself. I opened my mouth to speak just as the door opened and in walked Josephine DuMaurier.

Josephine strutted in, her shapeshifter wolf at her side. "I've been waiting for you to return. I would've come last night, but I saw Nicholas slip in. When he left, I assumed the worst. Good to see you're all still in one piece."

The white wolf watched me like hawk. I met its gaze. "I am not so easily dispatched."

Josephine rolled her eyes as I took a swig of my drink.

Valentina chimed in. "Come to kick us while we're down, have you? I hope you're not planning on ambushing us with a bunch of sexually frustrated Witches again. I am *so* not in the mood."

Josephine shook her head. "I had nothing to do with that attack on the docks. They acted out against my wishes."

Valentina chuckled. Not in a thousand years had a coven gone against their leader. It was forbidden. "Wow. How embarrassing for you."

Josephine's face fell. "They blame you for bringing the

Consilium down on us. I tried to reason with them, but they wouldn't listen. They demanded that I step down. I was outnumbered."

A coven leader without a coven was shameful. She would be shunned, but it wasn't my problem.

"The waves of attacks are growing. They burned our home down as well. They killed Aldric's aunt. Now the spells that once protected this place are gone. I'm sorry about your coven but I have my own mess to deal with."

Josephine smiled. "Perhaps we can help each other."

My patience was wearing thin. "What could you possibly have to offer us? You've lost your coven, you have a target on your back, and you don't even have a safe place to practice magic."

Josephine's eyes darkened. "Exactly. I have nothing left to lose. Which makes me a very dangerous ally."

She had a point. "I'm listening."

"I know the location of one of the Consilium's compounds. A location that you could strike, leaving them vulnerable. They would never see it coming."

Aldric perked up. "Keep talking."

Josephine swallowed hard and took a deep breath. "It's a fortress, just north of Scotland. It sits on a steep cliff and is heavily guarded. There is only one known path of access. They refer to it as *patria origo,* but its true name is Stonehaven."

I had heard that name before. "Stonehaven. Isn't it abandoned?"

Josephine sighed. "Not anymore."

"What's inside?" Valentina asked.

Josephine shook her head. "I don't know, but it must be important to Tobias. They paid me an obscene amount of money to deliver some rare herbs once. I wasn't let inside or told what they were for."

Valentina huffed. "You've got to be kidding me. You *think* it's important, but you don't know for sure. I don't think so. I don't trust it."

Josephine pressed on. "Look, *patria origo* in Latin translates to family lineage. Origins. It could contain some of those answers you've been searching for."

Aldric and I exchanged a puzzled look. "And what do you want in return for this information?"

Josephine's eyes met mine with spite. "Tobias's head."

Valentina snickered. "Like in a box?"

Josephine snapped, "Joke all you like, gypsy, but I will not be able to show my face in the Quarter until I hold his severed head in my hands. He has disgraced me to my coven and to the gods."

I clapped my hands together. "Alright. You can draw us a map. We'll leave tonight."

Josephine let out a sigh of relief.

"Oh, and Josephine, if you double cross us, it will be your own head that you'll hold in your hands."

Josephine nodded, her eye twitching. "You have my word."

Sometimes you had to make a deal with one devil to dispel another. A shiver ran through me as I prayed that I wasn't aligning with the wrong one.

SIXTEEN

STONEHAVEN WAS IN THE NORTH SEA. THE CLIFFS WERE STEEP, and the terrain was rocky. There was no safe place to dock, so we left Seven and his ship behind, swimming the rest of the way. The water was rough and icy, but the three of us glided through as if it was our natural habitat.

The castle was in ruins amongst the other buildings on top of the jagged cliff. The exact location we were looking for was called the gatehouse. It was connected to a series of underground tunnels and was the only structure still intact.

Night had fallen by the time we made it onto shore. Darkness gave me an advantage. It made my sight sharper. There were only two guards posted on either side of the stone fortress. Dhampir soldiers. Fledgling newbies that were ferocious in their hunger and quicker in their attacks, but they were unlinked and possessed no magical abilities. This would be an unfair fight...*for them.*

Dressed in all black, the three of us crept through the night like shadows. With weapons drawn, we slinked toward them. Valentina snuck up behind the two on the right and took them both out at the same time, slicing their throats open with a dagger in each hand.

I rushed over to the other two and ripped their hearts out of their chests with the same swiftness. The first two were still writhing around on the ground. I sped over and plunged my hands into their chests.

Their bodies went limp as I spun around to face Aldric. "The heart is where the life blood is."

He nodded and chuckled. "Nice work, ladies."

Inside, there were ten times as many soldiers. The gatehouse was a maze of darkened hallways, lit by just a few torches. We crept through, taking care to keep to the shadows.

I stole glances into the rooms as we passed them. They were all identical, filled with operating tables and medical equipment. This place could have been a hospital or a clinic, but it still didn't explain the security or the secrecy.

We turned down another corner and ducked into a room as two soldiers marched in our direction. Palms sweating, I held my breath. We crouched down low as the soldiers passed by. I let out a sigh of relief. It was only a matter of time before they would find the dead guards outside. I didn't want to fight them all if we didn't have to.

Back out into the hall, we were met with more corridors. There didn't seem to be any rhyme or reason to where they went. It would be easy to get disoriented.

With the corridor finally coming to an end, two double doors faced us. My pulse quickened as I pushed them open.

Aldric and Valentina both gasped in horror. I scanned the room, hands trembling. *They were everywhere. Hundreds of bodies.*

Humans on operating tables. *Were they dead?* I had to fight the nausea building in my belly and rising in my throat. A cold chill passed through me as I took a step closer.

Not dead, but they were hooked up to IVs. A wave of panic knocked the air out of my lungs. It hit me like a shot to the chest. These people were living, breathing...*blood bags.*

I reached for Aldric's hand to steady myself. Valentina panted, bordering on hyperventilation. None of us could tear our eyes away. Like being caught in a dream where you can't speak, or scream, or run away.

All these people had been taken from their homes, only to be ripped apart like animals and kept alive for the Consilium to feed on.

My heart sank. "Is this where *our* blood bags come from? Is *this* how it's done?"

Valentina's eyes were wide, glossy. "This is...monstrous."

Aldric pulled both of us back toward the door. "We need to get out of here right now."

He could barely finish his sentence when we heard voices. I nodded and sprinted out of the room. Glancing back at the bodies one more time, anger welled up in my chest. *Somehow, I would put an end to this.*

My mind raced. I wasn't sure which way to go. Aldric took the lead as we barreled down hallway after hallway, stopping only to hide every few feet. He charged ahead, retracing our steps, using his magic to get us out of there.

I honed in. "There, up ahead. I can smell the saltwater."

Valentina took a deep breath, tilted her nose, and nodded in agreement. We were almost to the door that would lead us back to the beach.

Another group of soldiers turned down the hall toward us. Aldric pulled us into the room closest to us, an office with a wooden desk and several filing cabinets along the wall.

The guards passed without detecting us. Aldric motioned for us to continue, but something gnawed at me. I couldn't walk out of here without answers. I ignored his plea and pried open one of the filing cabinets. Valentina shrugged as Aldric shot her a pleading look.

I rifled through the files. There were receipts, expense reports, and shipping manifestos. Nothing peculiar stood out. The second filing cabinet contained folders full of patient charts and biorhythms. Pointless.

Aldric sighed, waving his hands at me. "Gray, c'mon. Let's go."

"Hold on. I just need one more minute."

Valentina grabbed my wrist. "*We gotta go, Gray.*"

I ignored them both as I pulled apart the desk.

"Hurry," Aldric pleaded.

The desk was empty except for office supplies and more receipts. Nothing. They were right, we had to go.

Wait. A file peeked out, wedged between two drawers. I snatched it out from the desk, my pulse quickening. It was labeled *Patria Origo*. I tucked it under my arm as the three of us ran out and bolted down the last hallway. The alarms blared as we ran. We ran fast toward the stretch of shore where we first came in.

Drawing short breaths, I prepared myself to jump back into the icy water. But we weren't the only ones who heard the alarms. A crew member from the ship was waiting for us on a speed boat.

He waved his arms around frantically as we approached. "Let's go. Let's go," he shouted.

The three of us high jumped into the air and landed into the boat as it was moving.

My nerves were shot. I couldn't get the image out of my head. All those lifeless bodies, barely breathing but kept alive for their blood. It was stupid of us to think that the blood bags we survived on were given to us by voluntary donors. Naïve even. It weighed on me like a ton of bricks, making me sick to my stomach. Our need to consume caused this. We contributed to this. It was too much to take in.

Valentina shivered, staring out to sea. We were not affected by mundane things such as weather or exhaustion, yet our bodies sometimes mimicked the symptoms. As if we were still clinging to what once made us human.

Aldric's voice jarred me out of my reverie. "What's in the file?"

I had forgotten I still had the folder tucked inside my jacket. Valentina turned toward me, her eyes wide and bloodshot. The three of us stood there in anticipation as I opened it. I hoped that something in it would help us. Anything to get my mind off the atrocity we just witnessed.

My heart raced as I scanned the pages. It was a ledger. A list of names. It was a list of Consilium members. Names we already knew. I shook my head. This wasn't anything of importance.

Valentina grabbed it from me. "Let me have a look." Her eyes widened as she rifled through the papers.

Aldric stiffened. "What is it?"

She looked at me like she had seen a ghost.

I shivered. "Val, talk to me. You're scaring me."

She swallowed hard, her hands trembling. "These are bloodlines. *The* bloodlines. All of them."

"So? How does that help us?" I didn't understand what she was getting at.

She fixated on me, her eyes wild. "You're one of them."

"What are you talking about?" I thought my heart might burst out of my chest.

Aldric shook Valentina by the shoulders. "How is she one of them? You aren't making any sense."

Valentina's eyes welled up with tears as she handed me the folder. I was too afraid to look but I had to. I had to know.

As I looked at the names on the page, they began to blur together. I felt the air leave my lungs as if someone had just shoved a knife into them.

Aldric snatched the paper from my hands and read it aloud. "Tobias Wynter. First wife, Jezebel Wynter. Second wife, Pythia Wynter. Daughter, Arcadia Wynter. Daughter... Gray Wynter."

He could barely say the last words out loud. I couldn't stand to hear them. My knees collapsed out from under me as I hit the cold wet wood of the deck.

Aldric rushed to my side. "It doesn't change anything, Gray. It doesn't matter."

My eyes shifted from brown to black. I clenched my fists together, shoving them into my pockets for fear I might split the entire ship in half. Valentina cowered.

I knew it. Somewhere deep inside, I always knew it. I *was* a monster. This changed everything.

SEVENTEEN

LONDON WAS AS COLD AND RAINY AS I REMEMBERED. I HADN'T planned on returning so soon. I hadn't planned on any of this. Finding out that Tobias could be my father was the last thing I expected. It was a punch to the gut.

There was only person who knew the truth about my father: Jane. For once in her life, she needed to come clean. She owed me that much. Getting to her would be impossible, so I would have to get her to come to me.

Valentina and Aldric had been watching me constantly since we left the ship. The concern on their faces hadn't left for a second. They waited for my eyes to shift back to normal. Forty-eight hours later, and they were still as black as night.

Valentina broke the silence. "Gray, why are we back in London?"

I stopped dead in my tracks. They both nearly toppled onto me. I had been racing through the streets since the moment we docked. "We're going to pay Lucien a little visit."

Aldric furrowed his brow. "Who's Lucien?"

Valentina chimed in. "He leads the London Coven. Gray, what's going on?"

I took a deep breath. I didn't have time to explain myself, and I was growing annoyed with all the questions. "According to this file, Jane oversees the covens. If any of them were in trouble, they would send for her."

Valentina grabbed my arm. "What are you going to do?"

My eyes darkened as I smiled. "Cause some trouble."

Lucien's guards stopped us at the entrance. I rolled my eyes. "Get Lucien." The taller guard glared down at me, using his body to block my path.

My body tensed as I squared up with him. "It's not a request." I was prepared to rip his heart out without hesitation.

Aldric fell in step beside me in a gesture of solidarity. I knew he was prepared to fight with me, even if he didn't know what he was fighting for. I felt a twinge of guilt for shutting him out, but it passed as soon as I reminded myself why I was there.

After a few minutes of consideration, the guard nodded and motioned for us to wait. Watching the guard disappear down the tunnel, Valentina's heart beat fast in her chest. She stepped in front of me, revealing her fingers, firmly gripped around her dagger.

The guard returned minutes later and waved us through. We followed him through the dimly lit tunnel and came to a stop at a large oak door. Two more guards were posted on either side of it. I ignored them, pushing it open.

Inside, Lucien was seated in a tall chair resembling a throne. *Pompous prick*. Of course he would liken himself to a king. His arrogance astounded me. I wanted to slap him.

He looked ridiculously smug, sandwiched between two of his soulless guards. I chuckled to myself. All this security would not stop me from getting what I wanted.

In one swift move, I shut the door behind us, placed my hands against it, and whispered, "*Signatia claustrum*." A locking spell.

Lucien sprung to his feet. "What did you just do?"

I smiled and licked my lips as I turned to face him. "Making sure we have plenty of privacy."

Lucien's cheeks flashed red as he motioned to his guards. Aldric took three short steps as they approached and ripped out both of their throats.

He plunged his hands into each one of their chests and pulled out their hearts. He stood in front of Lucien, wild-eyed, with both of his hands dripping in blood and flesh.

"It seems you have the floor." Lucien sat back down and narrowed his eyes at me with contempt.

I circled around him like a lion stalking its prey. "You're going to call Jane. Tell her you need her help. That she must come immediately or have to explain to the Consilium why your body is no longer attached to your head."

Lucien snorted. "And why I would I do that?"

I leaned in close to him so he could see my eyes shift from brown and then back to black again. "Because if you don't, that is exactly what will happen."

Lucien winced and looked away from me. I grabbed his chin and pulled it back hard to face me again. "I have sealed you in here with us. Two of your guards are dead, and the others can't get in. I suggest you don't underestimate me."

He looked toward Valentina for help, but her eyes remained straight ahead.

Aldric's pulse raced, but he stood firm beside me. "We can do this all day, Lucien. The sooner you make that call, the sooner we can get out of your hair." His voice was steady, but his body was ready to pounce at any moment.

Lucien looked back and forth between us. "Very well. I will make the call. But you must know, you will never be welcome back here again."

I laughed out loud. "Best news I've heard all day. Now, make the call and tell her to come alone."

We sat in silence as we waited. Lucien drank an entire bottle of wine and mumbled to himself like a madman. The guards on the other side of the door hissed and shouted for us to let them in. They tried for hours to break it open. The spell was weak, but only a Witch could get past it. Still, Aldric stood in front of it, ready to tear down anyone who might get in.

Valentina put a stop to her incessant pacing to sit down next to me. "I'm worried about you. I've never seen you so upset. What if you're wrong? You said your father died before you were born."

I sighed in annoyance. "Yes, Jane *told* me my father was dead. She also told me that *she* was my mother."

Valentina nodded. "That would mean you have a sister. That might be nice."

I rolled my eyes. "Yes, the daughter of Pythia. I'm sure she's an angel."

I heard the bitterness in my own voice as I spoke, but I didn't care. My heart was tightening inside my chest, and I had to stay closed off or I would fall apart. Maybe someday I could let myself weep over the life they stole from me. But not today. Today, I was out for blood.

The guards quieted. Aldric shot me a look. We could both feel it. *Magic.* It was moving toward us. She was here. My emotions swirled through my blood like wildfire. I wrestled between the longing to look upon the face that once soothed me and contempt for the woman who had abandoned me for dead.

The door swelled and pulsed as the spell was stripped down layer by layer. Valentina stepped back and crouched down behind me. Lucien laughed like a maniac. My knees trembled. Images of my childhood flashed through my mind. Aldric planted himself in front of me. The door burst open and flew off its hinges. I held my breath as she emerged from the shadows. Like a thief in the night, in she walked.

Jane was more polished than I remembered. With her icy blue eyes and chestnut locks, she resembled a painted doll. The kind you put on a shelf because it's too pretty to play with. Her skin was fair and flawless with just a touch of pink on her cheekbones.

I drew in a sharp breath as she entered the room. Behind her, a trail of guards lay scattered in pieces.

Lucien was furious. "I called you to help me, not wipe out my entire security system."

Jane kept her eyes on me. "Leave us. All of you."

You could cut the tension with a knife. Lucien scowled and muttered to himself as he scurried out of the room. Valentina squeezed my arm and gave Jane a quick nod as she followed Lucien out. Aldric, however, would not move.

Jane cocked her head to the side and smirked at him. "Did you not hear me, handsome? I said everyone out."

Aldric was as still as a statue. "I'm not going anywhere. I won't let you hurt her any more than you already have."

She smiled demurely at him, but her eyes were as dark as the devil's. She was not the mother I remembered, but I knew she wouldn't talk unless we were alone.

I placed my hand on his shoulder. "It's all right. I'll be fine." His eyes pleaded with me as he gripped my hand tight.

"Aldric, please. I can handle her. Go."

His eyes darkened, shooting daggers in Jane's direction. "I'll be right outside."

After four hundred years, Jane and I were finally face to face. She snickered. "He's attractive. Loyal too. Quite the change from Dragos."

As the shock wore off, the anger boiled beneath my flesh. "I didn't summon you here to talk about my ex-boyfriend, or my current one for that matter."

She looked me up and down as if she were memorizing every inch. "Yes, I imagine not. You must have many questions."

I clasped my hands behind my back to stop them from shaking. "I want answers. I want to know *who* I really am."

Jane stared, a blank look on her face. Right in front of me, but a million miles away. "We never wanted this life for you. We tried to protect you for as long as we could." Her voice changed, sad and bitter.

Every muscle in my body tensed. "Protect me from who?"

Her eyes welled up with tears. "From your father, Tobias."

My heart stopped. I knew it was true with every fiber of my being, but there was still a small part of me that hoped it wasn't. That what I saw in that file was a lie. "You said 'we.' Who was helping you?"

Jane studied me for a moment before taking a deep breath. "Jezebel. She was my best friend, and she was your mother. *Your real mother*. I would've done anything for her, so when she asked me to take you and run away, that is exactly what I did. I cloaked us with magic and raised you as my own."

My head pounded. "Why did I need protection from my own father?"

Jane's eyes darkened. "Because he's pure evil. He was going to turn you into a Dhampir when you became of age and link you to a Bannister Witch. You were to be the first of our kind. Half-Witch, half-Dhampir, with the blood of the gods running through your veins. He was going to use *you* to create his army."

It was insane. I used to think of myself as a target, a pawn. If what Jane said was true, then that meant, I was the actual *game*.

Jane continued. "Jezebel was terrified of Tobias. We all were. We were his prisoners. Tobias believes that we belong to him. That he owns us."

The weight of her words crushed me until I could barely breathe. My voice trembled as I struggled to speak. "Why didn't she come with us?"

Jane smiled sadly. "To distract him. To give us a chance to run. She loved you more than she loved herself. She could live with never seeing you again if it meant you were safe."

Tears streamed down my cheeks. I felt like I was losing everything all over again. My blood was filled with guilt and shame. Jane had sacrificed so much for me, and I'd spent the last four hundred years hating her. Every emotion and every thought I'd ever had, had been wrong and misdirected. I never stopped for one second to even consider that she never had a choice.

My selfishness sickened me. I should have given her the benefit of the doubt. "When did it all go wrong?" I was almost afraid to ask, but I had to know the whole truth.

Jane's eyes hardened. "Over the years, the Consilium grew stronger. More powerful. My spell had weakened. Nicholas Bannister discovered where we were. He was sent to kill me and bring you back to Tobias. But Nicholas was threatened by you. He didn't want you to be found. He was going to kill you instead. He turned me into a Dhampir as punishment for my betrayal. I panicked. The only way I could protect you was to turn you too."

She paused to take a swig from one of Lucien's bottles of wine. "A cruel twist of fate. I turned you into the very thing that we were trying to keep you from becoming. Nicholas was furious. His soldiers took me back to Tobias. That was the last time I saw you alive until the day I was summoned by Valentina to break you out of the *Ligaveris* spell."

The world was closing in on me. My chest was tight, heavy. I couldn't breathe. I felt more lost now than I did then.

"My mother, Jezebel, where is she?"

Jane looked down at her feet. "When Nicholas returned, he told us you had died. Of course, I knew that wasn't true, but they believed it. I knew Tobias would stop looking for you if I let him believe it. Before I had a chance to tell Jezebel the truth, she took her own life. She had no reason left to live. I had failed her."

I gasped. Once again, a mother was being snatched away from me. The realization that I would never meet her or feel her embrace filled me with a sorrow I had never felt before. I was drowning in it.

My thoughts turned to Nicholas with a new and darker thirst to tear him apart. Jane watched every twitch and flutter that passed through my face. My mind flashed back to the day Jane left. I tried to convince myself that it was just a bad dream. I had never spoken about it with anyone until now.

"He *tried* to kill me that day. He tied me to a stake and set me on fire. I was scared. Confused. It burned everything except my flesh. I didn't understand why I wasn't in pain. Why I wasn't dead. He was as surprised as I was, so he fled. Then the thirst came. It scratched at my throat until I thought I would claw out of my own skin. I didn't know what I was. I was alone, and I hated you for it."

Jane stifled a sob. "I know. I wore that hate like a badge of honor because I knew you were safe. Even though it broke my heart."

All these years, my hatred toward her defined me. Fueled me. An hour ago, I wanted to rip her throat out, but now, I just wanted to find a way to make myself worthy of her love. She gave up her life for me. Jezebel literally lost her life because of me. I owed it to them both to see this through.

The quiet stillness between us was a refuge from the chaos that we had left in our wake. There was just one more thing that gnawed at me. "Did he buy it? Does Tobias think I'm dead?"

Jane sank into Lucien's chair. Her eyes were dark and glassy. "You already know the answer, Gray. You can feel him in your bones as he feels you in his. I can see him in you now as you stand across from me. You've always known. You just didn't know what it was. That thing pulling you toward darkness...is him."

EIGHTEEN

THE OTHERS WAITED FOR US NEAR THE ENTRANCE TO LUCIEN'S compound. Aldric was pacing back and forth. He let out a heavy sigh as I approached, searching my face for some indication of what was to come.

Jane acknowledged them with a nod before turning back to me. "We cannot meet again. It's too dangerous. I'm working on a way to end this, but I need you to stay out of it."

She was still trying to protect me after all these years. I felt even more guilty for spending the last four centuries despising her, but I was in too deep to stay out of it now. Tobias had to be stopped. That was the only way this would end.

I nodded to appease her. There was no point in wasting time arguing. Her eyes welled up with tears as she took a last lingering look at me. I pulled her into an embrace, drawing gasps from both Aldric and Valentina.

Lucien grunted in disgust. "How heartwarming."

Caught up in their shock of witnessing my rare display of affection, they didn't notice my sleight of hand as I plucked a tiny strand of hair from Jane's head, a necessary ingredient for a tracking spell. I clutched it in my hand so that no one else could see.

Jane squeezed my hand. "Take care of yourself, Gray. Trust that we will see each other again."

I nodded and squeezed back. Guilt stabbed at me. If she only knew it would be sooner rather than later.

———

It was good to be back in New Orleans. I felt more at home here than I had ever felt in England, but I couldn't stop thinking about the past. The memories I had tried so hard to forget flooded back. I had to let them in. The path to the truth might be locked in there.

It occurred to me that my intrusion at Lucien's compound would not go unnoticed by the Consilium. "We can't go back to the Three Blind Mice. I have secured us another location. We need to stay out of the city."

A car was waiting for us just like the first time Valentina and I had arrived. It seemed so long ago now. The new villa was isolated on a plantation about twenty miles away from the Quarter. It was dark, quiet, and surrounded by large oak trees. The air was damper out there, earthy and crisp. A welcome respite from the liveliness of the Quarter.

Inside, the furniture was covered with sheets and plastic tarps. The electricity had been shut off, but there was a tall stack of wood by the fireplace. Cobwebs and dust lurked in every corner. It wasn't what we were used to, but it was the perfect place to hide.

Valentina yawned and stretched her arms out over her head. "I need a drink and a dark room. Talk more in the morning?" Her eyes pleaded with me.

I nodded. Aldric and I were finally alone but he had questions in his eyes that I didn't have the answers to. I wanted to run into his arms and feel the weight of them around me. He was my safe place. My sanctuary. But I couldn't allow myself to feel safe now. There would be time to catch my breath later. For now, I needed to stick to my plan. Even if it meant pushing him away.

"Gray, you know you can talk to me about anything, right?"

I bit my lip and looked away. "I...I'm just...I need to process everything. Jane. My father. All of this."

Aldric nodded and folded his arms to his chest, but his eyes were full of doubt. I wanted to reach out and reassure him, but I couldn't. I had to track Jane tonight and I couldn't let him know. I would explain everything to him later, but for now I had to stay focused.

The air between us was layered with hesitation and uncertainty. He let out a deep breath and cupped my face in his hands. "It's been a long day. I'm going upstairs. Come up when you're ready."

I squeezed his hands, nodding. Knots formed in my stomach. I hated myself for lying to him. For shutting down. I waited till I could no longer hear his footsteps, and then I slipped out into the night.

Walking away from the villa, my thoughts drifted to what Jane had said last night. How Tobias wanted me to link with a Bannister Witch. How Jane turned me into the very thing she was trying to protect me from. I thought about The Keeper telling Aldric that our paths were meant to cross. That it was destiny. It seemed no matter what anyone did to try to change it, here I was, linked to a Bannister Witch. Tobias got what he wanted after all.

I was deep in the bayou when I realized the tracking spell was taking me toward the Wolf and Crescent. Why was she all the way out here? Was she looking for Josephine? Maybe she was on another errand for Tobias.

The knife in my heart twisted deeper. *I don't even know what my father looks like.* He could have walked by me a thousand times and I would have never known.

As I got closer to the ruins of the Wolf and Crescent, I heard voices. I strained to listen, but they were muffled just below a whisper. My hearing was impeccable, but I couldn't make them out.

I moved closer, remaining hidden. I heard two, maybe three voices. One was the deep tone of a male voice. The second voice was high pitched and almost shrill. The tones were hushed, but aggressive. They were having an argument.

I strained my eyes to see, but all my senses were dulled. The shapes were fuzzy. Magic surrounded me with the push and pull of two different spells, working against each other like a black cloud hanging over the sun. I had to get closer.

I was almost to the blackened door frame when I saw them. My stomach dropped and the blood rushed to my feet. Jane was tied to a chair and standing on either side of her were Pythia and Dragos.

Pythia's eyes glowed in the dark, gold and orange like two amber stones. She wore a hooded cloak of black velvet, half-covering her head. Her hair was thick, knotted, and the color of wet soil. She pranced around Jane, jumpy but graceful. Like a cat with the intentions of a lion. The stench of oleander draped the air.

Dragos hovered next to Jane like a shadow. My heart raced at the sight of him. His skin was smooth, golden brown. A striking contrast to his light grey eyes. His black hair was shorter than I remembered, with no trace of the boyish curls he hated so much. I used to love running my hands through them.

I shivered. It felt like a lifetime ago since we had been this close. He used to gather me up in his arms like I was made of paper. He was slender but strong, and he towered at least a foot above me. He made me feel small and fragile, like a tiny bird. I used to think that's what being safe felt like. I know now that it was just a cage.

I shouldn't have come, but it was too late to turn back now. They already knew I was there. I took a deep breath and walked through the door.

Dragos and I locked eyes. My heart fluttered and beads of sweat formed between my fingers. His lips parted, letting out a slight gasp. The corners of his mouth turned up into a devilish grin. He still affected me, and he knew it.

Pythia cleared her throat. "Well, look who decided to join us."

"Pythia." I swallowed hard.

Pythia circled me like a snake. "I see so much of your father in you. You have his *tenacity*."

Jane whimpered, struggling against her ropes. My heart sank. This was my fault. All this was because of me.

Pythia chuckled at seeing me in pain. "She cannot move, or speak for that matter. She's done enough talking for one day. Don't you think?"

"Let her go. I'm the one you want." I should've known they were going to use her to get to me.

Pythia laughed. "I'm afraid I can't do that. See, she violated the terms of our agreement. You were *not* supposed to wake up from that spell until *I* allowed it. In exchange, she would get to keep breathing."

Jane and I locked eyes. I tried to will my thoughts into her mind. To tell her how sorry I was for leading her into this trap. But there was no way of communicating this to her now.

Pythia continued to slither around the room with that smug look on her face, delighting in my struggle. "I knew you wouldn't be able to stay away once you discovered the truth. I was counting on it. I love it when a plan comes together. Here you are, right where I want you."

With my body temperature rising, I imagined what it would feel like to crush her bones between my fingers. "And what is it that you want, Pythia?"

She grinned from ear to ear. "Well, a family reunion of course. Tobias would like to invite you and Aldric to join us at Infitum. Where is your other half, by the way? I thought you two were *linked* at the hip." Dragos rolled his eyes.

A wave of possessiveness flowed through me. "Leave Aldric out of this." I clenched my fists to keep them from shaking.

Pythia chuckled. "You're in no position to make demands. I have the *Sang Magi*. Besides, my magic is stronger and much older than yours."

My blood was boiling. "Now that you mention it, you are looking a bit older these days."

Her eyes darkened. "Enough. I'm growing tired of your childish antics. You *will* join us. One way or another. You have until the next full moon to get your affairs in order. You and Aldric can come willingly or by another means that will not be so pleasant. Jane will stay like this until you do."

My lungs tightened. A rage grew inside me, replacing any fear. Jane's eyes bulged as she struggled to speak. I wanted to set her free. To break the ropes and wrap them around Pythia's neck. But I couldn't do anything. She was right. My magic wasn't strong enough.

"Fine. Thirty days. If anything happens to Jane, I swear you will regret it." I planted my feet to keep from collapsing.

Pythia pursed her lips and narrowed her eyes toward me. "Full moon, Gray, and not a second after. I'm known for many things. Patience is not one of them." Like a bolt of lightning, she swooped Jane up and darted out into the night, as if she were never there.

But Dragos still was. The tension between us unnerved me. I didn't fear him; I feared myself when I was around him. His eyes lingered over my body, drinking me in. I shuddered. I wanted to knock him over the head for taking such liberties.

"How's my sister?" His voice was melodic, the words dancing off his tongue. His Romany accent was faint, but still present.

"Like you care. You're lucky she still does. Otherwise, I'd kill you." My hands were trembling.

Dragos smirked and took a casual step toward me. "You don't want to kill me, Gray. You still want me. I can see it in your eyes. I can *hear* it in your breath. You want me with every fiber of your being."

I swatted his hand away as he reached out to stroke my cheek. "You don't get to touch me anymore. Don't be ridiculous. Valentina is the *only* reason you are still alive."

He grabbed my wrists, his eyes darkening. "Is that so? It doesn't have anything to do with your little Bannister Witch? See, I think you're afraid he's not going to satisfy you forever. In fact, you know he won't. You aren't going to kill me because you know I'm the only one who can." His breath was hot on my cheek as his lips lingered over my ear.

I sucked in a deep breath and was met with the familiar scent of clove and honey. "Get your hands off me." I ripped free from his grasp and took two steps back.

He shook his head. "Stop acting like a child, Gray. Everything has a purpose. Everyone has a role to play. *Even you*."

His words stung. I blinked back tears. "The only thing you were playing was *me*. You used me over and over again. Led me to believe that we were in love. All the while, you were plotting to destroy me. Where is the purpose in that?"

Dragos snarled, grabbing my shoulders. "You used me just the same. Your hunger for revenge poured into me like famine. You embraced it with every deviant thrust. Do not speak to me of love, darling. You have no idea what it is."

My arms ached as I wriggled free from him again. I bit my lip, fighting back tears. I would not let him see me cry. "You're right. How could I possibly know what love is? I was turned against my will, burned alive, lied to by everyone I've ever known, and left to rot for three years in a coma that *you* helped put me in. Not exactly a fairytale, so excuse me if I'm a little rusty in the love department." I was seething. The nerve of him, after everything he'd done, to turn it all around on me.

Dragos sighed and threw his hands up. "Poor Gray, always the victim. I had forgotten how much I loathed your incessant whining. It's a shame that your stamina in the bedroom does not follow you into the battlefield." He smirked, smug and pleased with himself.

I lost it. My hands were around his throat before he could react. He didn't break eye contact as I spat at him, "You disgust me."

Dragos smiled, our faces mere inches apart. My cheeks flushed as his lips moved closer to mine. Teasing, but not touching. He gently removed my hands from his neck but didn't let go.

"I didn't come here to fight with you, Gray." His voice softened.

My heart was beating out of control. "Then why did you come?"

"To see you. To remind you of who you really belong with. Forget about the past. You need me. You know you do." He whispered in my ear, seducing me like a demon. This was madness.

I shoved him away. "You don't know anything. I *never* needed you."

Dragos sighed. "So stubborn. Fine, I'll play along. But know this, when you grow tired of your new pet, you *will* come back to me. I can promise you that."

He turned to leave but paused in the doorway to give me a wink. "See you soon, Gray." I shivered as I watched him disappear into the night.

NINETEEN

It was already morning when I got back to the villa. Valentina was pacing around, frantic, as I approached.

"Where have you been? We have been freaking out. Aldric went out to look for you."

A lump formed in my throat. I never stopped to consider what I would be putting them through by leaving.

"I had to take care of something. I'm sorry. I didn't mean to worry you."

Her eyes bulged. "*Seriously?* After all we've been through? You can't just sneak off in the middle of the night like that. Of course we're going to be worried. We're being *hunted*."

I shook my head. "You're right. I should have just stayed here. Now, everything is more complicated."

Valentina huffed. "What do you mean? Where did you go?"

"She was with Dragos." Aldric stepped out of the shadows, his face twisted in disgust.

I lowered my head. "You followed me?"

Aldric clenched his fists. "No, I *tracked* you. We're linked, remember? You actually have to know someone is leaving to follow them."

His words cut through me like a knife, but I deserved every one of them.

Valentina's mouth dropped open. "You saw my brother? What's going on?"

My heart sank. "I'll explain everything."

I spent the next hour telling them how I tracked Jane through the bayou to the Wolf and Crescent. How I found her with Dragos and Pythia, and about the deal I made with them. I left out the sparring match between me and Dragos. Though, I was sure by the way Aldric was looking at me that he had heard every word of it.

Valentina shook her head, dumbfounded. "They could have taken you. Are you crazy? We *must* stick together. Promise me you won't do that again."

I nodded, guilt consuming me. "I promise."

Valentina pouted, but seemed satisfied with my response. Aldric, on the other hand, was glaring daggers at me. There might as well have been steam coming out of his ears. Valentina took one look at him, excused herself, and went inside.

The look on his face broke my heart. I couldn't look him in the eye. He was never going to understand. "How much did you hear?"

He rolled his eyes at me. "Enough to know you still have feelings for him. That he is a piece of shit that doesn't really love you. And enough to know I plan on ripping out his throat the next time I see him."

He was angrier than I thought. I had never seen this side of him before. He was coming apart at the seams. I had to find a way to calm him down. "The only thing I feel for Dragos is hatred. Nothing more. You have to believe me." I wasn't sure if I believed myself.

"I saw the way you looked at him, Gray. I *felt* it. He still has a hold on you. I believe that you hate him, but I also believe you still love him too."

My head was spinning. I felt sick. "It was never love. I thought it was, a long time ago, but I know now that it wasn't."

Aldric snapped, "Be honest. If he hadn't left you, you would still be with him."

The tears were welling up, but I blinked them away. "He didn't just leave me. He handed me over to the Consilium. That was his plan the whole time. How could you even think for a second I would still want to be with him?"

Aldric fumed, glaring at me with his fists still clenched. I didn't know what else to say. The anger was creeping up in my throat, threatening to explode all over him. I was used to Dragos pushing my buttons, but Aldric had never spoken to me like this before.

My head throbbed. "I can't do this. Believe what you want."

I turned to walk away when Aldric grabbed me by the arm and pulled me to him.

"Gray, *I'm in love with you.* I have never felt this way about anyone. Ever. But you keep shutting me out. And then I find you with your ex-boyfriend in the middle of the woods. What am I supposed to think? It's making me crazy. I hate what he did to you. I hate that you were ever with him."

His words hit me like a ton of bricks. I couldn't breathe. He was right. I'd been holding back. I wasn't giving him all of me. With Aldric, I felt safe. Loved. Complete. We were linked. It was time for me to let him all the way in. I didn't want to lose him.

My emotions swept through me like a hurricane. I took a deep breath and beckoned him in. I let his magic surge through me like wildfire. I stumbled as the rush took over, my knees buckling. Tears poured down my face. I collapsed into him, a trembling heap of sweat and sobs.

I clung to him for dear life as he wrapped his arms around me. "I love you too, Aldric. I love you too." He held me tight as I repeated it over and over again. And for the first time in my life, I didn't feel like I was in a cage.

Valentina perked up at the sight of us holding hands. She let out a sigh of relief. "I've been thinking. We should go back to the Hall of Secrets. The Keeper will know what to do about Pythia."

Aldric and I nodded in unison.

Valentina jumped up in excitement. "Good. I'll call Seven and tell him to get the ship ready."

I was exhausted, but we couldn't slow down now. "Tell him we need to leave tonight."

The journey back to the Hall of Secrets was a quiet one. Even Seven kept to himself. There seemed to be a dark cloud following me, affecting everyone around me. Would I ever be able to live free without looking over my shoulder?

Tobias would never let me be free, but could I kill my own father? A man I'd never met but was still my blood? I needed to understand what made him this way. I feared his evil lurked in me. What if it was my destiny to become just like him?

My stomach was in knots. Dhampirs from both sides would likely die in this battle. Of that I was certain. But I couldn't bear to lose anyone else. The ones I loved were in danger because of me. I hoped The Keeper could tell me how to protect them.

The ship was barely docked before I sped off toward the Hall. I didn't want to waste a second. I marched into his study with Aldric and Valentina at my heels.

It was empty. There was a fire blazing in the hearth and a bottle of wine open on the table. With the thirst for blood not a factor anymore, I helped myself to an old vintage of French Bordeaux. Aldric also poured a glass while Valentina slurped on a blood bag.

We waited in silence. I fixated on the flames, remembering the day I was engulfed by them and how frightened I had been. I wasn't scared anymore, but I would never look at fire the same. It didn't seduce me or enchant me anymore.

Maybe I was like the phoenix, reborn out of its ashes. Or maybe I was just a child of the devil, cursed for eternity to do his bidding. Either way, it didn't matter now. The physical thirst for blood might be gone, but the memory of it would always remain. Like humans, demons had nightmares too. The only difference was we were awake when we were having them.

The Keeper finally entered the study and all eyes turned toward me.

I raised an eyebrow. "Did you know about Stonehaven? About the human blood bags?"

Without hesitation, The Keeper nodded. "Yes, of course. I know everything."

If he didn't have the likeness of a monk, he would've almost seemed smug.

I was annoyed. "Why didn't you tell us about it?"

The Keeper sat down across from me, folding his hands in his lap. "It wasn't vital information. But I see now that finding it has led you to other things that are."

I was growing impatient. "You knew that Tobias was my father, but you didn't tell me. Why?"

The Keeper sighed. "It wasn't my secret to tell. It was something you had to find out on your own. Now you have."

My blood boiled beneath the surface. I had no right to be angry with him, but I was. "I think that piece of information was very vital. You should have told me. I would've liked to have known that the monster I've been hunting is my father."

The Keeper didn't flinch. "It would've changed everything. You would've been distracted. Conflicted. You needed to link with Aldric without that burden upon you."

He was right. I knew he was right. It *had* changed everything. "Pythia has Jane. She's going to kill her if I don't do as they ask."

The Keeper regarded me carefully, pursing his lips as he weighed my words in his head. "Pythia. She's a clever one. She took the *Sang Magi* from me. Her magic is hard to resist."

His voice trailed off and something flickered in his eyes. Something that was rooted deep.

"I need to know how to defeat her. A weakness I can use against her."

The Keeper rose and stood by the fire. He drew in a deep breath.

"Pythia is an Oracle. That's how she stays one step ahead of everyone. Except for you. She can't see your actions because you are linked to Aldric. A Wynter-Bannister blood link is powerful. Pure and protected by the gods. But you cannot fight her. The only way to stop her is to take her magic from her."

A chill swept over the room, sending shivers down my back. The Keeper's eyes darkened. "There is a spell, but it requires a Narcissus flower. Once you ingest its nectar, you will have the power to drain any Witch of his or her magic. But it has *never* been done before."

Growing up in Pendle with Jane, I had learned about various flowers and herbs. I would help her gather them from the forest so she could make her potions. In all those years, I had never heard of a Narcissus flower.

The Keeper continued. "To acquire a Narcissus flower, you must travel to the Underworld. That is the only place it grows."

His words hung in the air like smoke. This had to be a joke. The obvious way to get to the Underworld was to die. There were other ways of course, but if you went uninvited, you wouldn't be allowed to leave.

Valentina's mouth dropped open in disbelief.

Aldric shifted in his chair. "Um...I'm sorry, but the Underworld? That's not a real place, is it?"

I swallowed hard. "As in Hell? Yes, it is a very real place."

Valentina sprang to her feet. "No. It's impossible. You won't make it back."

After coming this far, I wasn't going to turn back now, but the thought of getting stuck there terrified me.

The Keeper motioned for her to sit down. "There is a way. I can show you, but it will be dangerous."

I had already made up my mind. Pythia had to be stopped. If this was the only way, then so be it.

Aldric grabbed my hand. "I'm going with you. We'll cover more ground together."

I tried to protest, but Valentina chimed in. "Me too. I'm not going to let you two have all the fun." She winked at me.

The Keeper placed his hand on my shoulder. "Gray, you must be aware of something. Draining Pythia of her magic requires you to take all of it in. It will become a part of you, like the blood in your veins. If you're not careful, the darkness could change you."

His words sent chills through me. I hadn't even thought about *where* her magic would go. Magic needed a vessel. It only made sense that the vessel would be me. But to hear him say it out loud was another thing entirely.

I shivered. I didn't want to think of what I might become with dark magic pulsing through my veins, but who knew what any of us would become if the Consilium succeeded. "I'll take the risk. I'm anchored to Aldric. He will pull me back from the dark." I had to hope that he would.

Aldric pulled me in close and whispered in my ear, "I won't let anything happen to you."

The Keeper approached Valentina, lowering his voice to just above a whisper. "There is something else. Something the Consilium doesn't know. There is another spell that is not in the *Sang Magi*. It has been committed to memory only, and it will be useful to you."

The hairs on the back of my neck stood up. "What is it?"

The Keeper remained focused on Valentina. "It's an ancient spell that links Dhampirs to Lupi."

TWENTY

A SPELL ALLOWING DHAMPIRS TO LINK WITH LUPI WAS A HUGE advantage. The potential strength and prowess would be limitless. A wolf, already quick and agile, would be even more ferocious with Dhampir powers. The sight, sounds, and smells would be heightened and amplified ten times over. The Lupi, as they are known, are stronger in wolf form. If one was linked to a Dhampir, their strength would be increased.

"Why is he looking at *me?*" Valentina spoke as if The Keeper was no longer in the room.

I remembered the way Valentina hadn't been able to take her eyes off Josephine's wolf, back at the Wolf and Crescent. At the time, I thought it was out of fear. Now I wondered if it was something else drawing her to it. Why else would The Keeper bring up the spell? He didn't make light of things like these, and this was the second time he hinted at her needing to link with someone.

The Keeper smiled. "You would be a fierce asset to the Lupi. Perhaps you should consider it. That's all I meant."

Valentina looked like a deer caught in a pair of headlights. "Well...um...okay. I'll think about it."

The Keeper pressed on. "You should start by speaking with Arcadia. She will lead you to the Lupi."

Hearing her name struck a raw nerve in me. "You mean my long-lost sister?" I couldn't hide the bitterness in my voice or deny that a part of me was jealous of her.

She was born without any secrets and raised by both her parents. As sick and twisted as they were, she still got to know them.

The Keeper continued. "Arcadia is a Wolf Charmer. She has taken control of the Lupi by enchanting their leader, Lycos. He never leaves her side."

Somehow, I didn't think that she was going to just hand over one of her wolves to us. "I don't understand what you want us to do. Arcadia is the daughter of Pythia. I doubt she wants anything to do with me."

The Keeper narrowed his eyes. "She most likely does not, but that's not the point. You mustn't reveal what I've told you about the spell. You just need to get close enough to Lycos. He has been under her thumb for decades. You will understand it only then."

More riddles. "What about the Underworld? We should be focusing on getting the Narcissus flower."

The Keeper shook his head. "You are not ready, and I need time to prepare your supplies. In the meantime, go to Arcadia. When you return, I will be done."

The Keeper revealed that Arcadia lived in Diana's Forest. It was in a realm that Valentina and I had traveled to many times. The forest itself, however, was cloaked in magic. We would need Seven's ship to get us there.

The Keeper addressed Aldric. "You will stay here with me. I need your assistance in the preparations."

Aldric sprang up from his chair. "Absolutely not. Out of the question. Gray, I'm not letting you go out there without me."

Valentina rolled her eyes. "Gray and I have been surviving on our own a lot longer than you have. I think we'll be able to handle this excursion without you."

Aldric's face turned bright red. "Unbelievable. You—"

I stepped in between them. "Stop, *both* of you. Aldric, The Keeper needs you here. Besides, Val and I already know the terrain. We can slip in and out faster without you."

Valentina beamed at Aldric victoriously.

"And Val, stop antagonizing him." Her face fell as Aldric smirked.

Aldric paced around the study while Valentina and I readied our things for the trip. I knew he was worried. I sensed his nerves in the pit of my stomach. "I'll be back before you know it."

His lip twitched, attempting to force a smile. I pulled him toward me and kissed him hard. His body tensed as he tightened his grip around my waist. "Be careful, please." I nodded and gave him one last kiss. Valentina groaned and sauntered out the door behind me.

Walking toward Seven's ship, a wave of uneasiness washed over me. I wondered how far our connection would reach. Would I still be able to feel Aldric from another realm? The look on his face told me he was wondering the same thing. The ache of being away from him was already starting to form. I kept my eyes fixated on him as we drifted out to sea. I stared until he was nothing more than a speck on the horizon.

The air was cool and salty, refreshing. Valentina's crimson hair flapped in the wind and whipped around her face. Her eyes were full of wonder as she gazed out at the waves. My mind was somewhere else too. I wasn't even sure what I was going to say to Arcadia. Would I feel a connection to her? A kinship?

I'd always wanted a family, just not this one. She was Pythia's daughter and I was Jezebel's. Sisters or not, I doubted she was looking forward to meeting me either. I took a deep breath and sucked in as much salt as my lungs could stand, hoping it would force down the lump that was forming in my throat.

My heart swelled as we approached. This forest was sacred. It was where it all began. Where *we* all came from. It was where Diana fled after Zeus cast her out. Where she built her empire of Crescent Witches. Where Apollo had forged the first Dhampirs. There was deep-rooted magic here.

I gasped in awe, gazing upon it. The trees were a shade of green I had never seen before. They shimmered like a forest full of emeralds. Blinding. The closer we got to the forest, the more my body changed. The magic was like a magnetic force, pulling at me. It spread into my veins. The air transformed into tiny silver stars, dancing in front of me. I had to blink fast to focus. My magic was remembering its connection to the source.

Valentina crept off the docks in a half crouch with her eyes peeled. Ravens crowed in the distance. My breath quickened. I stepped off the docks, surprised to find the grass was spongy. It gave way with each step I took. The air was thinner here, crisp, and smelled like thick soil after a heavy rain.

We took the only path that looked walkable. Lined with massive oak trees, their trunks were so smooth, you could run your hands over them without getting a splinter. In between each tree were bunches of hibiscus flowers. Their petals were an array of pinks, reds, and oranges, like the colors in a sunset. My eyes lingered on each one, inciting visions of cotton candy, tangerines, and...*blood.*

My stomach fluttered. *Where were these images coming from?*

I looked over to Valentina, who appeared unfazed as she kept her eyes on the path ahead. I shook off the feeling of dread and decided I should do the same.

An opening in the trees allowed for the sun to break through. It shone down, illuminating the ground like a spotlight. Everywhere else was dark as far as the eye could see. Valentina drew in a sharp breath and took a sudden step back. We were not alone.

Two figures emerged out of the shadows and stood directly under the sun like statues, stoic and poised.

I started forward, but Valentina pulled me back. "It's them."

I squeezed her hand. "I know. They appear to be waiting for us."

I lifted my shirt and showed Valentina my daggers. She loosened her grip on me as I continued forward.

Arcadia's cat-shaped eyes glowed blue like the base of a flame. She was striking with her pale skin and white hair. Not white like the hair of a crone, but bright like snow. She stood tall with her shoulders pressed back and her chin lifted. She had the air of a queen. *An ice queen.*

Her lips were full, with a hint of rose, as she smiled in amusement. This was a woman who was used to getting what she wanted. Who most likely believed she was better than me. Maybe she was. Looking at her, I felt nothing. No connection, no kinship, nothing. Just blank. Numb. We looked nothing alike and no doubt *were* nothing alike. The look in her eyes seemed to hint that she agreed.

Arcadia bowed her head in acknowledgement, lowering herself into a half curtsy. Her movements were slow but deliberate, like a demon trapped inside the body of a ballerina.

"Welcome, sister. I was wondering when you would finally grace me with your presence." Her high-pitched voice unnerved me.

"Well, I always did like to arrive fashionably late." Our politeness couldn't mask the bitterness in both our voices.

Lycos stood next to her, motionless and without expression. With his broad shoulders and piercing blue eyes, he resembled a Viking. His white locks fell into a knotted braid down his back. If I hadn't known they were lovers, I would have thought they were twins. Mirror images, guarding each other like lions.

Valentina muttered under her breath as she crouched down beside me, a tight grip on her daggers. Arcadia's frozen smile faded as she noticed her watching Lycos. Her eyes narrowed. "Who's the gypsy?"

"She's with me. Don't worry about it," I snapped.

Arcadia giggled. "Sister, this is sacred ground. We don't allow unlinked Dhampirs to enter."

Valentina snarled and bared her fangs. I placed my hand on her shoulder to calm her.

"We won't be here long. She won't be any trouble."

Arcadia sighed dramatically. "Fine. I'll let it slide this once. The least she could have done is brush her hair, though. I mean really dear, you are quite a mess." Her smile returned but her eyes shot daggers toward us.

Valentina chuckled and winked at Lycos, eyeing him like a piece of candy. "When you're done being her pet, you should give me a call. I can help you get that leash and collar off."

Arcadia was not amused. The little color she had in her face drained. "Call him my pet again and see what happens." Lycos remained still and quiet.

Valentina smiled devilishly. "What's the matter, Wolf Charmer? You afraid he's going to start thinking for himself one of these days? Oh wait, he can't."

I gasped and looked over at Lycos. Still no reaction.

Arcadia started toward Valentina. "I am going to snap your neck, you little—"

I stepped in front of her. "Enough. We didn't come here to fight. This is a waste of time." I shot Valentina a look. She giggled but stepped back and threw her hands up in mock surrender.

Arcadia continued to glare at her. "Looks like your friend is the one that could use a leash and a *muzzle*."

My eyes rolled. "She's only joking. Now, can we please move on and get to the matter of why we're really here?" I didn't know how long I could keep Valentina from opening her mouth again.

Arcadia huffed. "Fine. Why are you *really* here?"

I wanted to reason with her. Plead with her for help even. But this girl didn't have an empathetic bone in her body. I took a deep breath. "I need you to convince the Consilium to let Jane go. I have already agreed to do whatever they ask. They don't need her anymore."

Arcadia cocked her head to the side, eyes full of curiosity. "And why would I do that for you? We don't even know each other. Besides, the minute they let Jane go, you'll disappear. And I will look like a fool."

I had to go at this from a different angle. "You're right, we don't know each other, but I can sense that you don't exactly like to share.

So, what if I did disappear? Isn't that what you want? I'd be gone, and you would have everything."

Arcadia's eyes lit up. She tossed her head from side to side like weights on a scale. "As tempting as that sounds, I could never go against my father. See, you and I are nothing alike. I like our world the way it is. You want to destroy it. I can't let that happen."

Arcadia never had any intentions of helping me. She was only humoring me for her own amusement.

I erupted. "You have no idea what I've been through. I didn't want any of this. I never asked for it. But I wasn't given the choice that you were. And I see how you have made it. So, if you aren't going to help me, then I strongly advise you to stay out of my way." My eyes were black. I could feel it.

Arcadia took a step back. "I'm going to pretend you didn't say that to me, Gray. That was hurtful." Arcadia pretended to wipe tears from her eyes.

Valentina sighed loudly. "Let's get out of here before I make her cry for real."

I nodded and willed my eyes to turn back to brown. Lycos remained quiet, but very much alert. Valentina couldn't resist taking one more jab as she batted her eyelashes at him.

"Like I said, if you ever grow tired of her commands, look me up. I can be obedient too." Valentina winked and licked her lips.

Arcadia shrieked, stomping her foot like a child. "That's it. I'm going to slit your little gypsy throat."

Valentina moved into a cat-like stance, ready to pounce. I moved in between them just as Lycos swooped in. He picked up Arcadia and threw her over his shoulder like a rag doll.

"Lycos, put me down right now. Lycos! Are you listening to me? What has gotten into you? I'm going to kill that bitch. Put me down!"

Lycos gave Valentina a wink before he turned to leave, carrying a hysterical Arcadia kicking and screaming over his shoulder. Valentina blushed a shade of red so deep, it matched her hair.

TWENTY-ONE

WE WERE DUMBFOUNDED AS LYCOS DRAGGED ARCADIA AWAY OVER his shoulder. Valentina rubbed her temples. "What was that about?"

I shook my head in disbelief. "No idea. Maybe some sort of mating ritual? Who knows what those two are into."

Valentina snorted. "He *winked* at me. The man doesn't say two words the whole time and then he winks at me."

I chuckled. Valentina was no stranger to flirtation. "Oh, don't act so shocked. You're not exactly an ugly duckling."

She continued to feign surprise. "No, but I thought he was supposed to be under some sort of *Wolf Charm* or something."

I was at a loss on that one. "Who knows. Maybe it doesn't work like that. Or maybe your beauty is just too hard to resist," I teased. She rolled her eyes as I giggled.

The walk back to Seven's ship was quiet. Too quiet. It felt like we were being watched. Like there were creatures lurking in the shadows, watching our every step. If Lycos and Arcadia lived here, then the rest of his pack must live here too.

The Keeper suggested Valentina link with a wolf, but I wasn't sure how we were supposed to do that if Arcadia controlled them all. We couldn't tell her about the link. Even if we had, she would've never helped us. I had no idea why The Keeper sent us out here.

"Gray, you okay? You haven't said a word since we left the forest."

I bit my lip. The rocking of the ship wasn't doing anything to soothe the pounding in my head. "I was just thinking about what Arcadia said about not going against her father. She knows him. Loves him. Obeys him. I've never even seen what he looks like. Growing up, he was just a fantasy. Now that I know the truth, it feels like a nightmare. If my father is the monster, what does that make me?"

Valentina wrapped her arm around my shoulders and pulled me in. "You are nothing like them. The only thing you have in common with those people is blood." The weight of her words made my stomach turn. Blood was anything but common.

Seven emerged from his cabin just as we docked at the Hall of Secrets. He dashed over to The Keeper to discuss our next travel arrangements. His ship needed special preparations before taking us to the Underworld.

Aldric was waiting for me. I drew in a sharp breath at the sight of him. His hair was slicked back off his face and he was dressed like The Keeper. Instead of his usual designer suit, he wore black pants and a black sweater, fitted so it showed every curve of his chest. His face was clean shaven, and his eyes were clear and bright. He was armed with two daggers on both sides of his waist, and he had a bow strapped to his back. The sight of him fully armed and ready for battle took my breath away. He was every bit the fierce warrior I hoped to have standing by my side. He was beautiful.

"I see you've been busy since we left." I smiled warmly at him.

His eyes lit up. "Hi, darlin'." He pulled me in close and wrapped his arms around my waist.

"Get a room," Valentina teased as she charged past us.

Aldric rolled his eyes. "Well, she's just as delightful as always."

I laughed. "Don't worry about Val. She's still trying to figure out why Lycos winked at her."

The Keeper looked up from his conversation with Seven. "They made contact? Lycos and Valentina?"

"Um...sort of. There was an incident with Arcadia. He intervened."

The Keeper looked out into the distance. "So it has begun." Aldric and I exchanged a puzzled look.

Seven's eyes were full of shadows as he approached me. "Everything is set. Come aboard when you're ready to go."

My stomach was in knots again. "Seven, I don't know how to thank you. We literally could not do this without you."

He shrugged. "Don't thank me yet, beautiful." His voice was gentle, but skeptical. Seven was not a man who scared easily. His hesitation was unsettling.

The Underworld wasn't meant for us. It was a place for gods and demons. For the damned and the lost. We weren't welcome there. But there was a fail-safe. A series of trials, designed by the gods, that would ensure a way out.

There were five trials. Each one required a specific talisman or potion to complete. Except in the final trial, where we would have to come face to face with the Reflection Siren. She guarded the Narcissus flower under the Elm of False Dreams. Her tricks were cunning and seductive. She would feed off our hopes and fears, sending us into madness. A nightmare that no one has ever escaped from.

The Keeper explained the trials in detail. He mapped out what we would encounter at each stage and what we would need to pass through to the next. Not even the warmth from the fire could prevent the cold sweat from dripping down my back. The flames were casting an eerie glow on his face as he spoke.

"I have gathered most of the supplies you will need to descend. Your usual weapons will not be effective, so they have been replaced with ones that were spelled and blessed by Diana. These weapons have been guarded since the beginning of time. Archived and preserved for moments like these."

Valentina's nose twitched. "How will we know how to use them?"

A shadow passed across his face. "You won't. They will use you."

Aldric crinkled his brow as he studied The Keeper's map of the Underworld. He mumbled, tracing the lines of the rivers with his fingers. He was so entranced that he barely noticed my presence.

"Have you been staring at this all night?" My voice snapped him back to the present.

"Gray...do you really think we can do this?"

It seemed impossible, but I needed him to believe it wasn't. "Yes. And we will. We have to."

Aldric smiled and shook his head in amazement. "You're absolutely fearless."

I let out a deep breath. "No. Stubborn? Yes. But fearless, not at all. I'm terrified."

Aldric reached out and cupped my face in his hands. A warm tingle started to spread through my body. "I'm with you one hundred percent. We are going to make it back." My lips quivered against his as he kissed me.

It was our last morning with The Keeper. Our last chance to get what we needed from him before heading out. We were all aware that we might not make it back. Uncertainty blanketed the air like a thick fog, threatening to squeeze the air out of my lungs. Even Valentina was not her usual bubbly self this morning. Her head hung low as she entered the main hall.

The Keeper motioned for us to gather around. "It is time. You must rely on each other more than ever. That is the only way you will make it out alive."

I swallowed hard, looking back and forth between Aldric and Valentina.

The Keeper continued, "No matter what you think you feel or see, remember, it is only an illusion. No matter how real it seems, it is not. Hold fast to that truth."

My hands trembled as reality sank in. There was no more planning, no more talking about it. It was happening now. And there was no turning back. We headed out to begin our dark descent into the Underworld.

TWENTY-TWO

We were near the outer edges of the river Oceanus, a part of the sea where the mortal world ended and the Underworld began. The air was cool yet balmy, somewhere between winter and spring.

I stared straight ahead. "Last chance to turn back."

Valentina sighed. "What kind of friend would I be if I did that?"

"A safe one." I was having second thoughts about bringing my friends on a possible suicide mission.

"I'm not leaving you, Gray. I told you, you're stuck with me." She smiled through her fear. She was more stubborn than I was.

A surge of guilt shot through me. "I promise you, I will get us out of here."

She squeezed my hand. "I don't doubt you for a second."

I wish I had her confidence. Doubt was spreading through me like wildfire.

Many supernatural worlds existed alongside our mortal one, hidden behind a veil that could only be accessed through magic. The Underworld was no different. Seven's ship idled at the spot where the entrance should be, according to our compass.

All eyes were on me. I drew out one of my daggers and pricked my finger. Holding my hand over the side, I let my blood drip down into the sea. Aldric was as pale as a ghost while he watched me. "Your turn."

He raised his hands up and closed his eyes. The clouds darkened and the sky in the horizon cracked open, splitting vertically like an invisible curtain parting in two. The ship swayed back and forth. A magnetic force pulled us toward the opening.

The wind whipped at us, scratching my lungs. Aldric and I clung to each other as the ship picked up speed, turning the world around us into a hazy blur.

White light blinded me as we moved closer to the opening with a force that threatened to tear us apart, limb from limb. I threw myself over Aldric. "Everyone down. Now!"

Seven pulled Valentina down underneath him as the loud crack of thunder and splitting wood rang through my ears. We were being sucked in like a vacuum. Aldric wrapped his arms around me and held tight. Water sprayed up and over us from every direction. The wind howled as we plunged forward into the divide. I held my breath as it swallowed us whole, and then everything went black.

It was dark, but I could make out shapes and shadows scurrying around the ship. My face was wet, pressed against the wood panels of the deck. The water continued to splash up and over the sides of the ship.

I strained, trying to will my eyes to adjust. "Is everyone all right?"

Valentina grunted. "Ugh, I'm drenched."

A light flicked on like a spotlight, shining in my eyes. I blinked a few times to clear the spots out of my vision.

Seven held a lantern over Valentina. "You look like a wet mop."

She pushed out her lower lip. "Thanks for stating the obvious." Seven chuckled as Valentina rolled her eyes and gave him her back.

Aldric groaned beside me. His hair was drenched and matted to his forehead. His hands trembled as he attempted to sit up. "Did it work?"

Considering this was the first time Aldric and I had used our magic together, I'd say it worked too well. "Yeah, I think it did. We went through the veil."

Aldric's eyes were red and swollen. I reached out to brace him as he was still unsteady. Magic this powerful was draining. Especially at the level we were using it. Once we were both fully standing, I took my first look out into the abyss.

I swallowed hard, an effort to keep the contents of my stomach from bubbling up. The dizzying effects of this place were already starting to set in. The air was thick and chalky, like fog that you could taste. Every hair on my body stood at attention. Every nerve was on edge. There was no denying it. This place was toxic. Evil. I could feel it in my bones.

I shivered as the ship began moving again. The wind whipped through my hair, coating each strand with tiny ice crystals. I sensed Seven's eyes on me. He watched me, expressionless. He had a way about him that was both calm and alert at the same time. He took slow easy breaths while his stance suggested he was ready to fight at a moment's notice. I was grateful he was here. He nodded in my direction as if reading my mind.

There were five rivers in the Underworld, but we only needed to get across one—the River Styx. The entrance to the river was guarded by Charon, the Ferryman of the Underworld and the Taker of Souls. The souls of the dead would make offerings to Charon by placing gold coins underneath their tongues. It was the only way to ensure safe passage into the afterlife.

A faint beacon of light glowed in the distance. We were getting closer. The once-fierce wind transformed into a warm breeze. It would only get hotter from here. The black sky was behind us, but a different type of darkness was hovering in the water up ahead.

The Ferryman was hunched over his staff, covered in dirt and black sludge. His eyes glowed, fiery swirls of black and red. I shuddered as he looked in our direction. His limbs were like branches, twisting and curving around each other like snakes. Sharp, but smooth like obsidian. Whispers floated in and out of the air around us.

With gold coins underneath our tongues, Aldric, Seven, Valentina, and I joined hands and stood in a line to face Charon.

I took a deep breath and said a silent prayer to Apollo. *Would this work? Would the Ferryman let us pass?*

I closed my eyes and found my link to Aldric. I visualized the connection in my head. *Focus*. Aldric squeezed my hand just as his magic seeped in and danced alongside mine. Sparks of light flashed behind my eyelids as I summoned the power of *Dolum*. *Fox magic*. It bestowed the ability to trick and deceive. Its power was strong, but I still needed Aldric to help blanket the others inside the spell with us.

Sparks of light turned to shards, bursting inside my head as our magic pulsed between us. It whipped and sizzled before finally settling into a quiet rhythm. It hummed just below my consciousness, present but not distracting. I let out a deep breath and hoped the spell would work.

I opened my eyes to see Charon aboard our ship and mere inches from my face. His eyes were full of flames like two volcanoes erupting over and over again. I forced myself to hold his gaze. I tried not to tremble, but I was on the verge of losing control.

His long scaly fingers outstretched before me as he waited for my payment. With one swift motion, I opened my mouth and dropped the coin into his hand. Charon weighed the coin diligently, never taking his eyes off me. My hands began to sweat as I waited.

Satisfied, Charon moved over to Aldric and did the same. I was tempted to look to see if he was okay, but I couldn't move a muscle. My heart was beating out of my chest. I held my breath as he moved on from Aldric to Valentina, and then Seven.

With the spell still buzzing low in my ears, I thought I heard Valentina's soft whimpers as she dropped her coin into Charon's hand, or maybe those were my own whimpers. Lastly, Charon faced Seven. The thought of a pirate giving away gold coins almost made me chuckle. If I hadn't been so terrified, I would have laughed out loud.

Seven grunted, spitting out his coin. Charon lingered in front of him, longer than he had with the rest of us. My stomach dropped. *Was the spell wearing off?* The tension was thick around us. All four of our hearts were beating hard and fast. My eyes were shifting. I felt them changing color. I started to pull my hands away from the others. *I needed to reach my daggers.*

Aldric gripped my hand tighter. "Don't do it, Gray," he whispered.

The buzz was fading. I could barely hear it as black clouds formed in my eyes. I couldn't wait any longer. The spell would break soon. *I had to do something.* Just as I was about to break free from Aldric's grip, Charon closed his hand around Seven's coin. He looked at each of us one more time before disappearing into a patch of barren trees.

Aldric spun around at me. "What were you doing, Gray? You almost broke the link."

"I know. I'm sorry. I couldn't help it. It was like something was making me do it. I can't explain it." My chest was tight and heavy.

Aldric looked at me wild-eyed. "You couldn't control it?"

Seven stepped in between us. "No, she couldn't. It's this place. It affects everyone differently."

Aldric fumed at Seven. "And how do you know so much about this place?"

Seven chuckled. "A story for another time, mate. Another time."

Seven was right. I felt different here. Darker. I was on edge, and Aldric was too. Valentina, on the other hand, was full of sorrow.

"Val, you ok?"

She trembled. "It's like there's this ache in my chest. Like I'm missing a part of me. I feel nauseous."

I wrapped my arm around her shoulders. "We have to keep moving. The sooner we get out of here, the better."

Everyone nodded in agreement. We had made it past the first trial, but it would only get more difficult from here.

Seven steered us down the River Styx in silence. Everyone seemed lost inside their own thoughts. Prisoners in our own minds. I suddenly felt unprepared. All my training seemed so trivial now. We worked so hard to get here together, but this place threatened to pull us apart.

Aldric touched my arm. "I'm sorry I snapped at you. I...I don't know what came over me."

"Aldric, promise me that we won't ever turn on each other. No matter what. I couldn't bear it."

He pulled me to him and wrapped his arms around my waist. "Nothing will ever come between us. I promise."

I felt warm for the first time since entering this place. My heart was swelling and bursting with love for him. I couldn't imagine a time when that would end.

Everything ends.

A lump formed in my throat. *Did I think that?* No. I would never. Not when it comes to Aldric. I shook it off. "Seven, *faster*."

His eyes narrowed as he nodded. The ship sped fast toward the Ninth Gate.

TWENTY-THREE

WE WOULD BE DEAF SOON. NO SCREAMS, NO HEARTBEATS, NO sound. Silence would take on a whole new meaning.

The potion would shield us from their cries. It was the only way to keep our ears from bleeding. A knot formed in my chest at the sight of the willowy figures up ahead, guarding the Ninth Gate.

Banshees. There were twenty-five of them. I reached into my pocket and pulled out the vial that The Keeper had prepared for us. *Silentium*. It was the antidote to their madness.

"Bottoms up." I took a swig and passed it on to Aldric.

Valentina was next, then Seven, who hesitated but gulped it down.

Like a blow to the head, all sound left my ears. Valentina clung to Seven as he clutched her to his chest. Aldric and I stood still next to each other. His fingers reached for me and I clasped his hand.

This was insane. I couldn't hear a pin drop. I couldn't even hear my own breath. My knees wobbled as we inched closer to the gates. All my other senses were amplified. Bile rose in my throat as the stench of sludge and opium pinched my nose. The banshees were all around us as we sailed through, hanging off the gates like animals.

The banshees' mouths opened wide, contorted as they screamed at us. They whipped their heads around revealing black empty holes where their eyes should have been. A wave of panic washed over me. I looked away from them.

Aldric was wide-eyed and as pale as a ghost. Valentina's eyes were shut tight as she held onto Seven with an iron grip. He glared defiantly at them. The more we resisted their screams, the more they flailed around. They reached for us in hysterics.

The potion was working. We couldn't hear a thing, but it was still just as terrifying as if we could. It was chaos. The banshees screamed at each other in a fit of agony, pulling at each other's hair and limbs. They craned their necks up and screamed at the sky like they were pleading to the gods to let them have us. But the gods weren't listening, and neither were we.

As we passed them, the wood rumbled under my feet, threatening to break apart.

I mouthed to Aldric, "You okay?"

He nodded, grinning from ear to ear. He looked back at the banshees and waved goodbye. This sent them into more of a frenzy as they lunged over each other, struggling to break free from their post. But they couldn't reach us. We had made it.

The spell was wearing off, but the effects made me feel like I was underwater. Voices were muffled as we tried to speak to each other. After a few more minutes, my ears popped and opened. I let out a huge sigh of relief. The Keeper told us it wouldn't last, but the fear of being deaf forever was very real.

My moment of satisfaction quickly faded. We got lucky. How many poor souls had been tortured by them? We were prepared. We knew what to expect. But my heart suddenly ached for those who had no idea. For those still to come. I wished I could save them all. But I knew that I couldn't. I was immortal, but not everyone else was. That was my curse. To watch those around me perish. The humans deserved better than this.

"We shouldn't be here. This place is damned." Seven was a man of few words, but when he spoke it was wise to listen. He was right, but it was too late now.

I blinked back tears. "We had no choice."

Seven looked at me, eyes full of sorrow. "There is always a choice, Gray."

His usual charm was gone, and in its place was something much darker. It cast shadows over his eyes in a way I had never seen. I had no answer for him. For me, there was no other choice. I had to get the Narcissus flower. To defeat Pythia.

Aldric came to my defense. "Well, it's too late to turn back now, buddy."

He couldn't hide the bitterness in his voice. He never liked Seven, and he would jump at any chance to put him in his place.

Seven shot him a defiant look. "We can turn back anytime you want, Bannister. But you and I both know that's not going to happen. Just try not to get yourself killed."

We spent the next few hours chewing on pieces of willow bark to keep the nausea at bay. It got harder to breathe the further we went. The ship glided like a bird downstream, maneuvering gracefully through jagged rocks and thick marshes.

There was some comfort in being on deck, but we would have to dock soon and go the rest of the way on foot through the Mourning Fields. It stood between us and Erebos, where we would have to face our last challenge before meeting the Reflection Siren.

The Mourning Fields were pain and desolation personified. It was where the lost souls roamed with no end to their suffering. Their unrequited loves and failed endeavors kept them in a state of limbo. A torture they would have to endure for all eternity. The only brief respite was the occasional offering of a blood sacrifice. Blood would temporarily alleviate their misery. And they didn't care where that blood came from.

"This is as far as I go, my lovelies." Seven turned to Valentina and embraced her. "I will wait here until you return. I cannot go any further."

Panic struck me. I thought he would accompany us all the way through. I'd already asked enough from him, but the thought of him staying behind filled me with dread. "You're not coming?"

Valentina shot me a look that seemed to say, *don't ask any more questions*. Aldric stiffened as Seven took my face in his hands.

"I *cannot* go any further. You don't need me, Gray. The gods are with you."

I was dumbfounded, but one look at his tortured eyes and I thought it better not to push. There was so much I didn't know about him.

"No. I am grateful you came with us this far. We'll try not to keep you waiting."

Seven winked and reached out to shake Aldric's hand.

He hesitated but took it. "Just keep the engine running."

Seven pulled Aldric in for a hug, which caught him off guard as he chuckled and awkwardly patted his back. "May Apollo guide you and keep you safe, my friend."

As happy as I was to see them getting along, I couldn't help but worry that I was leading us all to our deaths.

The ground was black, jagged, and colder than ice. A gaseous steam rose between the cracks, blurring my vison. The terrain stretched on for miles in every direction. It was impossible to get my bearings. I pulled out the compass that The Keeper had given me. Not an ordinary compass, but it was from his realm and blessed with magic.

There were no directional indications of north or south on it. Instead, the device was marked with the twelve signs of the Zodiac. We were instructed to follow the constellation Virgo for the rest of the way. Apollo created Virgo as a tribute to our fallen kind. It made perfect sense that the Reflection Siren would be waiting at the other end of it.

My skin tingled. "We're almost there. Can you feel it?"

The Mourning Fields were not yet in sight, but I could *feel* the anguish. My chest was heavier and filled with an unexplained sadness. The sorrow had been collecting here. It wafted through the entire perimeter, pricking the back of my throat like nettle thorns.

Aldric and Valentina nodded, their heads drooping and slumping as they walked. *Was I dragging my feet too?* I couldn't tell. Everything was hazy. The trees were bare, like skeletons, arching and twisting in agony without leaves or grass to comfort them.

The ground shifted, and we began walking uphill. The swelling in my chest grew with each step I took. The skeleton trees were disappearing the higher we climbed. The desolation was unbearable.

As we neared the top of the hill, my chest tightened. Their moans blasted through my ears. My knees buckled. Valentina let out a yelp as she toppled over, her hands slamming out in front of her. Aldric collided into me, covering his ears as we hit the ground right next to her.

Every fiber of my body burned as the Mourning Fields' moans turned to screams. Valentina's eyes glowed red. She dug her nails into the thick soil. Saliva dripped from her fangs as she gasped for air.

"Gray—the blood—make the offering."

The blood. Yes, the blood should make it stop.

I fumbled for my pouch. Pain seared through my head as I struggled to get it open. Aldric writhed around on the ground, clutching his head. My heart beat faster as I dumped the contents out in front of me.

A ceremonial dagger, willow bark, and honeycomb spilled out. My head buzzed as the screaming intensified. All their anguish and sorrow were accumulating into one giant ball of torture. I shoved a piece of honeycomb into each of their mouths before taking one for myself.

Valentina came close to biting me as I pried her mouth open. Aldric snatched the dagger and sliced open his hand without hesitation. I did the same as he was already dripping blood onto the willow bark. We clasped hands, trembling and bracing each other.

The ground shook as we willed our magic to thread together. Valentina flopped on the ground, her eyes threatening to roll back.

C'mon. Take the sacrifice, dammit. I squeezed Aldric's hand tighter. *"Focus."*

We tried again, this time using every ounce of energy we had. I forced my mind into his and imagined tiny golden threads, interlocking and dancing together. He thrusted back. White and blue sparks, like stars, rained down. A calm settled in. *It was working.* The screams turned to soft whimpers, then whispers, and then silence.

"Val." I could barely move my limbs as I crawled over to her.

"I...I'm okay." She was as pale as snow.

"Here, drink this." She eagerly took the blood bag and gulped it down.

"Aldric—"

"I'm good. My head almost exploded, but other than that, I'm good."

Relief washed over me. Then dread. We almost didn't make it. And these trials would only get harder from here. What if we're not ready for this?

"What have I gotten us into?"

Aldric shook his head and knelt beside me. "Stop. Don't doubt yourself now. Look how far we've come."

I choked back tears. "We almost *died*. I should have started the offering right away. I shouldn't have waited."

Aldric sighed. "Darlin', they got in your head. You were disoriented. We all were. But you did it just like I knew you would."

I couldn't take that chance again. I needed to focus. To be better prepared. I shrugged and backed away from him. He meant well, but I could not shake this feeling of dread. Maybe it was residual feelings from the Mourning Fields. Maybe it was something else. But it was nagging at me like an open wound.

The guardian demons would be coming soon. They paroled the outer edges of the Elm, protecting the Reflection Siren. There was no way to slip past them. We would have to fight with weapons we had never used before. Our magic would be useless.

We finished off the last of the honeycomb to heal any damage that might have been inflicted on our minds. Valentina slurped down another blood bag while Aldric readied his frost bow. The arrows were designed to shatter on impact, inflicting shards of glass into their targets. Valentina and I were both armed with daggers and throwing knives. We stashed them in every crevice we could find. She also chose a battle axe while I settled for a longsword to carry in my dominant hand. It felt strange and unfamiliar, but it would have to do.

The Elm was far off in the distance, but visible. It was a straight shot through an open field that would soon be littered with demons. The ground rumbled as we marched. It was faint at first but shook harder the further we went. They were coming.

"Get ready," I whispered.

Valentina nodded, her eyes glowing a vibrant shade of red. I took a deep breath and felt mine go black, like a switch. Aldric's were a milky shade of white. I drew in a sharp breath. I had never seen his eyes change before. It was magnificent.

The rumbling was louder than thunder. The ground started to crack and separate. With weapons drawn, we held our positions. The wind picked up as the guardian demons came into view. They charged toward us like a stampede of wild horses. But these things were not horses.

With two heads and the bodies of lions, they moved with a speed unlike any other creature I had ever seen. They growled and snapped their jaws as they inched closer to us. I swallowed hard. There were only six of them. They were either over confident, or I had underestimated their strength.

We scattered as they crashed toward us, barely dodging the first attack. I spun around as one lunged at me. I ducked and slid underneath it, its slimy skin just barely grazing my cheek. I leaped up as it came back around and slammed into it, knocking it backward. It growled and charged at me again, sending me flying.

Pain shot through by back as I hit the ground. I rolled quickly to the side as it sprang up in the air. Moving behind it, I thrust my sword into its back and ripped in and sliced its body completely in half.

One down. It was like a dance and I was finding my rhythm. The sword was a part of me, like another limb. I flowed through it without effort. It knew my moves before I did.

Everything became a blur of blood, slashing, and snarls. I scanned the field for Aldric. He had one in a headlock as he stabbed it in the eye with a dagger. The demon lunged at him when he backed away, right before he shot it with a frost arrow. Shards of glass exploded out from its body, spraying blood and chunks of flesh all over the ground.

The next one came at me faster. I dodged to my left, but not quickly enough. Its jaws clamped down on my wrist, flinging me forward to my knees. With my free hand, I swung my sword around and slashed into its neck. I pulled my wrist out just as it was about to tear it from my body. It came at me again, its head barely connected to its neck. *Just die already*.

It charged again, but this time I slid out of the way and brought down my sword on what was left of its neck, slicing its head clean off.

Valentina was on her back, a demon snarled over her. I sprinted toward her but stopped as she pulled out two daggers and gutted open its stomach. She grunted and pushed it over before it could fall on her.

A frost arrow sped past me. I spun around and braced myself for another attack. The demon sprang up and the arrow pierced its eye. Blood and flesh rained down upon me as it exploded in mid-air. Trembling, I spun around again, ready for another attack.

Aldric jogged toward me. "It's over. We got all of them."

I couldn't breathe. My heart was beating out of control. My arms were stiff and sore. I could barely lift my sword. I scanned the field. It was completely still. The rumbling was gone. The stench of rotting demon flesh singed my nostrils. I had to force down the bile that was rising in my throat.

Valentina huffed, wiping at the blood covering her arms and chest. "Ugh. I am *so* ready for a shower."

Aldric looked at me with concern, his eyes now back to their usual shade of blue. "Are you hurt?"

"I'll live."

My wrist was throbbing, and my body ached with exhaustion, but other than that, I was still in one piece. Aldric looked more handsome than ever. Sweat glistened down his face, casting a fresh glow on his skin. His cheeks flushed the same way they did in the bedroom. Fighting looked good on him.

I shot him a grateful look. "Thanks for having my back out there. You were amazing."

He winked at me. "I learned from the best."

My face flushed. Even covered in demon blood, he still managed to send tingles up my spine.

"Wow. Really? In this mess you two are *still* flirting?" Valentina shook her head at us in disbelief.

My cheeks grew hotter. Aldric smirked and winked again. For a moment, I almost forgot that we were in Hell.

"We need to keep moving." The Reflection Siren was already calling to us.

A sweet melody hummed in my ears, luring me to her. *Could they hear it too? Did it sound the same?*

She was the bringer of dreams and nightmares. She would drag out your highest hopes and deepest fears and bring them to life. I had many, but what I feared the most was myself.

TWENTY-FOUR

THE SIREN'S MAGIC WAS ALL AROUND US. HER BEAUTY RADIATED, soft and willowy like an apparition surrounded by flowers. The ground was blanketed in thousands of petals from deep reds, ambers, and golds to emerald greens, violets, and chocolate browns. But there was only one flower I wanted, and it was at her feet.

"You ready for this?" Aldric didn't look like he was.

I nodded. "Remember, we have to stay together or we'll get lost in our own minds."

Valentina crinkled her nose. "What if all three of us get lost?"

My chest tightened. That was the last thing I needed to think about. The Keeper warned me it could happen.

"We need to stay focused. If we work together, we'll find our way out."

Aldric turned toward Valentina. "Gray's right. Let's just stick to the plan and get out as quick as we can."

Valentina shook her head in agreement, but her eyes told a different story. A fear I had never seen in her before.

I took a deep breath and faced the Siren. Her face contorted into a sinister smile. Behind her were the bones of the ones who tried and failed before us. Once they were completely lost in their own minds, she fed on their flesh. I shivered, forcing away images of being eaten alive. I couldn't fall apart now. Everyone was counting on me.

We clasped hands, with me leading and Aldric in between us. My free hand trembled as I reached for the Narcissus flower. The Siren's wicked smile widened as we moved closer.

I glanced back at Aldric once more. "Don't let go."

My whole body trembled as I wrapped my hand around the stem. Everything went black.

I was falling. Free-falling through endless space. *Were those stars twinkling in the distance?* The darkness gave way to sparks of light flashing by me as I tumbled down. I clenched my teeth, afraid they might shatter. My skin was thin like paper. Like it might slide right off. *This wasn't real.*

I couldn't feel Aldric's hand. Panic clawed at my chest. The wind whipped around me like a hurricane. I was being sucked into a tunnel. *Was I dying?* My chest rattled in its cage while my lungs struggled with each breath. I flailed out my arms in every direction, but my limbs weighed me down. It was like trying to run underwater.

Endless falling. The wind picked up more speed, sucking me further into its embrace. *Where was I?*

On the brink of madness and close to losing consciousness, I stopped fighting it. I couldn't endure this black hole any longer. It was empty. A void that sat in the pit of my stomach like a gnawing ache. It burned my insides, threatening to rip me apart, limb from limb. I fell faster, tumbling down. Nausea set in.

Debris flew past me. *What was that?* My heart dropped. *Bones.* I opened my mouth to scream, but nothing came out. Then, everything went still.

A white light pierced my eyes. A reflection. White sand. I was hovering above a desert. There was movement below. People fighting. Blood ran through the sand like a river. Bodies missing limbs. Heads scattered in disarray. *So much blood.*

The bitter stench stung my nose and filled my mouth. I held my breath. I was moving further down, slower now. Hundreds of soldiers crashed into each other without mercy. Faceless creatures against three warriors.

I gasped. *It was us.* All three of us. Me, Aldric, and Valentina. We were there, fighting. *How could this be happening?* How could I be down there and up here at the same time? Were they seeing this too?

We were outnumbered. *Run!* They couldn't hear me. I screamed again, but I was invisible. My voice did not exist. *I can't watch this.* I cried out. One of the faceless came down on Aldric and sliced him in two. Valentina's head flew off as another faceless attacked her from behind. *No.* I was sick. Tears streamed down my face as I choked on my own screams. My throat turned to sandpaper. *This can't be real.*

The Siren hummed a sweet tune, coating my ears like honey. I closed my eyes, taking deep breaths. I was still floating down. My feet hit the ground. I opened my eyes. Everyone was gone. Vanished. The blood, the bodies, everything. I was completely alone. *What have I done?*

I wanted to lie down and die with them. I did this. I killed them. They died because of me. *Fighting for me.* I didn't deserve them. I deserved to be alone. To wander this desert for eternity with no one to blame but myself. This was my punishment.

My legs collapsed from under me and my knees hit the sand hard. I feared the tears would never stop. They ran down my face like heavy rain. But no one would cry for me.

"Poor Gray. Always feeling sorry for herself." His voice was dark and raspy.

Dragos.

I looked up as he towered over me. "How...how are you here?"

His lips formed into a smirk. "Because you wanted me here, Gray. I'm in your head. They've all left you, except for me. I will always be with you."

I shook my head. "No. You aren't real. None of this is real. I don't want you. Get out of my head."

He laughed. "This is *your* dream, Gray. You brought me here. We belong together."

No. This was the Siren, messing with me. I didn't want him. I couldn't. I would not.

"Get away from me." I scrambled to get off the ground.

Dragos laughed harder as he grabbed me by the shoulders. His breath on my face smelled of honeysuckle and tobacco. Why did he always smell *so* good? *No. Stop it, Gray.* You *have* to get away from him.

"You remember how good it was, don't you, Gray? How you never wanted me to stop."

Heat radiated from his lips, just inches away from mine. He was pulling me in. The Siren sang louder. My head was spinning, our lips almost touching. The sweet scent of honey lingered between us, teasing my senses.

I could just...let go. Surrender. *Was this what I wanted? To close my eyes and melt into...Dragos?* My hands trembled as I looked up at him. A chill ran through me. His eyes, they were *hollow*.

I shoved him hard and ran. There was a tiny light in the distance. I ran toward it.

"Aldric, where are you? Aldric?" I screamed his name as loud as I could.

I would not give up. I had to fight.

"Please, Aldric. Don't let me go." My tears turned to sobs but I kept running.

"Gray, come back to me. I need you. Gray."

My heart raced. *Aldric.* He could hear me.

"I'm coming. Aldric. Wait for me. I'm coming."

Aldric's voice shook with desperation. "Gray! Where are you?"

Where was I? I'm in a desert. No. That's not right. Then it hit me. I was still in the Siren's song. None of this was real. It never was. It was time to get out of here.

I looked around wildly. Where was he?

"Gray, focus. Use the link. Find me."

I spun around in circles. His voice was getting louder.

"I'm coming, Aldric. I'm coming."

I shouted as I ran in the direction of his voice. I pictured the link, a silvery cord connecting me to him. I focused on it and nothing else. I charged ahead, ignoring my aching limbs. My blood rushed to my head as I clung to the link for dear life. I screamed his name as I ran. I had to live. I had to get back to him. It was the only thing that mattered. His love was in my bones. I hungered for it like blood.

The desert faded away, peeling back like the layers of an onion. The ground was now jagged and sharp. My heart sank. *I was running toward a cliff.*

A lump formed in my throat. I would have to jump. There was nothing behind me anymore. I took a deep breath and said a silent prayer to Apollo. Inches away from the edge of the cliff, my stomach dropped. I screamed as I leaped out into the abyss. It roared out of me like thunder.

I braced myself for the fall, but in one quick swoop, he caught me. Aldric's strong arms wrapped around me.

"I got you."

A fire, hotter than the sun, spread through me. Our eyes locked and everything went black again.

Daylight blinded me when my eyelids fluttered open. Aldric's arms were still around me. I looked around the meadow, my head throbbing. It was still and quiet. The Reflection Siren was gone, and in my hand was the Narcissus flower.

We did it. Delirium set in. I couldn't stop laughing. We passed her test. Aldric helped me up, laughing with me. We stood face to face. I kissed him without warning. He pulled me in tight, running his fingers through my hair. My lips physically ached for him. My heart beat fast as we broke away, gasping for air.

His eyes were glassy. "I thought I lost you."

Guilt stung me. Pushing images of Dragos out of my mind, my stomach turned. "You could never lose me."

He smiled but shot me a concerned look. "Gray, the visions... what was it like for you? What did you see?"

A chill came over me like a dark cloud. I shook my head. "I don't want to talk about it. Not now. Not here. Let's just get Valentina and get out of here."

A shadow passed through his eyes as he stared at me. "Later then."

I nodded, but I had no intention of telling him anything that I went through in there.

I ran over to Valentina. She was on her knees, completely still, expressionless. As if she was in a trance. "Val, it's time to go. Are you okay? Val, get up."

Nothing. No response. She stared straight ahead, but she wasn't staring at anything at all. *She must have let go of my hand.* No. This couldn't be happening. I fell to my knees in front of her.

"Aldric, do something. She's not getting up."

Aldric shook her shoulders. "Val, you're scaring us. C'mon, snap out of it."

She was there, but she wasn't. She didn't even blink. Dread washed over me.

My voice was hoarse. "We have to get her back to the ship."

⸻

Seven sprang into action. He lifted Valentina out of Aldric's arms as if she weighed nothing. He was already calibrating our way home before we were even on deck. I swung my leg over the railing as the ship lurched forward.

Seven took Valentina below deck to the sleeping quarters. A few minutes later, he returned with panic in his eyes. This man did not fear anything, but he was genuinely scared for her.

"What happened? How did she get like this?"

I lowered my head. "It's all my fault. I let go of her hand. I promised her..."

Aldric cupped my tear streaked face in his hands. "This is not your fault. We don't know what happened. Val is strong. She is going to come out of this."

The tears would not stop. "You don't know that. What if she is like this forever? I need her. I can't do any of this without her."

Seven placed a gentle hand on my shoulder. "You need to be brave. Aldric is right. Valentina is the strongest woman I know. She would not want you to blame yourself."

With the Narcissus flower clutched to my chest, I stared out at the horizon. We made it past the Ninth Gate, the banshees, the Mourning Fields and the vicious guardian demons. I resisted the Reflection Siren and lived to tell about it. I should've been happy. Relieved even. I felt nothing.

As we flew past the skeleton trees, Aldric raised up his hands and cracked open the sky. It sucked us in and pushed us out and back into our world. The first of our kind to ever travel to Hell and back, but it would mean nothing if my best friend didn't wake up.

TWENTY-FIVE

MY SCREAMS ECHOED THROUGH THE HALL OF SECRETS AS WE RAN.
Seven clutched Valentina's lifeless body to his chest. The Keeper
ushered us into the healing clinic where Seven laid her down on one
of the beds. The room was bare and sterile. There were three beds
covered in white linens, a small lamp, and no windows.

Across the room, there was a table covered in herbs, amulets, and
tonics. A healing station with a collection of tools that would be used
to bring her back. *What if she didn't come back?* I shivered, seeing my
breath exhale out before me. The Keeper shoved us out of the room
and closed the door behind him.

I slumped down against the nearest wall. Aldric and Seven pacing
in front of me only added to my apprehension. Hours went by as we
waited. Devastation filled me like a disease. It stretched into every
corner of my mind, tugging at my sanity. To me, this was worse than
the Mourning Fields.

It was almost morning when the clinic door finally opened. The
Keeper emerged, pale and gaunt. I jumped up and rushed over to

him. Aldric and Seven darted over, almost colliding into each other. The Keeper seemed so small and childlike in that moment. He stood before us with shoulders hunched and dark circles under his eyes.

"I'm sorry. I cannot bring her back."

His words sucked the air out of my lungs. The room was spinning. Aldric reached out an arm to steady me as my knees buckled. I hunched over, heaving and gasping for air. *This can't be happening.*

Seven punched the wall and stormed out, causing all of us to flinch. The sound of his fist hitting stone was louder than thunder. It reverberated down every corridor. I shoved Aldric's arm away and jumped up.

"I...I need to see her."

The Keeper nodded. "Of course, but I must ask, did you get the flower?"

I stiffened. "I did. But I would take it all back if it meant that I could save her."

Valentina's chest moved up and down as each breath filled the space between us. Her eyelids fluttered. She was still in there. Lost in her own nightmare. It should have been me. I should be the one lying there, not her. *I was supposed to protect her.*

My heart throbbed. What had the Siren done to her? She looked peaceful, but a war waged on inside her head. If I didn't pull her out soon, she would be lost in there forever.

"You should get some rest. I will keep watch."

My body tensed. Of course, he would keep watch. That is what he did. He *kept* things.

"I'm not leaving her side."

The Keeper sighed. "I am sorry to say this, but it is not you, nor I, who can help her."

I snapped, "You know everything and yet you know nothing. I am *not* giving up on her. If the roles were reversed, she wouldn't give up on me. I will find a way."

I clenched my fists into her bed sheets, choking back tears.

The Keeper's eyes widened. "You're angry. You have every right to be. I admire your tenacity, but do not forget why you went to the Underworld to begin with. Valentina would not want you to forget. She knew what was at stake, and for you, she would do it again. No matter the risk."

He was right. Valentina knew the risk. We all did. But she was lost because of me and I needed to fix it. The answer was taunting me this entire time. It called to me quietly, but I had been pushing it away. Now, it hit me like a ton of bricks. I knew what I had to do.

I would do anything to get her back. Even dance with the devil. I couldn't avoid it any longer. The Keeper's eyes darkened as he watched the wheels spin inside my head.

I looked him straight in the eye. "Only blood can save her now."

The Keeper shook his head, confused. "Gray, feeding is not going to bring her back. Don't you think I tried that already?"

I drew in a sharp breath. "You don't get it. I'm not talking about feeding. I'm talking about blood...*her blood*. The blood she shares with only one other person."

The Keeper's eyes lit up as my words sank in. "Yes...he is the only one who might be able to reach her."

A lump formed in my throat as we both thought what neither of us wanted to say.

Dragos.

If I had to make a deal with the devil, I might never see my soul again. After everything, I wasn't even sure if I still had one. When I was a child, I believed in fairytales. I dreamed of princes charging in to save the day. Champions of good who would slay the monsters under my bed. I knew now that fairytales did not exist...but the monsters did.

They lived and breathed and walked amongst us. They cursed us and poisoned us with their very existence. We had to be our own heroes. Our own champions. No one was coming to save us. And to beat them, I had to join them. I said I would do anything to save her and I meant it. I only hoped that Aldric would still be there when it was done.

The horizon was calm and peaceful. I, on the other hand, was anything but. I stood on the hill outside the Hall, gazing out at the Sea of Magia. My insides twisted and turned as the reality of what I had to do began to sink in. *What was I going to say to Aldric?* He already sensed something was off, back in the Underworld.

After he pulled me out of the Siren's song, he was anxious about what I had seen. We were linked, but I did not see him until he pulled me out. What if he had been there the whole time, watching me and my visions of Dragos? If so, he would never forgive me for it.

Seven sloshed up the hill, shaking me out of my reverie. "I assume you have a plan."

I shot him a look. "I do. But not everyone is going to like it."

Seven scoffed. "Aldric doesn't need to like it. He just needs to be on board. Saving Valentina is all that matters right now. He can work out his jealousy issues with your ex-boyfriend after she wakes up."

I sighed. This thing between me and Dragos was becoming a thing between me and Aldric. The tension around us was thick and it was spilling out for everyone to see. But Seven was right. It wasn't about us.

"I take it you're up for a little adventure?"

He smirked. "I've already prepared the ship."

I found Aldric in the study. I watched him from the doorway as he sat in front of the fire, swirling a glass of whiskey in his hand. He was pensive, his gaze lost in the flames. With my stomach in knots, I took a deep breath and sat down next to him.

"Aldric, I'm going to tell you something that you aren't going to like. In fact, you're going to hate it."

I waited to get a reaction, but he said nothing. "I need to find Dragos and bring him back here. I believe he is the only one who can help Val. And I need you to be okay with it."

The silence between us was deafening. A faint flicker of contempt flashed in his eyes, but his face remained blank. This was the first time I was unable to read him. His thoughts were closed off to me.

My hands trembled when our eyes finally met. His expression was cold and vacant.

He let out a deep breath. "I know. I knew the second it happened that he would be the one. I've been going over it in my head for the last three days. You're right. *I hate it.*"

"Aldric..." I didn't know what else to say.

He leaned in close and gently took my hands in his. His breath was warm on my face, but it sent shivers up my spine.

"Gray, I trust you. I know that this is about saving your friend and nothing else. But...I don't trust *him*. So, I've made up my mind. I'm going with you."

The look on his face told me there was no talking him out of this. If this was how he was going to be okay with it, then I had to let him come. I let out a deep breath, slightly relieved, but more surprised.

I was expecting more of a fight, but I was grateful that he didn't give me one. Today, I needed all my energy for the dark road ahead. Today, I would have to open a door that I had spent the last four years barricading shut.

TWENTY-SIX

THE ONLY SOUND IN THE NIGHT WAS FROM THE WAVES CRASHING against the sides of the ship. I kept my distance from Aldric and Seven, lost in a riptide of my own thoughts.

I hadn't seen Dragos since that night in the ruins of the Wolf and Crescent. Looking back, a part of me tingled with excitement when I first laid eyes on him. All those familiar feelings came flooding in, only to be quickly clouded with anger for what he did. Then came the sorrow and the grief from the broken shards of my heart. The twisted agony of being ripped apart from the inside out.

He seemed to revel in it. My pain made him stronger. And then came the realization that he never loved me. Like a cold, hard slap in the face, leaving me forever stunned. All the while, Aldric had watched from the shadows. He watched me flinch, and cower, and agonize. And I was so caught up in my emotions for Dragos, I didn't even sense Aldric there.

Tonight, Aldric watched me like a hawk. His eyes searched my face for answers I didn't have. I didn't know what to say to him. My past was my burden, but it was driving a wedge between us and I didn't know how to make it stop.

I needed Valentina more than ever. She would have known what to say. My heart sank. I kept hoping a sign would come from The Keeper, telling us to turn back. Telling us that she had woken up and we could turn the ship around. Anything to keep me from going after Dragos. But there were no signs. No messages. Only the sound of the waves, mocking me with each splash.

My anxiety was building as we neared the edge of Diana's Forest. Seven and I had both agreed that the safest way to get to Dragos would be through Arcadia. Aldric remained quiet as we discussed our plans. Seven made it clear that his opinion was not wanted. My focus was on the task ahead, not on Aldric's feelings. Though, I would have to face them eventually.

I dreaded the walk through the forest for many reasons. The main one being that Seven would hang back with the ship while Aldric and I would have to suffer in awkward silence. I hated this rift between us. Things were always so easy and smooth with him. This new distance was strange, and it left a hole in my heart. We were linked, but we were closed off to each other.

The air was crisp, and the leaves crunched under our feet like broken glass. I sucked the cool air deep into my lungs, hoping it would help calm my nerves. Aldric came to a halt and put his hand out in front of me. His pulse raced as they came into view. Arcadia and Lycos appeared out of nowhere, just a few feet ahead of us.

"Hello, sister. I see you have come to pay me another visit. You're not getting sentimental on me now, are you?"

I nearly choked. "Don't flatter yourself."

Her eyes glistened with amusement. "You must be Aldric. My, you *are* handsome. Come to join us finally?"

Arcadia licked her lips and looked him up and down. It was all I could do to keep my eyes from rolling back in my head.

I gritted my teeth. "You know that's never going to happen. I'm here for Dragos. I need you to summon him."

Arcadia's eyes widened. She squealed with delight. "Gray, I didn't realize you two had an *open* relationship. I don't think Dragos will want to share, though. He's rather possessive over what belongs to him."

Aldric stiffened and clenched his fists. The more she spoke, the more I wanted to punch her in the face.

I shook it off. "Enough with the jokes, Arcadia. Valentina is sick. She is...she needs Dragos. He would want to know."

Lycos stepped forward. "What happened to her?" His voice was deep and raspy.

Arcadia shot him a look of annoyance for speaking.

I shook my head. "It's complicated. Let's just say she's trapped inside her own mind." I couldn't let them know we had the Narcissus flower.

Arcadia huffed. "What? I've never heard of that."

I snapped, "Well, it must not exist then. Seriously, do you ever get sick of listening to your own voice?"

Arcadia gasped, covering her mouth in disbelief.

Aldric intervened. "That's why we need Dragos. Maybe he knows something we don't." He shot me a look, daring me to read between the lines.

Lycos stood tall and firm, like a statue. Yet there was a warmth emulating from him that I hadn't noticed before. A genuine concern. "You are right. He would want to know. We will contact him."

Before Arcadia could protest, Lycos put a gentle finger to her lips to quiet her. It was hard to tell who was controlling who at this point. Either way, I was grateful for his influence.

Arcadia's smirk returned. "Yes. We'll get Dragos for you. I'm looking forward to witnessing your heartfelt reunion." She chuckled, looking back and forth between me and Aldric.

I wasn't going to let her have the last word. "Lycos, thank you for your help."

Lycos gave a quick nod and turned to leave. Arcadia rolled her eyes. She spun on her heels and stomped off after him, leaving me and Aldric alone in the forest.

Words unspoken held more power than the ones that leave your lips. In silence, there was truth. It was louder than thunder and lasted longer than the eternal night. I didn't know what to say to Aldric because I didn't know what to say to myself. Our love for each other was not in question. It was the unseen forces that hovered, just beyond our reach, that made me uncertain. It was the past spilling into the present. We were in a constant state of war. With ourselves, with each other, and with our enemies. Our link was weakening, and we both could feel it.

"What happened to you in the Siren's song?" I was hoping he wouldn't ask me that, but I knew it was all he could think about.

I hesitated. "I don't want to talk about it. Not here. Not now."

His face turned red. "When then? I almost lost you in there. Something had a hold on you. I need to know what I'm dealing with."

My hands were shaking. I didn't want to think about those visions. "But you didn't lose me. *You* brought me back. That's all that matters."

He took a deep breath and ran a hand through his disheveled hair. "He was there, wasn't he? In your head. Dragos. He was the reason I almost lost you."

A pang of guilt stabbed at me. "Aldric...it wasn't like that. Please, can we talk about this—"

I cut myself off when I heard them approaching. It had only been a few hours, so I was surprised to see them back so soon. Aldric stiffened at the sight of them.

Dragos and I locked eyes. With nostrils flared, he charged toward me with lightning speed. The ground shook with each thunderous step.

Aldric grabbed my wrist and pulled me closer to him. "If he lays one hand on you, I will rip out his throat." His voice was cold and full of malice. My whole body shuddered.

In one quick stride, Dragos moved in between us and grabbed me by my shoulders. "Where is she, Gray? How could you let this happen? You were supposed to protect her."

He shook me hard as he shouted. I had never seen him so angry. So frightened for his sister.

His voice got louder as he continued. "I let you *live* because of her. I let you run around, playing your little games so that she could have a companion. She wasn't supposed to get hurt," he spat at me.

I was dumbfounded. He squeezed his fingers into my flesh as his eyes bulged, crazed and bloodshot.

Aldric pounced on him like a wild animal. Dragos knocked me to the side as he came crashing down on him. Aldric snarled, his eyes turning white. He sank his fangs into Dragos's neck. They rolled around on the ground, clawing and snapping at each other.

They were going to kill each other.

I charged forward without thinking. I wedged myself in between them just as Dragos's hand flung at me with a force that sent me flying into the air. I gasped for air as my back slammed into a tree. Panic rose in my chest as I struggled to breathe. I was on the verge of blacking out.

Aldric growled louder. I jumped to my feet and looked around. They were both covered in blood, their clothes shredded as they took turns pouncing on each other.

Lycos and Arcadia looked on with blank expressions, and no intentions of jumping in.

A burning sensation formed in my chest. My blood pressure rose as they continued to hiss and snarl at each other. *This wasn't about them.* Like a tidal wave, everything hit me. My pain, my anger, *my magic.* It welled up inside me like one gigantic ball of hate. I threw my head back, flung my arms at the sky, and unleashed all of it.

Magic coursed through my veins, down to my fingertips, and out of me as I shouted, "*Disparo.*"

Dragos and Aldric were thrown backward with such force, it was as if an invisible hand had reached down and pulled them apart. With their eyes wide and their breaths heavy, they glared at each other. It was the opening I needed. I let them have it.

"How *dare* you behave this way. Both of you. Valentina is fighting for her life and all you two care about is whose bite is bigger. You disgust me."

Aldric looked away, uncomfortable, while Dragos continued to stare daggers at me.

I charged at Dragos but stopped inches from his face. "And *you*. This is just as much your fault as it is mine. You abandoned us. You were supposed to protect us both. But you were too busy playing house with the Consilium to care. And it is because of her that I let *you* live. So stop with this temper tantrum and help me wake her up. If anything happens to her, there will be nothing stopping me from ending your life."

Dragos eyed me carefully. His breath was hot and quick. "Fine, let's go. But this conversation is far from over, Gray."

Aldric got up and stood between us. "You will not speak to her like that. You will not put your hands on her ever again. Do you understand me?"

Dragos's face twisted in contempt. The animosity between them ran deep.

Arcadia huffed. "As entertaining as watching your little love triangle unfold has been, I am ready for all of you to leave."

I rolled my eyes. "For once, we agree on something."

A devious smile formed across Dragos's face. "I'm not going anywhere with *him*. You want my help, he stays."

Aldric charged at him again, but I gripped his arm, holding him back.

"Out of the question. I am not letting her go anywhere with you alone."

Dragos knew me well. He knew that I would agree to his demands. He knew that I would do anything to save Valentina. And he knew that it would drive Aldric crazy to watch me go off with him.

Dragos snickered. "Afraid she'll choose me instead? Well, you should be."

Aldric puffed out his chest and clenched his teeth. "I'm going to kill you."

He grunted as he started toward Dragos. This time, I couldn't hold him back. Dragos laughed, waving him over for round two. I took a deep breath and braced myself.

Lycos dashed over and placed a strong, but gentle hand on Aldric's shoulder. "I will go with them."

Aldric looked at him, puzzled.

Lycos pleaded. "I give you my word that no harm will come to her."

Aldric relaxed, slightly, as he weighed his options.

"You can't possibly think I will let you leave with her." Arcadia pouted.

"I'm not asking your permission, Arcadia." Lycos was gentle, but firm.

She let out a squeal as she stomped her foot.

Aldric looked around, helpless.

I cupped his face in my hands. "It has to be this way. I will be fine. I promise. *Trust me.*"

Aldric nodded, but he didn't look convinced. "It seems I don't have much choice."

Dragos chuckled.

Arcadia sauntered over and draped an arm around Aldric. "Don't worry, sister. I will take good care of him while you're gone." She snickered as Aldric shoved her arm off of him.

Arcadia shot Lycos a defiant look, which he ignored. Something was happening between them. It seemed like she was losing her power over him and she knew it.

I didn't look back as the three of us made our way toward Seven's ship. I couldn't bear to see the hurt look on Aldric's face.

Like a band of misfits, Seven regarded us cautiously as we approached. He shot me a look. There was just one last thing to do. I spun around and placed a hand on each of their heads.

"*Obscuro.*"

Dragos gasped. "I...I can't see."

Lycos remained calm and silent.

I chuckled as I pushed Dragos on board. "You didn't honestly think I was going to let you see our location, did you?"

Dragos swore under his breath as he stumbled onto the ship.

As we set sail, my heart ached for Aldric. *What have I done to him?* I prayed he would still be the same man I loved when we returned.

TWENTY-SEVEN

DRAGOS WHINED AND COMPLAINED THE ENTIRE TRIP. ONCE WE were safely inside the Hall, I lifted the spell. His eyes darted around the room, half expecting an ambush. Lycos, on the other hand, was calm as he methodically took in his new surroundings.

Dragos spun on me. "Where is she? Where is my sister?"

The desperation in his voice was real. It puzzled me. After all he had done to her, he was now concerned about her well-being?

The Keeper emerged from the study and met us in the main hall. He regarded Dragos with quiet contemplation before approaching.

"Follow me. We haven't got much time."

My heart sank. She was slipping further and further into her own mind. I said a silent prayer to the gods as we followed him to the healing clinic. I still blamed myself and I begged for their forgiveness.

Dragos stormed into the clinic behind The Keeper and slammed the door shut, but not before throwing me one more menacing glance. I shook my head. He had a lot of nerve being angry with me. It was so typical of him to lash out at everyone else.

Time seemed to drag on. Seven paced around the room as he had done before. He was beside himself. He and Valentina shared a special bond. I didn't know all the details, but I knew she had gotten him through a difficult time. With her life hanging in the balance, there was nowhere else he'd rather be.

But why was Lycos here? Why did he volunteer himself for this journey? He could have easily stayed with Arcadia in the forest, leaving Aldric and Dragos at each other's throats. Yet here he was. He planted himself in one of the chairs next to me, across from the clinic door. He didn't move a muscle.

I didn't waste any time. "Why are you here?"

Lycos didn't even flinch. "My people have a long and complicated history with your kind."

I was intrigued. "I don't know much about your people."

Lycos tore his eyes away from the door to look at me. It seemed to pain him to do so. "Do you believe in destiny? In prophecies? My people do. We live by it. That is why I am here."

I was still confused but mesmerized by the smokiness of his voice and the careful, yet deliberate way his lips formed words.

I shrugged. "My kind only knows blood. We take what we want regardless of who suffers. If that is my destiny, then I have truly been forsaken by the gods."

His eyes sparkled. "The gods didn't forsake you, Gray. They are testing you. We are always exactly where we are supposed to be."

His words lingered in the air between us, clinging to me like a dream. Every hair on the back of my neck stood up. *The prophecy.* Valentina. The wolves. *He knew.* His eyes lit up as he saw the realization sink in for me.

He leaned in close and whispered, "*Vulkodlak.*"

My whole body trembled.

Sometime in the middle of the night, the clinic door finally opened. A pale and disheveled Dragos came stumbling out. I held my breath as I waited for him to speak. I tried to search his face for some indication, but all I could read was exhaustion.

Lycos and Seven stood on either side of me, like two warriors who had spent all night on the battlefield. Their patience was holding on by a thread and threatening to snap if they didn't hear what they wanted.

Dragos's eyes were sunken in and covered in dark circles. He turned only to me. "She's awake."

I could breathe again. Tears streamed down my face like rain. I threw my arms around Dragos's neck and sobbed into his shoulder. He was as surprised as everyone else. I forgot for a moment who he was. So many emotions flooded through me, but mostly relief.

Dragos's arms tightened around me, snapping me out of my delirium. I jumped back. *What was I doing?* We locked eyes and his face softened.

My cheeks were burning up. "Sorry. I...I just got caught up in... I'm just happy she's awake."

He smirked and nodded as I brushed past him to go to Valentina's bedside.

Her face lit up when I walked into the room. Her skin was moist and pale, but her eyes were clear and alert.

I squeezed her hand. "How are you feeling?"

A hint of color was starting to return to her cheeks. "He saved me." She smiled, childlike.

A pang of guilt shot through me. I put her here, and Dragos saved her. The irony was not lost on me.

I smiled back. "I knew he would. He loves you very much."

She reached for my hand. "He loves you too, Gray. He always has."

Here it comes. The truth that I could never see until now. She never gave up on him. On us. She had been clinging to this hope, all this time, that we would be one big happy family again. I didn't have the heart to tell her otherwise. Not in this moment.

"Val...what did you see in there? In the Siren's song?"

She turned her head away, her eyes welling up with tears. "I don't want to talk about it. Ever."

I understood. The things I saw and felt were...unspeakable. "I'm sorry. You must be exhausted. I'll let you get some rest." My knees trembled as I walked toward the door.

She called out. "It wasn't your fault, Gray. Everything happens for a reason. We are all exactly where we are supposed to be."

The floor nearly fell out from under me.

I stumbled into Lycos while he waited directly on the other side of the door. "May I see her?"

It was more of a statement than a question. My head hurt, and I didn't have the energy to question him. Something beyond my control was happening between them. I stepped aside and gestured for him to go in.

The Keeper raised an eyebrow at me.

I shrugged. I needed a moment to myself. "I'll be in the study if you need me."

With just one foot in the study, Dragos was already nipping at my heels.

"Gray, can we talk?"

I sighed. "Not now, Dragos. I'm too tired for your mental warfare."

His eyes darkened. "Very well. Another time then."

For the first time ever, he didn't put up a fight. He just let me be. I didn't care to think about his reasons. I was just happy to be alone. I poured myself a glass of whiskey and settled in by the fire.

I was so entranced by the flames, I hadn't realized how much time had passed. Lycos's heavy footsteps shook me out of my daze.

He cleared his throat as he stood in the doorway. "Seven has prepared the ship for departure. It's time for you to go back."

I almost choked on my whiskey. "Don't you mean *us*?"

A gleam of mischief twinkled in his eye. "I'm not going back."

Great. This day just keeps getting better. "What I am supposed to tell Arcadia? We made a deal with her."

His voice was firm but gentle. "No, you made a deal with her. I simply promised Aldric that you would not be harmed. I think it's safe to say that you are not."

I let out a deep sigh. Arcadia was going to flip out. How did everything get so complicated?

My heartbeat quickened. "Arcadia is going to come after you."

Lycos smiled softly. "She cannot control me. She will soon see the truth."

The only thing Arcadia was going to see was red. "And what is that truth, Lycos?"

He leaned against the side of the door frame as a playful grin spread across his lips. "Balance. Like the scales of Libra and the changing of the seasons, it is a time for balance."

He was no longer under Arcadia's control. He was free, and it was all because of Valentina. He was drawn to her from the moment they met. It was more of a mystery than Lycos himself.

I raised an eyebrow. "How did you know about the Dhampir-wolf link? About *Vulkodlak*?"

Lycos chuckled. "My people created it. Much like the Helm of Awe that is burned into my back, it is a form of protection. We have been waiting for the red-eyed one since the beginning of time. Valentina *is Vulkodlak*. Once we link, my people believe we can never be controlled by the magic of the Wolf Charmer ever again."

Everything clicked into place. The prophecy. Valentina's fascination with wolves. The Keeper telling *her* about *Vulkodlak*. My head was spinning. This war was not mine alone. It stretched far beyond my need for revenge. There was so much more at stake than I could have ever imagined.

———————

Dragos struggled to keep up with me as I bolted toward the ship. I wanted to avoid him like the plague.

"Gray, slow down please. You are being ridiculous. I just want to talk."

Why did he insist on badgering me? I just wanted to get back to

Aldric. I missed him more than ever. I longed for his calm, soothing voice and tenderness. Unlike this maniac behind me who insisted on driving me insane.

"Oh, I think you've said enough."

Dragos sighed heavily as he followed me aboard ship. Seven shot me a puzzled look as he was most likely wondering where Lycos was.

I rolled my eyes. "It's a long story." He shrugged and disappeared below deck.

Dragos moved in front of me. I couldn't shake him. "Gray, forgive me. I was harsh with you back in the forest. I was scared and upset, but I meant none of it."

A quiet rage had been building just below the surface, and now he was pushing me over the edge. I lost it. "Which part? The part where you blamed me for everything? Or was it when you finally admitted to wanting me dead?" I turned to face him, fists clenched.

"*None* of it. You know how I feel about you. It was just...seeing you standing there, next to *him*. It made me angry. It should have been me, not him."

I couldn't hide the bitterness in my voice. "You had your chance to stand beside me many years ago. Instead, you chose to stand *behind* me, so you could stab me in the back. Yes, you made it very clear how you feel about me."

Dragos threw his hands up in the air. "I made a mistake, Gray. I know that now. But you can't honestly tell me that you would rather be with him, over me. You were hurt and wanted to get back at me. I understand. You made your point. Now drop this charade and come back to me. We belong together."

I gasped, almost falling over. "*We* are not doing anything together. Aldric is better than you in *every* way. You and I are done. Let it go."

His eyes flared. He grabbed the back of my waist, pulling me toward him and pinning me against the rail. I tried to wriggle free, but his grip was too tight.

His lips brushed my cheek as he whispered, "*You and I will never be done.*"

I pushed him hard, sending him flying backward. He chuckled as he regained his footing and waved his hands up in mock surrender. I marched over to him and placed the blinding spell on him again.

"Don't speak to me for the rest of the trip, or I'll make you a mute as well."

A chill ran down my back. I could still feel the trace of his lips on my skin.

TWENTY-EIGHT

ARCADIA'S SCREAMS ECHOED THROUGH THE FOREST, THREATENING to crack the ground we stood on. Birds scattered, and branches snapped all around us.

"*Where* is Lycos?"

I bit my lip and lowered my head. "He's not coming. He's chosen to stay with Valentina. I'm sorry."

Arcadia's eyes widened and her lower lip quivered. I did feel bad for her, slightly. Regardless of the circumstances, I believed that she loved him.

"What do you mean he's not coming? He has to...he's my..."

As the weight of my words hit her, I could see all traces of sanity leaving her.

Dragos chimed in mercilessly. "Another one bites the dust, my dear. Don't worry, I'll comfort you." He shot me a wicked smile.

Arcadia shook her head, dumbfounded. "I don't understand."

Was she really that clueless? "You can't control everyone."

Her eyes narrowed as she glared at me. "This is all your fault. You brought that gypsy here. You've ruined everything just as I knew you would." Her voice was shaking. "Tell Lycos his days are numbered."

Dragos trailed after her as she stomped off. I was about to

breathe a sigh of relief when he paused to get in one last, snarky comment. "See you soon, love."

He blew me a kiss and ran to catch up with Arcadia.

Aldric stiffened and moved to go after him. I grabbed him and pulled him back. "Don't. He's not worth it."

He tightened his jaw as he looked back and forth between me and Dragos's direction.

Aldric snapped, "Can we be done with this now?"

His tone was sharp, and I didn't blame him. I nodded and gently stroked his cheek.

"Let's get out of here. Together."

Aldric softened and pulled me in close. "I'm never letting you out of my sight again."

On the way back, I filled Aldric in on everything that happened. Well, almost everything. I told him about Lycos and the prophecy and how it involved Valentina. I told him about the war that was brewing between the wolves and the Consilium. I left out the parts about me and Dragos. I had already put Aldric through so much, there was no need to further agitate him. He sensed there was more, but he didn't push. I don't think he wanted to hear much more about Dragos either.

For the next four days, we trained. Aldric never left my side. There was still some uneasiness between us, but our magic grew stronger. Valentina's spirits had lifted, and she agreed to not mention Dragos. She and Lycos were inseparable. They teased and flirted and couldn't keep their hands off each other. Her spunkiness returned, and I was pleased that she was back to her old self again.

Today was an important day. It was the day that Lycos and Valentina would become linked. He would take in the blessings of Apollo, becoming half-Dhampir, and she would embrace the earth and the moon as half-wolf. They would be the first of their kind. A new breed. A new force to be reckoned with.

That morning, I managed to pull away from Aldric to meet The Keeper in the catacombs. He asked me to come alone.

"Did you get what I asked for?"

I nodded and pulled out the carefully wrapped herb. "You were right, there was no shortage of wolfsbane there."

The Keeper had told me it grew rampant in Diana's Forest. I managed to clip some and shove it in my pocket while everyone was arguing. It was necessary for the *Vulkodlak* ceremony.

"What will happen to her? As a wolf...will she still be...herself?"

The Keeper smiled. "No more than you are still yourself after linking with Aldric. Different, but the same. She will have her own pack after today. A loyalty like you have never seen. They will die for her. But she will always need you, Gray."

Would she? The more she changed, the more I stayed the same. It could tear us apart. I feared this more than anything.

I left The Keeper to his work and found Aldric in the study. The sight of him was breathtaking. He had showered and changed back into his usual attire. He wore a pair of dark slacks and a gray cashmere sweater that fit tight over every muscle in his chest. His hair was combed back off his face, revealing his piercing blue eyes. He smelled of sea salt and sandalwood, mixed in with a bit of musk and tobacco. I let it fill my lungs as I entered the room.

He caught my eye and gave me a wink. A playful smile returned to his lips as I joined him by the fire.

"We need to talk, Gray." His voice was warm, but full of anxiety.

My stomach tightened. Was this it? All my past indiscretions came barreling through my mind. He must be growing tired of me. With everything I'd put him through, I was almost surprised he hadn't left me sooner. A lump formed in my throat as I waited.

"I'm all in, Gray. I am absolutely and ridiculously in love with you. I know you have a past and I know I'm not the only man you've ever loved, but I'm the man who is with you now. And...I'd like to be that man forever. If you'll let me."

I was stunned. My heart beat like a drum in my chest. I grabbed him and kissed him hard.

Aldric chuckled. "You seem surprised."

I let out a deep breath. "I thought you were going to leave me. I wouldn't have blamed you after all I've done."

He took my hands in his. "Leave you? That would be like cutting off one of my own limbs. I could never do that. When I made the commitment to link with you, I made it forever. I told you, I'm never letting you out of my sight."

My heart swelled and burst with happiness. I was so scared that I was pushing him away. I should have known not to doubt him. He was different. He *loved* me.

"Aldric, I choose *you*. I don't want you to ever think any different. I love you. And I plan on showing you every day just how much."

He grinned wide and pulled me onto his lap. His fingers rested on the small of my back, warm and tingly.

I winked. "Starting right now."

Our lips locked in urgency as we clawed at each other like animals. His hands were hot, moving all over my body. He let out a soft moan. Our bodies swayed, up and down like a symphony, slowing down, then speeding up. I cried out as he burst into me.

Breathless and trembling, I nestled into his heaving chest. He wrapped his body around me tight, caressing my back. I couldn't stop smiling. I felt warm and safe and loved. This was the only place I wanted to be. With Aldric.

We curled up around each other on the floor in front of the fire. I rested my head on his chest as he ran his fingers through my hair.

"It will always be you, Aldric. Never forget that."

He tilted my chin up so he could look into my eyes. "I'm going to hold you to that."

We lay in each other's arms for the rest of the night.

As morning came, so did a new dawn. Magic. It was all around us. It flowed down the hallways and twisted up into the cracks above us.

My blood pumped fast through my veins as we walked to the ceremony room. It was time. Lycos and Valentina were waiting.

I furrowed my brow. "Are you nervous?"

Valentina giggled and shook her head. "A little. What if I'm a terrible wolf?"

I snorted. "Are you kidding me? You're going to make a fierce wolf. Besides, Lycos worships the ground you walk on."

Valentina beamed. "He's great, isn't he? I can't explain how my heart feels right now. It's like it's...full."

I knew exactly what she meant. I winked at Aldric who was across the room, chatting with Lycos. "You, my friend, are going to be one lethal wolf."

"I have to be. Lycos is so strong. Resilient. I need to be that for him."

I shook my head. "You don't need to be anything but yourself. If he loves you, that's all he'll ask of you."

Valentina smiled demurely, looking down. "Yeah, you're right. I'm not sure what's happening to me. I'm getting soft."

I chuckled. "That's because you're in love. It's a sickness."

She took a deep breath. "Well, I'm almost up. Any last words?"

I pulled her in for a hug. We held each other tight. "I'll be waiting for you on the other side."

She gave me one last squeeze and then disappeared with Lycos and The Keeper into the ceremony room.

I let out a deep breath. I had no idea who was going to walk back out. Valentina, my best friend and sole companion for the last four hundred years, or a stranger?

We were so used to only depending on each other, but now we had Aldric and Lycos helping us carry our burdens. It was wonderful, but at the same time, it made me nostalgic for the old days. The days where it was just us. I was happy for her, but I was also mourning an era that had passed and would never come again.

Valentina emerged from the ceremony room like a lioness. With Lycos beside her, they stood glowing in each other's golden light. She looked different. Radiant. Strong. Powerful. Her eyes had changed to a shade of amber, mixed with flecks of gold. A shade that matched Lycos's new eyes like a mirror.

They belonged together. Her prowess with his cunning would be unbeatable. They complimented each other like thunder and lightning. Valentina beamed with pride and love for him. My heart burst for her as I knew this was what she had always wanted. To belong to something. To be linked to someone the way I was with Aldric.

The four of us should be unstoppable. We had the Narcissus flower. We had a Bannister Witch, I was a Wynter Dhampir, and now, we had the power of *Vulkodlak*. Soon we would control the Lupi, the *Sang Magi*, and even Pythia herself.

The Consilium had no idea what was coming, but they were about to find out. Tonight, we would celebrate, but tomorrow we would have to prepare. Soon we would bring the fight to them. This war was just beginning.

TWENTY-NINE

THE KEEPER BURST INTO THE STUDY, HIS FACE COVERED IN SWEAT. "Tobias has come out of hiding. He's in London." He doubled over, struggling to regain his breath.

My heart raced. "Are you sure? He hasn't shown his face in centuries."

"I'm sure. A trusted source saw him entering Lucien's compound."

I shivered, cold sweat dripped down my back. After all these years of living in the shadows, he's resurfaced. *Why now?*

"I need to leave at once. Aldric, tell Seven to ready the ship."

Aldric grabbed my hand. "Whoa, slow down. How do we know this isn't a trap?"

"We don't." I had to see for myself. Without bothering to pack, I sprinted toward the ship.

Valentina stormed after me. "Gray, slow down. You aren't thinking this through."

I slowed my pace enough for her to catch up with me. "This is my chance, Val. I need answers. I *have* to do this."

"You have no idea what he's capable of. Let me go with you. If it's a trap, you'll need all the help you can get."

I knew she meant well, but there was no way I was putting her in danger again. I just got her back.

"No. I have to do this alone. Val, he's my father. I can't run from him anymore. For Apollo's sake, I don't even know what he looks like."

Valentina flew in front of me. "No, but *I* do."

"What about Lycos? He's not going to let you leave without him."

She folded her arms and pursed her lips. "And you think Aldric is going to let you?"

"Let me? I'm four hundred years old." I was seething.

Valentina cocked her head to the side. "Oh, and I'm not? Look, Lycos and Aldric are right behind us. They promise to stay out of your way. We'll just follow you anyway."

There was no use arguing with her. She was right. They would follow me, regardless. Why did they constantly insist on putting themselves in danger for me? At least Valentina would be there to point out Tobias.

"Fine, but once we get there, Aldric and Lycos need to stay back with the ship. If something goes wrong, they will need to get help."

Valentina shrieked with delight. I didn't know why she was so happy to risk her life again. A part of me understood. I knew I would do the same for her. Still, bringing them so close to Tobias made me uneasy. Valentina was right. I didn't know what he was capable of.

Lycos and Valentina huddled in a corner for most of the trip. Deep in conversation, she giggled while he caressed her face. They were so easy around each other. Aldric and I were like that once. Until everything got complicated. I hoped for Valentina's sake that they would always be that carefree with each other. There was a light in her eyes that wasn't there before Lycos. I prayed to the gods that it would remain.

Aldric hesitated before coming over. I was lost in thought but saw him watching me out of the corner of my eye.

"I hope you aren't angry with me for being here."

Angry? It saddened me that he felt that way. I didn't want my past to be a burden to him. I wanted to protect him from it.

"I'm not angry with you, Aldric. I wanted to go alone because I can't bear the thought of anything happening to any of you."

His eyes softened. "Darlin', we are in this together. I told you, I'm all in. I'm a grown man. I can take care of myself."

He always knew the right thing to say. I nestled up against his chest. "If anything goes wrong, I need you to get Valentina out first. If anything happened to her..."

Aldric sighed heavily.

I turned to face him. "Aldric, promise me."

His eyes glistened, beads of sweat dripping down his temple. "Okay, but if anything happens to you, I *will* kill him."

The fog draped over London like a heavy blanket. It was dense and damp, and just as eerie as I remembered it. The thought of Tobias and I being in the same city, let alone the same room, terrified me. All this time, the monster I had been hunting was the father I never knew.

What made him so evil? Was he born that way? Or did someone hurt him the way he hurt me? I hadn't let myself think about him in this way until now. I was too busy planning his demise and trying to put an end to his organization.

Aldric cupped my face in his hands. "Be careful out there. If you're not back before morning, we're coming after you."

I squeezed his hands, giving him the best smile I could muster. "I'll see you soon."

Aldric and I embraced, tighter than we ever had. I broke away before I could change my mind and walked over to Valentina. Lycos was whispering something in her ear. She nodded and caressed his cheek.

She turned to face me. "You sure you're ready for this?"

I took a deep breath. "Not at all, but I have to be."

With one last look back, Aldric blew me a kiss right before we scurried out into the night.

Valentina and I crept through the streets like shadows. We dashed and darted down alley after alley, staying hidden. There were humans in our path, but no sign of the Consilium. If this *was* a trap, we would have to fight our way out, and dozens of innocents could get caught in the crossfire. Either way, I wasn't about to let Tobias win.

As we rounded the corner, a block away from Lucien's compound, the scent of blood hit my nostrils. *Witch blood.*

I stopped dead in my tracks. "Do you smell that?"

Valentina nodded, her eyes glowing. Flecks of gold flickered through them like flames.

The wind shifted, and the scent was gone. We exchanged a puzzled look. The back of my neck tingled. I spun around, and everything went black.

THIRTY

THE GROUND WAS COLD UNDER MY CHEEK. MY HEAD THROBBED. *Where was I?* I tried to move, but my limbs wouldn't budge. Panic washed over me. *Where was Valentina?* Voices, soft and muffled, echoed from somewhere in the building. Forcing my eyelids open, I recognized the room. My heart dropped. We were in Lucien's compound.

Valentina was crouched in front of me, her fangs out. "They're coming back."

The feeling returned to my legs, but I was still too weak to stand up. "Who's coming back, Val?"

"He's here. Tobias is here and he's not alone. Samuel is with him."

I shook my head, confused. "Samuel. Josephine's son? Why would he be with Tobias?"

Valentina went rigid. "He's helping him. He's pissed off at us and blames us for his mother losing control of her coven."

It was starting to make sense. Josephine set the trap. A very strategic trap that she planned from the moment she told us about Stonehaven. I should have known not to trust her. She wanted me to find that file. She wanted me to know who Tobias really was. I felt sick.

"Val, you have to get out of here. You knew Josephine couldn't be trusted and I dismissed it. This is my fight."

Valentina growled. "I am *not* leaving you. None of this is your fault."

"Ah, I see our guests have awakened." Tobias glided into the room as if walking on air.

I jumped to my feet, adrenaline pushing me up. I reached for my daggers. The sheaths were empty.

Tobias's face lit up in amusement. "You'll get those back when I feel like you can be trusted."

He was mocking me. His eyes were as black as my hair, like two gaping holes of darkness. I shivered.

Tobias towered over us like a giant. He was slender, but with broad shoulders and a square jaw. Valentina hissed as he approached. He chuckled and ran a hand through his dark brown hair. It was bone straight and hung just below his ears.

"I have dreamed of this moment for so long. This is cause for celebration. Welcome back, daughter."

Anger spread through me like wildfire. "I'm sorry to disappoint you, but this will not be the happy reunion that you were hoping for. You will answer my questions and then you will let us go."

Tobias's eyes darkened, but his smile remained intact. "I will oblige your questions, dear. But I can't let you go. You belong to me. Your place is with the Consilium, at Infitum."

I was shaking.

Samuel emerged from a dark corner of the room. "She'll see things your way soon enough. She's had her fun, running around like a rebellious teenager. Your havoc ends now, Gray." He looked at me with pure hatred.

Valentina snapped, "Finally stepping out of your mommy's shadow, I see. Only to step into another's. You're so pathetic, even your own coven wants nothing to do with you."

Samuel's eyes flared as he started toward her. Tobias threw up a hand and stopped him in his place.

Tobias glared at Valentina. "You, my dear, have something that belongs to me as well."

Valentina snorted. "And what could that possibly be?"

Tobias smiled. "You have my wolf. You will return him to me."

My heart raced. I should have known Arcadia would go to Tobias. Everything was unraveling. Nausea enveloped me.

Valentina drew in a sharp breath. "Lycos does not belong to you or anyone else. He has chosen to be with me and until he decides different, that is where he will remain."

Tobias chuckled to himself. "I think you will have a change of heart soon."

He snapped his fingers. "Bring him out."

My breath quickened. What was he up to? Lucien entered the room as if on cue. He was not alone. Valentina cried out. It was Dragos.

With a snarky gleam in his eye, Lucien shoved Dragos over to Tobias.

"I have no more use for your brother. You may have him back, but only upon Lycos's return. A fair trade, wouldn't you agree?"

Valentina's mouth dropped open.

Lucien erupted in laughter. "I told you two to never return here. Now the joke's on you."

I couldn't wait to kill him. That spineless bastard was going to get what was coming to him once and for all.

In the blink of an eye, I sped toward Lucien. I was behind him in half of a second. I wrapped both of my hands around his neck and squeezed.

Samuel raised his hands toward me, but Tobias motioned for him to stop.

I whipped Lucien around and thrust my hands into his chest. His heart went still. I ripped it out, holding it over my head as the blood dripped down my arm.

Everyone froze, eyes wide and mouths hanging open. Everyone except Tobias.

Tobias beamed with pride. "You see, Gray, we are more alike than you think. You did me a favor. Lucien has always been a nuisance."

My whole body trembled. "I did not do this for you. Now let my friends go. *All of them*. I will do as you ask. You can take me to Infitum."

Tobias grinned from ear to ear.

"Gray. *No*. Don't do it." Dragos's voice was hoarse, his eyes glassy.

Valentina let out a low snarl and lunged at Tobias. With one flick of his hand, he sent her flying across the room.

I cried out. "Stop. Everyone, just stop."

Tobias nodded at Samuel. He had Dragos pinned to the floor. "Only you can make this stop, Gray. Leave with me at once and your friends are free to go."

I had no other choice. He was too strong. I couldn't let anything else happen to Valentina because of me. I nodded and started toward him, my entire body numb. I glanced at Dragos as he struggled to get out from Samuel's grasp. I had never seen him look so weak, so helpless.

Valentina whimpered. "Gray, please. Don't go. We can find another way."

I couldn't even look at her. I feared I would change my mind.

Every fiber of me trembled as I walked closer to the door. Tobias and Samuel were flanked on either side of me. Valentina screamed. I couldn't look back. I would find a way out, but for now, I had to give him what he wanted.

I was almost through the door when a loud crash erupted from behind. Tobias grabbed my arm as I spun around. *There was another door*. I hadn't even seen it. It had been two feet away from us the entire time.

The door began to swell and shake. It rattled on its hinges. *Magic*. After one final thrust, the door burst open and in walked Seven, Lycos, and Aldric.

THIRTY-ONE

"GET AWAY FROM HER."

Aldric. My heart skipped. They had come for us.

Tobias's eyes were wide. "I'm taking my daughter, and you can't stop me."

He held me with an iron grip. Valentina dragged Dragos to the other side of the room and crouched down next to Lycos. Both of their eyes glowed like flames, their wolf link strengthening between them.

Aldric and I locked eyes. He was channeling me. Samuel sprang forward just as Seven threw up a deflection spell, sending him crashing into the wall and knocking him unconscious. Tobias roared, tightening his fingers around my arm and cutting off my circulation.

I squealed. "You're hurting me."

He spun me around to face him. His black eyes burned into mine. "You are hurting *yourself.*"

Aldric's magic was fighting with Tobias's inside my head. A power struggle ensued like a deadly game of chess.

How was Tobias able to get inside my head?

"*You have to fight it, Gray.*" Aldric's voice was calm and steady.

I swallowed hard and focused. I summoned everything I had

until it threatened to explode. I took a deep breath and shoved Tobias as hard as I could, breaking free as he stumbled backward. It barely phased him, but it was just the opening I needed.

Aldric reached for me, and at the same time that I bolted toward him, Tobias released his own blast of magic. I could feel it tickling the hairs on the back of my neck as I ran. *He was too strong.* Desperation set in as it gained on me. I threw myself to the ground as it sailed passed me and stopped.

Seven had thrown up a shield. "Get behind me, all of you."

Tobias's face twisted in rage. He sent another blast only to watch it fall against Seven's shield, just as the last one had.

We may not have been able to hurt Tobias, but he couldn't hurt us either. Tobias pounded his fists on the ground, causing it to rumble and crack, but Seven stood strong, immovable.

"Go, now. I'll seal the door."

I was stunned. His shield was holding.

Dragos ran out first, followed by Valentina and then Lycos. Aldric pulled me toward the opening as Tobias called out.

"Gray, wait. You don't know everything. You need to know the truth about your mother."

His words knocked the wind out of me.

Aldric kept pulling me. "Don't listen to him. He's just trying to manipulate you."

I knew this. This man was sick. I couldn't believe he was my father.

"How dare you speak of her. I no longer have any interest in what you have to say. I've heard enough. You *will* see me at Infitum, not to join you, but to *destroy* you."

Tobias pounded his fists again and let out a deep roar as we slipped out with Seven sealing the door behind us.

The dark corners of my mind taunted me as we ran toward the ship. Was Tobias right about me? Were we more alike than I realized? I killed Lucien in a fit of rage, without hesitation. I had always clung to my humanity and tried to keep my predator nature at bay, but the closer I got to the truth, the further away I got from who I thought I was.

Through all the commotion and chaos, I hadn't had time to think about the extra passenger that was now on deck with us. He held a spot in my mind that was the darkest place of all.

"What are we going to do with *him*?" Aldric sneered at Dragos with bloodlust in his eyes.

Dragos returned the look. "*Do with me?* Soon as Gray throws you overboard, I'm sure she will find lots of things to do with me." He snickered.

Aldric charged toward him. I stepped in front of him just as Valentina moved in front of Dragos. Looking back and forth between them, I secretly cursed Tobias for putting me in this position.

"He stays with us."

Dragos flashed Aldric a smirk.

I snapped, "Don't get too excited. You're only here because you can't be trusted out on your own. We'll discuss your future when we arrive at the Hall of Secrets."

He rolled his eyes and this time, it was Aldric's turn to smirk.

We sailed into the Sea of Magia in a silent divide and I was drowning in a sea of regret. If I had just listened to Aldric to begin with, we wouldn't be in this mess. I've painted targets on all our backs now. Even Seven would be in Tobias's war path. My selfish desire to catch a glimpse of my father put the people I love in danger. I couldn't rest until I fixed it.

The Keeper looked relieved to see us but raised an eyebrow toward Dragos. "Are we calling him a friend now?"

I snickered. "Let's just call him a prisoner of war."

Valentina winced. "Gray, we need to talk...in private."

I knew what was coming. She was going to make a plea for her brother. "We can talk, but I must warn you, my mind is made up."

Aldric watched Dragos like a hawk. "Seven and I will take him down to the catacombs for now."

The Keeper nodded and motioned for them to follow.

Dragos struggled. "Where are you taking me? Val, don't let them lock me up."

Valentina looked away, blinking back tears.

I sighed. He was always so dramatic. "Relax. No harm will come to you."

I was talking to Dragos but looking straight at Aldric. I knew he couldn't wait to torture him.

Valentina was fierce and spirited, but she always fell apart when it came to her brother. Her lower lip quivered as she spoke. "I know he has done some terrible things, but I believe he *has* changed. You saw it yourself with Tobias. Dragos was trying to help us."

I chuckled. "Dragos was just trying to not get himself killed. Self-preservation has always been his number one priority. Look, I get it. He's your brother and you want to see the good in him, but he betrayed us, Val. How can you be so sure that he won't do it again?"

Valentina shook her head in frustration, tears streaming down her cheeks. "I can't be sure. I just have to believe it. He is *done* with the Consilium. He knows that he picked the wrong side and he wants to make amends."

My heart broke for her. She was so desperate to believe in him, after everything. It was killing me to see her so distraught.

"He could still be working for them, Val. You have to consider that. He didn't have a scratch on him when they brought him out."

"I know. I've thought of that. That's why I will take full responsibility for him. I won't let him out of my sight." Her eyes blazed and I could see that she meant every word.

I sighed, already regretting this entire conversation. I would be taking a huge risk by granting her this.

"Fine, but he can't have *any* weapons and I want him accounted for at all times."

Valentina breathed a sigh of relief. She threw her arms around me, almost knocking me over. "Thank you. I promise, you won't regret this."

A pit of uneasiness formed in my stomach. Aldric was not going to like this.

THIRTY-TWO

ALDRIC STOOD GUARD AT DRAGOS'S CELL. THE MOONLIGHT beamed through the stone cracks, highlighting the shadows in his eyes. Dragos stiffened when he saw me. It was hard to look at him.

Aldric sighed when he saw me. "You're going to let him out, aren't you?"

I met his gaze. "Yes."

He looked disappointed, but not surprised. "If he even looks at you wrong, I'll kill him."

I knew he meant it. "Thank you for understanding. This isn't what I want, but I made a promise to Val. Besides, we can use him to our advantage."

Aldric's face hardened. "That's exactly what we are going to do."

He kissed my cheek before turning to leave. The pounding of his footsteps echoed down the hall. Once I knew he was out of ear shot, I took a deep breath and entered the cell.

Dragos looked like hell. His eyes were red and swollen. Beads of sweat matted his hair down against his forehead.

"Today's your lucky day. I've agreed to let you out, but there are conditions."

Dragos nodded. "I'm listening."

"You will not leave any room without permission or without Valentina accompanying you. You will not carry weapons and you will not antagonize Aldric. Are we clear?"

Dragos chuckled. "Whatever you want, Gray. I'm done fighting with you. I won't be a hindrance. You'll learn that in time."

His voice was scratchy and full of defeat. I wasn't expecting him to be so agreeable.

"I'm only doing this for Valentina. No other reason. I want to make myself clear on that. If for some reason this proves to be a mistake, you will not be given another chance."

Dragos's eyes burned into mine. "I understand."

I waited for his complaints, but they never came.

"Good. Follow me. The others are waiting. We have work to do."

We joined the others in the war room, located deeper inside the catacombs. The Keeper was there waiting, ready to fit us with weapons and armor. Like the ones we took with us to the Underworld, they were ancient and blessed by Diana. Lycos, Valentina, Aldric, and I loaded up on blades, swords, and crossbows. I tucked daggers into my boots and shoved two more inside my shirt.

Seven had returned with his band of pirates. All ten of them scurried around him, adorning themselves with weaponry. Aldric and Lycos discussed strategy in one corner while Valentina talked with her wolves in another. It was happening. The dark night was upon us.

Looking around the room at the hodgepodge of misfits gathered around, it hit me. The people in this room were my true family. Not Arcadia, not Tobias, not even Jezebel. A new sense of purpose rose in me. It reverberated in my bones. These people were willing to risk their lives for me. For my cause. For their own freedom. We all knew that if the Consilium continued to exist, we would always be looking over our shoulders.

The Keeper caught my eye and motioned for everyone to gather round. I stood in the center of the room and cleared my throat.

"We will discuss the details of our plan throughout the night, but first, let me make my intentions clear..."

I waited for everyone's undivided attention, then continued. "I don't care about Arcadia. The wolves can decide her fate. The Consilium must be destroyed, the *Sang Magi* needs to be recovered, and Jane must be rescued. In case there's any confusion, I want Tobias taken alive. He has much to pay for, but he also has much to answer for. We cannot falter. We cannot fail."

I swept the room, lingering on each face. Everyone nodded in agreement.

Except for Aldric. "Long as it's clear that Nicholas Bannister is mine. And Val, keep your brother out of my way."

Valentina's nostrils flared. I shot her a look.

"Now that we're all in agreement, let's discuss strategy. Dragos and Lycos have both been inside Infitum. They're going to map our way in."

Lycos stepped forward. "Infitum will be heavily guarded, as you can imagine. The entire perimeter is lined with Consilium soldiers—Dhampir fledglings that are very strong. Tobias starves them so they are in a constant state of bloodlust. This makes them erratic and unpredictable. Don't let your guard down for a second."

Dragos chimed in to describe the entrance, various chambers, towers, and hidden exits. Together, he and Lycos had drawn a detailed map of the structure. Infitum was a fortress and impenetrable to most.

Tobias, no doubt, was expecting us, and I'm sure Pythia and Nicholas couldn't wait to tear me apart. They would most likely dangle Jane as bait again. They were over confident, sitting in their tower of darkness, thinking they had the upper hand. We had so much more.

We had the wolves, the pirates, and even one of their own. Most importantly, we had the Narcissus flower. It was time to take in its power.

The Keeper had steeped the flower and brewed it into a potion. There was no antidote. No turning back. I only had one shot at this, so I had to get it right. I had no intentions of going back to the Underworld.

I had no idea what I was going to become, and it terrified me. The power of the Narcissus flower would give me an advantage that would change everything. It could be disastrous in the wrong hands. The Keeper trusted *me* with it, but I wasn't sure that I trusted myself.

The Keeper handed me the vial. Everyone held their breath. "May Apollo guide you."

The room pulsed with nervous energy as I put the vial to my lips. Aldric reached out. Pulling me in close.

He whispered in my ear, "No matter what happens, I'm always with you."

I studied the lines in his face, trying to memorize each one. I didn't ever want to forget the love in his eyes. I feared there may come a time when he would have to break that promise.

I forced a smile. "Bottoms up."

I put the vial to my lips and knocked it back. The liquid burned my throat as it rushed down. It was tangy and sweet but stung as it entered every single vein, pushing its way into my bloodstream.

I closed my eyes as the room began to spin. Or was I the one that was spinning? I couldn't tell. My skin was on fire. Like it might peel right off.

Images flashed through my mind. Memories. Burning at the stake. Feeling the heat of the flames as if it were yesterday. Free-falling through the darkness while the Siren hummed in my head. *Was she singing to me again?* Her song would always exist in some small part of me. Being trapped in my own body without escape. Feelings of helplessness rushed through me and out.

My beating heart slowed to a steady rhythm. I drew in a deep breath. The images turned off. My mind went quiet and still.

I opened my eyes. Everything looked different. *Everyone* looked different. The shapes and sounds were sharper. Clearer. Like looking through a blurred lens that slowly shifts into focus.

I could *see* their magic. There was a red wolf hovering inside of Valentina and a white wolf in Lycos, covered in Dhampir blood.

A golden light shot out of Aldric, like rays of sunshine, casting a warm glow over the space around him and outlining his silhouette.

The Keeper's face flashed, changing from old to young and back again. Like a shapeshifter, clutching to his former self.

Seven was encased in a shield made of iron and stone. Tiny sparks catapulted off it, blocking his energy.

Nausea set in. The magic was bombarding me all at once. I couldn't stop shaking.

Aldric took a cautious step toward me. "Gray, are you still...you?"

I didn't know how to answer. I was, but I wasn't. How could I explain what I was seeing? That looking at them was making me sick.

Valentina stepped forward. "Gray?"

Waves of light bounced off my eyelids, pulling me down like vertigo. My head pounded. *Stop. Turn off.*

And it did. It just stopped. The Narcissus magic responded to my simplest command. My vision returned, clear. The nausea subsided. I breathed out a sigh of relief.

I rubbed my temples. "I'm all right."

Valentina eyed me, unsure. "I don't know, Gray. You seem...strange."

I had to admit, I felt strange. But I was still me, just different. Every thought and emotion was amplified by a thousand, but my intentions were still the same. I felt euphoric.

Valentina's nose crinkled up at me. "I'm a little off, Val, because I literally just drank the potion from Hell. Not quite the same effect as a whiskey hangover."

Her body relaxed, a smile returning to her face.

Aldric sighed in relief. He cupped my face in his hands. "You had us worried there for a minute, darlin'."

His voice was comforting, but his words struck a nerve. My chest tightened. *They should be worried.* I had no idea what I was capable of.

There was a push and pull of emotions happening inside of me, a raging storm. I shook it off. It was time to focus on the battle ahead.

With all the chaos and commotion, I neglected one thing. Panic rose up in my chest.

"Where's Dragos?"

THIRTY-THREE

"I KNEW HE COULDN'T BE TRUSTED," ALDRIC FUMED, DISGUSTED.

My blood was boiling. I glared at Valentina.

She shook her head. "I'll find him. He couldn't have gone far."

I rolled my eyes. "Let's split up. The Keeper and Aldric will take the upper levels. Val, Lycos, you scan the outside perimeter. Seven, you're with me."

I needed to have a few private words with him.

Everyone nodded in agreement and took off in opposite directions.

Seven followed close behind as I flew up the catacomb stairs, taking two at a time. My heart raced as I ran. I could not let Dragos leave the Hall of Secrets and risk the Consilium finding out our plans.

Seven cautioned me to slow down as we reached the main hall. "He's still here. I can feel it."

I closed my eyes and focused on my breath. I felt it too.

A wave of relief washed over me, followed by rage. "I don't know what kind of game he's playing, but I don't have time for it."

Seven's voice was gentle. "I'm not going to defend him by any means, but you need to look deeper into his actions. He's losing the woman he loves. He's hurt and afraid."

I snapped, "He lost me *because* of his actions. You expect me to feel sorry for him now that he's had a change of heart?"

Seven's eyes couldn't hide the hint of sadness creeping in. "No. He wouldn't want you to. He's proud. Most men are. All I'm saying is, be patient with him. Trust me, he is harder on himself than you could ever be."

Seven's words weighed down on me as we searched the rooms of the Hall, but something else was nagging at me more.

"How did you do it?"

Seven raised an eyebrow. "Pardon me?"

"Earlier, when I drank the potion, I couldn't see your magic. You were the only one shielded."

Seven's eyes lit up. "Ah, yes, about that. I knew what was happening to you. The others didn't. Shielding is like breathing for me. It was nothing personal."

I wanted to press, but his dismissive look told me it was best I left it alone. There were so many secrets. So much sadness bubbling beneath his surface. But it wasn't my place to ask.

Dragos's scent grew stronger as we neared the study. The hairs on the back of my neck prickled as we entered the room.

Dragos sat by the fire, gazing into the flames, as if in some sort of trance. Seven was right. He wasn't trying to escape. He was too busy beating himself up.

Seven placed a gentle hand on my shoulder. "I'm going to go tell the others we found him. Give you two some time to talk."

I shuddered at the thought of being alone with him, but I needed to make myself clear. I opened my mouth to speak. He cut me off. "I'm sorry I ran off."

I couldn't figure out if he was talking about today or before. Maybe it was both.

"I know. It doesn't change the fact that you did. You will not be going with us to Infitum. I can't risk it."

Dragos lowered his head. "I should've protected you. I should have...made different choices. But I didn't. So here we are...together but apart. You did nothing wrong, Gray. Don't ever forget that."

All these years, I had longed to hear those words leave his lips. Now that they had, it wasn't enough.

Aldric came bolting into the study, the rest of our group at his heels. He charged toward Dragos, who didn't move a muscle. Stepping in front of Aldric, I placed a firm hand on his chest.

"Let it go. There's nothing you can do to him that he hasn't already done to himself."

I caught Seven's eye and nodded.

Aldric huffed but relented.

I kissed him softly on the lips. "Thank you."

I addressed the room. "Dragos will remain here under The Keeper's watch. It's not up for discussion. Get yourselves ready. We leave for Infitum at dawn."

Readying myself for battle, a quiet calm came over me. I took comfort in the mundane act of putting on armor. It was cold and heavy as it pressed down upon me, helping to clear my mind.

"Everyone is just about ready." Aldric watched me intently as I sharpened my blades.

My eyes flickered toward the window. The sky was a radiant shade of amber as it embraced the rising sun. Its warmth filled the room. I closed my eyes and basked in it.

Aldric knelt beside me. I gazed into his eyes and felt his love surge through me. He had come so far from when we first met. He was no longer the lost frightened boy I stumbled across in the Three Blind Mice, cowering at the sight of blood. He was strong, resilient, and braver than anyone I'd ever known. And he was mine.

I kissed him hard on the lips. He wrapped his arms around me, lowering me to the floor. I cried out as he entered me, our bodies intertwining. His magic surged into me with the force of a hurricane, collapsing into mine. I clung to it with a fury, allowing it to fill every vein and crevice.

His kisses deepened, and I met them with wild abandon. We pulsed inside each other, hungry. I thought we might explode. Warmth and light flooded through me, washing away everything else. The rest of the world fell away and the only thing that existed was us.

The light coming in from the window was an unwelcome guest. I wanted to stay in this moment for as long as I could, but the day had other plans. With the dawn approaching, I was reminded that it was time to go. Aldric knew it as well.

He turned my face toward his. "Are you ready for this?"

I had been waiting for this moment for four centuries. Now that it was finally upon us, I hesitated. With the Consilium defeated, who would I be? The day I became a Dhampir, revenge and hatred drove me forward. It shaped me and defined me. Without that, what would be left?

Aldric pulled me tight to his chest.

I shivered. "Only one way to find out."

THIRTY-FOUR

A TREE BRANCH SNAPPED IN THE DISTANCE. IT WAS THE ONLY sound amidst the howling wind. It felt like a storm was brewing.

Infitum stood tall and sturdy, a fortress made of stone.

Not for long. I would take it apart, piece by piece if I had to.

It was eerily quiet as we made our way through the front gates. There were no signs of the guards Lycos had spoken of. With shields and weapons drawn, we moved into formation in front of the entrance.

Lycos and Valentina flanked my right. They led a pack of a dozen snarling wolves. Seven moved up on my left, accompanied by ten of his pirate-Dhampirs, all armed with an assortment of axes and scythes.

I nodded to Aldric, who stood at my side. He drew his bow and fired a frost arrow into the castle doors. They burst open on impact. We waited. I braced myself for an onslaught of soldiers to charge forward, but no one came.

Those bastards were drawing us in. I took a deep breath and flipped on the Narcissus switch. Deep inside the castle, Dhampir soldiers were getting into position. Their bodies glowed like heat signatures. I used only my hands to signal their locations to the others.

In silence we crept, moving closer to the entrance. My heart beat louder with every step I took. No doubt, they could sense us moving in. It was time. I raised my voice over the wind and charged forward. "*Fight!*"

I stormed into the courtyard with the others right behind me. Their roars and battle cries pounded in my chest, spurring me on. We crouched down and raised our shields over our heads just as the soldiers rained arrows down upon us. The wolves tore through, lunging and ripping out throat after throat.

I darted around the castle, meticulously spinning and dodging every soldier that came at me. My sword came down faster and harder as each one crossed my path, slicing through their flesh like butter. Blood seeped through the cracks in the stone ground like a river. All I could see was red. It dripped down my face and ran down my sword as I pushed my way further into the castle.

My speed increased with my rage. Another two came at me. I whipped out one of my daggers, taking them both out at the same time. A third one came up from behind. I spun around and sliced off his head with my sword, clean and sharp. An orchestrated dance of dagger, dagger, sword, dagger. The stench of blood and flesh stung my nose like a sickness. It only made me angrier.

Out of the corner of my eye, I spotted Aldric. He released his arrows with the swiftness of a tiger, sending bits of Dhampir flesh spraying out in every direction. Valentina brushed past me, growling as she ripped soldiers apart with her teeth and claws. Seven shot bolts of lightning out of his hands as his pirates used their own bodies to shield him. They sliced and ripped through anything that dared to get too close to him. The air was full of wails and cries, echoing through the stone walls, louder than thunder. It was chaos.

After dispatching the last of their soldiers, I led the way to the back of the castle. There was still no sign of the Consilium. With my face covered in blood, madness took over.

My voice erupted like a volcano. "Tobias, show yourself. You coward."

I surveyed the room as I waited. Still, nothing. A few minutes passed before I heard it. The door in front of us creaked and rumbled. It opened outward, lowering itself by iron chains. It wasn't a door at all. It was a drawbridge. On the other side of it was a sprawling field. I clenched my fists. There they were, waiting for us.

The Consilium were scattered throughout the field. I spotted Pythia first. Magic coursed through her fingers and extended outwards. She played with it in her hands. Nicholas was not far from her. He stood still, like a statue, except for his face. It twisted and snarled in my direction.

Down the middle of the field was Arcadia. Her eyes glowed as they burned into mine. Valentina and Lycos moved from behind me, exposing their new shape. Arcadia hissed at the sight of them.

And at the far end of the field was Tobias. With a sword in one hand, the other was firmly wrapped around Jane's throat. He smiled as I gasped. He was going to kill her.

I charged forward. Consilium soldiers spilled out from the trees. I slashed through them as I made my way toward Pythia. I lunged at one and darted right as his blade grazed my face. I jumped back as he swung again. I ducked at the last second and pushed him off balance. I pounced on him, knocking him to the ground. In one quick motion, I plunged my hands into his chest, stretched his skin back and ripped him apart. His eyes rolled back into his head as he went limp.

Everywhere I looked, Witches, Dhampirs, and Lupi were tearing each other apart. I could barely see through all the blood. But Tobias stood stoic in the distance, never flinching. He watched, motionless, as we massacred his followers.

He almost looked amused as Jane struggled to get out of his grip. I felt sick. *I had to get to them.* I ran like the wind, pushing and shoving soldiers out of my way. Desperation filled me as I zeroed in on Tobias.

A force sent me flying backward. My back hit the ground hard, knocking the wind out of me. Pythia stood over me. Her eyes twitched, and a devilish smile formed across her lips. I jumped up. She raised her hands, releasing a second wave of magic at me. It was like a bolt of lightning. I staggered back and fell to my knees. She laughed, releasing another bolt. This one only clipped me as I darted sideways, but it was strong enough to throw me off balance. Again, she laughed as I struggled to regain my footing.

"You can't beat me, Gray. I am better than you. Tobias will realize that soon enough."

Her voice was thick with bitterness and contempt. She thought she was invincible. That would be her downfall. Madness took over, sending me into a state of delirium. My laughter caused her to take a few steps back.

"You're right, Pythia. I am not going to beat you. I am going to *be* you."

Confusion and panic flashed across her face. Before she had time to realize what was happening, I sprang on her like a rabid dog. I wrapped my hands tightly around her wrists and clamped my teeth down on her neck.

Blood flowed into my mouth as I willed her magic out of her. I imagined it leaving her body and entering mine. She struggled, but her body weakened with each drop of blood I consumed. *It was almost done.* I could feel it coursing through my veins. It was dark and toxic. My body regurgitated. I gasped for air as she crumbled.

The look in her eyes went from surprise to sheer terror as I stood over her. It was done. I had drained her of all her power. I licked my lips and smiled wickedly. I had left her just enough blood to remain a Dhampir. A fate she considered to be worse than death.

Pythia screamed, shaking her hands at me. Her face twisted in agony, realizing her magic was gone.

"*What did you do to me?*"

I snapped, "Magic is a privilege. One that you do not deserve. I have relieved you of that burden."

Her eyes darkened and she lost it, flailing at me. I stepped back as Seven rushed in to bind her in chains. Her whimpers turned to screams as he dragged her away from me. "This isn't over, Gray. You will pay for this."

I already was. This new magic slithered around my veins like a slow burn. It gnawed and carved out holes in me, eroding my insides. Like a dimming light, it took everything I had to not close my eyes and drown in it.

I shook it off, looking around to assess the damage. Lycos and Valentina tended to each other's wounds. A few scratches, minor cuts, but nothing life threatening. They huddled close.

Aldric stood over Nicholas's contorted body, a look of satisfaction on his face. His chest had been ripped open, exposing bits of flesh and bile. A smirk, still frozen on his lifeless face. Even in death, he mocked us.

I should have gone to Aldric's side to check on him. To see if he was all right. Instead, I scanned the field for my father.

My heart raced. Tobias was still there, watching us with his hand wrapped around Jane's throat. I broke into a sprint toward him. Rage and adrenaline shot through me. He didn't flinch. They were standing on the edge of a cliff. He moved backward with lightning speed.

No.

He was going to get away.

I ran faster, but he was too quick.

A bank of fog passed over them and he was gone, taking Jane with him. They vanished like ghosts. My heart beat out of control. I dashed over to the side of the cliff and looked down. Nothing. Just an empty valley.

I snapped back around toward the field, searching for Arcadia. My resolve was crumbling. She was gone too.

I cried out. How could I get so close, only to have him fall out of my grasp? I was supposed to rescue Jane and capture my father. He had been toying with me this whole time. He was never going to let me get close to him.

Like a switch, Pythia's darkness turned on and moved through me like a river. I let the thick sludge permeate my insides, coating every crevice. Filling up every emotional hole, only to leave me hollow. The rage surged and billowed out. I pounded my fists on the ground and split it open.

Everything went black.

THIRTY-FIVE

DEMONS HAVE MANY FACES. THEIR SHADOWS CAST REFLECTIONS that were ever-changing. They twist into different forms and shapes that you will never see coming. We were all demons once, but not all of us were monsters. The lines were blurred today. I no longer knew what I was.

Everyone one was watching me, but no one dared to speak. I couldn't remember how we got back to the Hall of Secrets. All I knew was I was still covered in blood. With my magic amplified, I smelled their apprehension. I didn't dare move for fear I would break something. I didn't know what I was capable of. I sat in the middle of The Keeper's study and willed myself to remain as still as possible.

I couldn't discern how much time had gone by before the Keeper returned. It felt like hours, but it could have been days. There was a resounding sigh of relief from the group as they scurried out and left me alone with him. Except for Aldric, who remained cautious in the doorway.

The Keeper stood calm before me, wiping the sweat from my brow, slow and steady. I flinched at his touch. Afraid my flesh might turn him to stone or set him on fire. It didn't. I let out a deep breath I hadn't even realized I'd been holding.

"Gray, can you hear me? Everything is all right. You are safe here."

His voice was soft and soothing. I opened my mouth to speak but could only muster a hoarse whisper. "Yes, but are *you*...safe?"

The Keeper smiled, soft and warm. "Your magic responds to your intentions. You aren't going to hurt anyone that you do not wish to. Trust me. Take a deep breath and switch it off. You are in control."

Every muscle in my body ached. My head pounded. I was overcome. My body trembled as the tears flowed down my cheeks.

"Drink this."

My hand throbbed as I took the vial from him. The tonic was bitter. I had to force it down. Within seconds, I felt my body relax. My throat no longer burned. I looked at up at him, stunned.

"Holy basil leaf. It quiets the mind. I have prepared more for you to take home."

Home. I wasn't sure where that was anymore.

"What happened? Did we win?"

It was a question I was afraid to ask. The Keeper's eyes could not hide his hesitation.

"Yes and no."

He went on to tell me how Pythia was now imprisoned in the catacombs, that Nicholas Bannister was dead, and that Arcadia was never found. He had recovered the *Sang Magi* from Pythia and had it locked away somewhere safe within the Hall. The memories came flooding back as he spoke.

"Tobias got away. I remember. He took Jane and they...vanished."

He nodded, reluctant, but urging me on.

"And then I—I almost killed everyone."

I remembered everything, and it made me sick. *How could I lose control like that?*

"Gray, you are nothing like Pythia. You can fight this darkness."

I wasn't so sure. I didn't even know what I was doing before I did it.

"How?"

"With me at your side, darlin'." *Aldric*.

My heart burst at the sound of his voice. It washed over me like a warm bath. My fear subsiding, I ran to him, throwing my arms around his neck. I pressed my cheek to his as he pulled me in tight. I closed my eyes, letting his magic envelope me. Golden light, warm like the sun.

He whispered in my ear, "Let's go home."

I understood. Home was anywhere he was.

The Consilium were scattered, but Tobias would surely rebuild. With Pythia imprisoned and the *Sang Magi* back in The Keeper's possession, they could not make any more hybrids, though, this didn't bring me any comfort. Tobias was cunning. He still had Jane, and Arcadia was unaccounted for.

Then there was the issue of the human blood bags. Would they use them to make more Dhampir soldiers or let them die? Either way, it had to be stopped.

"We should travel back to Stonehaven soon. Find out if those people are still alive."

Aldric nodded. "If they are, we'll free them."

I smiled and squeezed his hand. "Thanks for being on my side."

He winked. "Always."

While Aldric gathered our things, I made my round of goodbyes.

Valentina and Lycos decided they would stay with The Keeper for a while longer to learn more about the prophecy. Dragos would remain with them, much to my relief. He would be their burden now. I was done with him coming between me and Aldric.

"Take care of yourself, Gray. You know where to find us." Valentina and I embraced, tears streaming down our cheeks. This was the first time in four centuries that we would be apart.

I squeezed her hand. "This isn't goodbye, just a see-you-later thing. Okay?"

Valentina nodded, her lower lip quivering. My voice choked in my throat, sadness filling me. I was never any good at goodbyes.

She hesitated. "Gray, before you leave, Dragos has something he wants to say to you." Her lashes fluttered and she shrank back, unsure of what my reaction would be.

I let out a deep sigh. What could he possibly want now? "Fine. Where is he?"

A part of me was curious. Another part of me still wanted to rip his throat out. And a secret part of me wanted to see him one last time. Valentina led me to one of the bedrooms. Dragos stood at the window. I took a deep breath and shut the door behind me.

"You wanted to see me?" My stomach was full of butterflies. His skin glowed in the firelight and he had let his hair grow just enough to reveal his curls, half-slicked back away from his forehead.

"I'm on your side too, Gray."

My heart raced. "You were spying on us?"

A soft smile formed across his lips. "I went to the study to see if you were okay. I overheard you and Aldric. I didn't mean to intrude. He does love you."

I swallowed hard. "I know. I love him too."

There was a quiet tension in the space between us. A space full of regret and unanswered questions. Even now, he was the only one who could do this to me. Make me feel a hundred different emotions at once, both toxic and electrifying.

Dragos walked over to me. He cupped my face in his hands. I drew in a sharp breath but did not move away. "I will win you back someday. I don't care how long it takes. I will spend eternity making up for what I did. You belong *with me*."

His eyes were clear, focused. No sign of mischief or trickery. He meant it. And it terrified me.

"Dragos...we can never be together. *Ever*. You and I are too dark. Too toxic. Aldric is my light. We balance each other. Lift each other up. You and me...all we do is tear each other down."

Dragos frowned, shaking his head. "No. We challenge each other.

You make me better, Gray. I make you stronger. Aldric holds you back. He makes you complacent. You will realize this in time."

I sighed again. Dragos was relentless. A wave of a nausea hit me. He was never going to give up.

"I have to go. Try to stay out of trouble."

I don't know why, but I stopped at the door and turned back around to look at him.

He winked, his face lighting up. "Farewell for now, my love. I'll see you soon."

A pang of guilt stabbed me in the chest as I made my way back downstairs. I didn't do anything wrong, but that exchange didn't feel right. Not where Aldric was concerned.

Downstairs in the study, Seven was taking his leave. Our small victory at Infitum had given us a window of time to rest and regroup. We would call on him again, but for now, he had his own matters to attend to. Besides, we no longer needed him to navigate the Sea of Magia. The Keeper had given us one of his ships, so we could come and go as we pleased.

And now it was time to go.

New Orleans was a welcome sight. We had changed, but the city was just as enchanting as we had left it. Bright and vivid, it coursed with energy. Laughter and dancing filled the streets over the scents of sugar and bourbon.

However, as news of what I had done at Infitum began to spread, so did fear and unrest among the covens. Witches murmured in the shadows as we passed, crossing to avoid us. We were outcasts now.

Josephine was nowhere to be found. Considering I failed to bring her Tobias's head, I wasn't in too much of a hurry to meet up with her. I suspected she was with Samuel, who was surprisingly missing from the battle. I could only imagine what he had poisoned her mind with.

Walking into the Three Blind Mice, I felt like I could relax for the first time in months. Aldric jumped behind the bar and poured us each a glass of whiskey. I took a deep breath and closed my eyes, savoring every drop.

Aldric studied my every move. "Talk to me, darlin'. What's on your mind?"

I didn't know where to begin. I didn't know how to describe what I was feeling. From the pity and shame that came over me as I felt Pythia's magic leaving her body to the darkness I felt as it entered into mine. How do I explain the explosion of emotions that caused me to break the ground in half? I didn't quite understand it myself.

Everything was amplified and quiet at the same time. The duality within me was fighting its own war with itself. He couldn't possibly understand. No one could. Exhaustion was setting in just thinking about it.

"Can we talk about what happened tomorrow? Right now, let's just enjoy being together."

Aldric nodded and kissed my cheek. He took my hand and I let him lead me upstairs.

The loft looked just as we had left it. Aldric's clothes were scattered around the room, along with half-smoked cigars and empty whiskey bottles. I chuckled as I surveyed the mess. It made me feel normal, something I thought I would never feel again.

Aldric took me in his arms. As I leaned in to kiss him, I spotted something out of place.

There was an envelope on the coffee table. It was propped up against an empty bottle, much like the one I had left for Aldric. Except this one had *my* name on it.

My chest tightened as we exchanged a puzzled look. I opened the envelope with caution, pulling out a slip of paper.

Aldric tensed. "What does it say?"

I shook my head, puzzled. "I don't understand."

It was a drawing, one I wasn't familiar with it. I handed it to Aldric. His brow furrowed as he turned the paper over.

"Look at this."

On the other side was another drawing. A serpent. And it was signed with only one letter.

"J."

Aldric looked up at me. "A message from Jane?"

I shook my head, uncertain. "Possibly, but how and when would she have left this for me? And what does it mean?"

My pulse was racing.

Aldric took the note out of my hands and set it on the table. He sighed, running a hand through his pale blond hair.

"Let's not worry about this now. We're here together and far away from Tobias. That's all that matters."

He took my face in his hands and kissed my lips, soft and sensual. I let myself surrender to it. I felt strong. Safe. Loved. For the first time in a long time I felt like I had a real family. A home. Despite Tobias getting away, everything else had fallen into place. It was a small victory, but a victory nonetheless.

But as happy and content as I was, I couldn't ignore the nagging in the back of my head. Tomorrow would bring more questions. More uncertainty. More blood would be shed. More enemies made. And then there was the darkness inside me, dormant, but simmering and waiting at the core of my soul.

The future was uncertain.

They were all waiting for me to die, but I was still very much alive.

There was only one thing that I was certain of. This war was just beginning.

THE END

Thank you for reading! Did you enjoy?

Please Add Your Review! And don't miss book two, FLESH AND BONE

Don't miss book two of the Blood and Darkness series with FLESH AND BONE and discover more from Melissa Sercia at www.melissasercia.com

Three months after the victory at Infitum, Gray's dark magic has grown stronger and threatens to consume her. She fights against it at every turn. But when her partner Aldric mysteriously disappears, she must rely on her powers to find him.

With zero leads and nothing but a strange drawing to go on, Gray seeks allies in the Hall of Secrets. During her search for Aldric, she discovers a mysterious cult, an ancient curse, and a family secret that is darker than she could ever imagine—an organization deadlier than even the Consilium.

In the wake of this new threat to humanity and her kind alike, Gray must rely on the one person she distrusts the most—Dragos. As her former lover and recent enemy, he knows more than he lets on. Traveling through the streets of New Orleans to the shores of Scotland, to the Romanian woods, and all the way back to the Underworld, Gray must find new magic and raise an army.

With the fate of humanity and Aldric's life hanging in the balance, Gray shall embrace her dark side once and for all, but in doing so, she may have to make a choice between love and survival of the species—or risk losing both.

your favorite social media and book buying sites.

For books in the world of romance and speculative fiction that embody Innovation, Creativity, and Affordability, check out City Owl Press at www.cityowlpress.com.

ACKNOWLEDGMENTS

When I first conceptualized Blood and Magic four years ago, I had no idea where it would end up or if it would ever make it into your hands. It has been an incredible journey. There are so many wonderful people I would like to thank for helping me take Blood and Magic from a dream to a reality.

First, I'd like to thank my amazing editor, Amanda Roberts. Thank you for championing my book and for putting up with all of my commas! You have been instrumental in bringing Blood and Magic to the world and I will forever be grateful.

Thank you to Tina Moss and Yelena Casale, my publishers at City Owl Press. You are patient, intuitive, and so supportive. I couldn't ask for a better team for Blood and Magic.

I'd also like to thank these amazing writers and innovators, who have taught me so much about the craft of writing and the joys of being part of such an amazing writing community. Thank you to Faye Kirwin, Kristin Kieffer, Jenny Bravo, Katie Golding, Zoe Ashwood, and all of the wonderful writers I've met through Storycrafter, Story Social, and Authors 18, and my fellow City Owl Press authors. You all inspire me.

To my mom, Linda Campbell, I'm so proud to be your daughter. You taught me how to be strong, independent, courageous, and to never give up on my dreams. You've always supported my passions and I love you with all of my heart for everything you do. I couldn't have done any of this without your love and support.

To my dad, Giovanni Sercia, thank you for always believing in me. It's not easy having daughters, but you handle it with grace, love, and a lot of patience. I'm also happy that my book will get you to start reading again! And thanks to Marji Sercia for putting up with all of us!

To my sister, Jennifer Sercia, you are amazing. Thank you for being the best sister and friend. I love you so much and I just know all your dreams are going to come true. Just remember, people change...Love you sis.

Thank you to my aunt, Charlene Deaver, for showing me the literary classics as a child and for your endless support. To my uncle John Deaver, for keeping Aunt Charlene happy and keeping us all entertained. To my cousin, Kathleen Dunagan, your journey has inspired me and taught me that anything is possible.

To my family across the pond in England, thank you for your love and support! I love you all! To my family in Sicily, grazie and ti amo tutti. I hope to see all of you soon.

To my extended family, Jenny, Morris, Fiona, and Joanne Driels, thank you for always being in my corner and encouraging me to go after my dreams.

I want to say a special thank you to my best friend Renee Infelise. You believed in Blood and Magic from the beginning and there are not enough words to express how grateful and blessed I am to have you in my life.

I also want to thank some of my dearest friends, Julie Brooks, Serena DeWinter, Brennan Kennedy, Jessica Such, Tiffany and Randy Werner, Joe Manuguerra, Ben Lawley, and David Protelsch. Thanks for your support and for always being there even if we don't see each other every day.

And finally, I'd like to save the best for last, and thank the love of my life, Christopher Driels. You have stood by me through thick and thin. You have supported every endeavor and every passion I've had with unwavering loyalty, strength, and love. You make me laugh everyday and I'm so lucky to have found you. I love you so much. Thank you for loving me too.

ABOUT THE AUTHOR

MELISSA SERCIA writes all things Fantasy and Science Fiction. She is the author of Blood and Magic, book one in the Blood and Darkness series. Melissa lives in California with her man and her cat. When she's not building whimsical fantasy worlds and slaying demons, you can find her in the kitchen cooking with a glass of wine in her hand.

Website: www.melissasercia.com

Facebook: www.facebook.com/melissasercia11

Twitter: www.twitter.com/fluidghost

Instagram: www.instagram.com/melissaserciawrites/

ABOUT THE PUBLISHER

City Owl Press is a cutting edge indie publishing company, bringing the world of romance and speculative fiction to discerning readers.

www.cityowlpress.com